THE ARRIVAL OF AN HOUR

Charles J. Schneider

THE ARRIVAL OF AN HOUR

DOUBLE DRAGON

THE ARRIVAL OF AN HOUR
is a sequel to
TIME'S FICKLE GLASS

Dedicated to Dessi:
My love and my inspiration

O gentlemen, the time of life is short!
To spend that shortness basely were too
long.
If life did ride upon a dial's point,
Still ending
THE ARRIVAL OF AN HOUR

William Shakespeare
Henry IV, Part I
Act V scene 2

FACT AND FICTION
IN ALL THINGS
'COURBET' AND 'CAILLEBOTTE'

Fact: *Jean Désiré Gustave Courbet (known by the second of his two middle names: 'Gustave') gained notoriety for his suggestive nudes—especially, his explicit depiction of an anonymous model's genitalia in his controversial erotic painting The Origin of the World, created in 1866.*

Fact: *Courbet's erotic painting entitled Sleep depicting 2 female lovers was the subject of a police report for obscenity in 1872. Sleep, Woman with Stockings (which shows a lascivious woman exposing her genitals), and The Origin of the World were all deemed inappropriate for public display and were thus banned from exhibition.*

Fact: *The Origin of the World was never viewed publicly until 1988. It is currently part of the permanent exhibition at Musée d'Orsay in Paris.*

Fact: *The model for The Origin of the World remains a mystery to this day, although long presumed to be one of Courbet's numerous secretive mistresses who doubled as artistic subjects, with the top contender until recently being Courbet's Irish mistress and model Joanna Hiffernan. Authorities now believe that the model may have been the Parisian ballet dancer Constance Queniaux: the mistress of Ottoman diplomat Halil Şerif Pasha (aka Khalil Bey) who actually commissioned the creation of the painting* *in 1866 by Caillebotte for his erotic collection of artwork. The same uncertainty exists surrounding Courbet's other nude models, whose identities were kept secret and never revealed, in order to protect their reputation.*

Fact: *Not much is known about Courbet's personal life. He was never married but had a mistress with whom he had a daughter in 1847. This mistress left with her child in the early 1850's and Courbet never maintained contact with them after the separation. He had countless physical relationships with various women and could have very well had other illegitimate children with these other mistresses.*

Fact: *Courbet also gained notoriety for his political views during the rule of the Paris Commune. He was forced to flee France in 1873, in order to avoid a large financial penalty for the key role he played in the destruction of the Vendome Column. He resided in Switzerland until his death on December 31, 1877 of liver disease exacerbated by heavy drinking.*

Fact: *Courbet was an inspiration to many of his contemporaries and a laughingstock to others. He was openly admired by Ferdinand Victor Eugene Delacroix and James Abbott McNeill Whistler, and was a role-model and teacher to many younger aspiring Impressionists, including Edouard Manet and Edgar Degas. His relationship with Jules Joseph Lefebvre was likely antagonistic since Lefebvre was accepted by <u>La Salon</u> as a legitimate artist notwithstanding his propensity for painting semi-explicit nudes, and Courbet was not.*

Fact: *There were three Caillebotte brothers: Gustave (the oldest), René (the middle sibling), and Martial (the youngest).*

Fact: *Gustave was a famous painter, and Martial was a renowned photographer. Not much is known of René, who died suddenly in 1876 at age 25 of an undisclosed and mysterious illness presumably cardiac in nature. Given the artistic creativity of his two brothers, it is conceivable that he had similar talents as well, though never documented.*

Fact: *Gustave and Martial both inherited millions, and spent most of their leisure time collecting stamps and devoting their energy to their various other hobbies (music and photography for Martial; gardening, yacht building and collecting paintings for Gustave).*

Fact: *Gustave, although trained as an attorney and painter, gave up his professional efforts to become a recluse, dying alone in his garden when he was 46 on February 21, 1894 of 'pulmonary congestion'. The true cause of his sudden and unforeseen death is unknown, and could have very well been the result of foul play.*

Fact: *Martial lived with his brother Gustave in Haute-de-Seine prior to Gustave's purchase of his country home that he named <u>Petit Genevilliers</u>.*

Fact: *Charlotte Berthier was an alias for Anne Marie Hagan: Gustave's long-time companion (from a lower class) and the eventual heiress of his estate. It is rumored that Gustave insisted that Anne Marie use the fictitious name in order to disguise her identity and distract attention from the fact that*

11

she had worked as a prostitute before becoming his mistress.

Fact: *Marie Minoret was Martial's wife, and had tremendous animosity towards Anne Marie Hagan aka Charlotte Berthier, to the point that Martial's relationship with Gustave was eroded by restrictions placed by his wife on how often he could see his older brother.*

Fact: *Martial Caillebotte and Marie Minoret had two children: a son, Jean, and a daughter, Geneviève. Geneviève, rather than Jean, inherited the majority of unsold paintings in Gustave Caillebotte's collection from his estate. There is no evidence that Jean had been disinherited, in contrast to his fictional portrayal in this novel.*

Fact: *Gustave only painted two female nudes: <u>Naked Woman Lying on a Couch</u>, 1873; and <u>Nude on a Couch</u>, 1890. The brunette model for the first piece was anonymous and unidentified, while the second redheaded model is incontestably a depiction of Anne Marie Hagan (aka Charlotte Berthier), pictured in the early years of her relationship with the artist.*

Fact: *Gustave painted a handful of male nudes—unconventional subject-matter at the time, leading to rumors that he was homosexual. His reclusive behavior and the fact that he remained a bachelor until his death added to this unfounded conclusion.*

Fact: *Francois Salle was a slightly younger contemporary of Gustave Caillebotte with only one notable painting of historically consequence, of a male model posing nude for a group of art-school* students (_The Anatomy Class at the Ecole des Beaux Arts_, 1888). Gustave and Francois (or easily the male model) could have very well crossed paths given their interest in depicting the naked male form on canvas.

Fact: _Gustave was an art collector and had a vast collection of Impressionist paintings. There is admittedly no documentation of whether or not he owned any Courbet pieces._

Fact: _Pierre-Auguste Renoir (known by his second-hyphenated name 'Auguste') was a close friend of the Caillebotte family, spending much of his time with Gustave at his estate at Petit Genevilliers. He was the executor of Gustave's Will and the 'caretaker' of Gustave's vast collection of Impressionist paintings until they were eventually passed on to Genevieve Caillebotte: Martial's daughter, after Renoir's death. Caillebotte had donated these paintings to the French government, but Renoir was unsuccessful in his attempts to facilitate Gustave's wishes since the Republic, unbelievably, declined the generous bequeathal. Many of these paintings were eventually purchased by Dr. Albert C. Barnes of Philadelphia and reside at the Barnes Foundation Museum, including_ _Woman with White Stockings_.

Fact: _Auguste Renoir was a womanizer who had affairs with virtually all of his nude models (including the infamous Suzanne Valadon). He eventually married Aline Charigot, whom he had depicted nude in some of his most famous pieces._

Fact: _Erotic photography as a genre was conceived in the mid-nineteenth-century, and was_

13

practiced by the French portrait photographer Felix-Jacques Antoine Moulin, among others. In 1851 his explicit photographs were confiscated, and he served a one-month prison sentence because of the obscene nature of his nude portraits.

Fact: *N-methylaminophenol (also known as Metol) is a developing powder used in black and white photography. It was developed in 1891, and was widely used in the late nineteenth and early twentieth century by both amateur and commercial photographers. Ingestion of even a small amount leads to the formation of met-hemoglobin in the bloodstream: a 'poisoned' form of hemoglobin that cannot bind oxygen. The disorder leads to rapid death by 'hematologic' asphyxiation.*

Fiction: *Everything else.*

For a comprehensive **PARTIALLY FACT,
LARGELY FICTION
CHARACTER GENEALOGY** please refer to
the **FOOTNOTE** section located
after the **EPILOGUE** *

** WARNING:
The Bruante-Berthier-Courbet-Caillebotte foot-
noted family-tree contains
<u>identity 'spoilers'</u> and is best studied after reading
the entire novel first
in order to preserve suspense*

PART ONE

What is ***PAST IS PROLOGUE***

William Shakespeare
The Tempest
Act 2 scene 1

CHAPTER ONE

"I'm here to see Dr. Lefebvre."

"Oh yes!" the attractive administrative assistant bubbled, just as Dr. Thierry Duvalier was about to offer his name; adding: "She's expecting you." The pretty brunette eyed him unsubtly while ushering him with an inviting smile into a back hallway which was home to a line of offices. He noticed that the door of the last one on the right: their apparent destination, had been pushed open in anticipation of his meeting with the occupant inside.

Dr. Thierry Duvalier had arrived in Paris last night at half-past ten, on the train originating from Brussels. He had checked into the hotel, ordered a late night snack that would double as his dinner, and settled down to wait for room-service after undressing and slipping on the terrycloth robe embroidered with the *Ritz Carlton* logo that had been left for him hanging on the bathroom door-hook. When his food arrived, he had stretched out on the king-sized bed with the platter beside him and his lap-top on his legs, opened to the intriguing case summary authored by the mentally-afflicted subject's treating physician: Dr. Genevieve Lefebvre, the chief of psychotic disorders at *L'Hôpital Universitaire Pitié-Salpêtrière* Psychiatric Institute.

Dr. Lefebvre was more than just an impressive physician with an equally impressive professional title to Thierry, though. 'Gennie' (as she liked to be called) had been one of his interns fifteen years ago

19

when he led a resident-team on the general medicine floor; and he would never forget the sweet yet bitter taste of their short-circuited romance. At the time, they were star-crossed due to Gennie's whim-like romantic obligation to another—unwavering one moment and faltering the next; but now, more than fifteen years later, he hoped for a more decisive alignment of fate's starry-eyed constellation.

He thought nostalgically about her while re-reading the medical treatise, typed out by the same fingers that had briefly entwined with his, a decade-and-a-half ago—her words on digital-paper describing the patient who called herself Susanne Bruante: a woman who claimed to be a time-traveler, allegedly stepping into a distant relative's life and living as an imposter for a full ten years, from 1886 to 1896. Thierry took a bite of the *jambon-beurre* corresponding with each of Gennie's many insightful talking-points: the same ones which had ultimately convinced him, after his initial review of the mini-treatise two weeks earlier, to accept the consultation job in his native city. The professional opportunity to study such an intriguing case was compelling, although his concurrent goal was to cautiously stir the simmering coals of a prematurely-arrested love-affair—this latter aspiration spurred on by the subtle encouragement he had heard in her voice when they had spoken of the potential consultation, more than once, on the phone.

Tomorrow, he would step into his role as visiting scholar—the endeavor solicited by a thoroughly perplexed Parisian psychiatric team led by a woman who had been committed amorously to someone else in their medical training days. Her faithfulness to 'Marc': her college sweetheart who was working for the Peace Corps in far-off Senegal at the time, seemed half-hearted at best—her irresolute promise of chastity bent if not completely broken in an impromptu *tête-à-tête* one night with Thierry while they were both staying overnight in the hospital, on call.

There was no question in his mind that their one intimate encounter had been fueled by shared passion; but the engine promising to propel them from an aborted one-night-stand into a long-lasting, meaningful relationship had been cruelly sabotaged by Gennie's one-sided guilt. From what Thierry had been able to infer from the tidbits of information offered up rarely by the woman of his dreams, Marc's true intentions were as confused as Gennie's—a circumstance that cheapened Gennie's grudging sense of accountability to a long-distance lover, making her maddening sense of allegiance seem naïve and foolhardy rather than admirable and stoic...*especially* in light of her conflicted but seemingly powerful feelings for Thierry.

"I wasn't supposed to fall in love with you," she had whispered in his ear that night-of-nights—the very words suggesting she had done just that. The indirect confession hung in the non-existent space between them expectantly as they lay naked together, their bodies pressed tightly against one-another on the narrow call-room bed. "I can't; I just *can't*," she added softly, her meaning unclear; but a

21

moment later as she gave him clear permission to continue with an impassioned, pleading, and almost desperate kiss, it seemed obvious that she was struggling with an existential, emotional dilemma rather than a physically-restrictive one. Her eyes were closed as if not seeing...not *looking* at what she had started would magically erase her fervor and make the reality of the moment disappear; while from behind closed lids she offered Thierry her intimacy without a hint of equivocation—and he responded in-kind.

Before he knew it they had repositioned themselves head-to-toe and toe-to-head in a smooth choreography—hands replaced by lips and tongues, mutually executing the most primal of pleasurably drawn-out dances, the wild performance ultimately climaxing with the feminine half of their reciprocity exultantly satisfied. The masculine, however, remained patiently unfulfilled, but stood firm— hopeful and ready. *May I?* he had asked with soundless action, lying expectantly now on top, his hips pressed tentatively against hers in preparation for full consummation should she give him leave.

The moment of uncertainty hung in the air with the heady, sweet aroma of 'her' that wafted into his very being with every insinuating breath. She would say 'yes'...of *course* she would—after coming this far, to the very brink of dual gratification promising to bind their destinies together, forever. But, no...her answer was 'no'—the shock of her unexpected rebuttal reinforced when she gently pushed him away with two palms on his chest.

He rolled away to give her space, dumbfounded by her rejection and feeling embarrassed by presumption—but really, could anyone blame him for assuming? She sat on the edge of the bed, her expression hard to read in the muted light but seeming to reflect a chaotic mixture of regret, sadness, and determination. "I can't," she repeated dully, even though what had already transpired almost certainly counted as 'you already did.' There could have been more...*should* have been more—but there wasn't; and Thierry's quiet, personal tragedy was reinforced as Gennie dressed in awkward silence, slipping into her hospital scrubs and closing the door with finality behind her. So it was that she left him, that night and forever (he thought)—to sleep in the adjoining call room while he lay awake, nursing a perplexed and injured sorrow.

He didn't push it, since it was stingingly clear that her mind was made up. He put on a brave face, for sure—outwardly smoothing things over, even going so far as to praise her decision as morally correct, while on the inside he nurtured a profound disappointment that she hadn't 'picked' him but rather, chose someone else. When the rotation ended they went their separate ways, saying a stilted, 'friendly' goodbye—she to a psychiatry residency, and he to neurology; and 'that was that'...until now.

To say he was surprised when she phoned him out of the blue, fifteen years later, would be an understatement. She needed his help, on the surface; but below-decks, the tenor of her voice implied that she might be interested, in a parallel agenda, in revisiting their unfinished past. The unsolicited reunion with Gennie and all of the potential for life-changing repercussions aside, Thierry was equally curious about the 'other' woman: the mysterious patient who called herself Susanne Bruante—the key, perhaps, to unlocking and proving a career-making scientific theory. Tomorrow he would have a chance to hear the 'subject' of his trip to Paris recount, in her own words, the far-fetched accounting of her delusional albeit 'memory-based' (Thierry theorized) experience.

Indeed, Gennie's unwillingly-committed convalescent alleged that she had originally become a time-traveler slightly-less-than ten years earlier, in 2011, when she had intentionally 'hijacked' a portal opened by another chronologic-journeyer: a misplaced relative from 1876 named Nicole Bruante. This family-member's confabulated genetics had enabled her to transform Gustave Courbet's erotic painting *The Origin of the World* into some kind of a '*Time-Tunnel*' that she referred to as a *Virtual-Hole*. The fascinating mental-patient asserted with distinct psychotic zeal that she had subsequently been conveyed *back* to present-day 2021 precisely a decade later (time passing here and there at the same second-by-second speed) by some type of science-fiction-like trickery executed by an entirely *different* meddling ancestor named Elle Bruante, on the 'other side' of the connection between 'today' and 'yesterday'.

Of particular interest to Thierry's medical specialty, *and* the specific reason he had agreed to

24

function as a consultant in the case, was the often-times true-to-history nature of the patient's descriptive experience that seemed to validate her 'memories'—which, he postulated, were actually the recollections of her long-deceased relatives. The proposed triad of paranoid schizophrenia, a probable mixture of more than one personality disorder, and a suspected memory 'ailment' made the case unique, and particularly relevant to Thierry's career-long research-focus, striking a chord in his training as both a neurologist and a psychologist.

His plan was to conduct a lengthy conversational interview with the afflicted subject, beginning immediately after his debriefing first thing in the morning with Gennie; and, if his evaluation led to the preliminary impression that he fully expected, he would arrange the patient's transfer to his facility in Belgium for intensive therapy under his care—an endeavor that would be well worth the administrative hassle if the subject under scrutiny eventually yielded the proof he needed to validate his neuropsychiatric research.

Before agreeing to take the consulting job, Thierry had thoroughly reviewed the at-first perplexing medical records accompanying Gennie's professional plea for his involvement, which he ultimately felt certain he understood when viewed in the context of the unique variant of an uncommon psycho-neurologic syndrome that he had formulated as a preliminary diagnosis. After drawing his tentative conclusions a few weeks ago, he had confirmed in a lengthy telephone conversation with

Gennie that the patient's ailment did indeed appear to fall under his area of expertise—*if* his hypothesis was confirmed.

So, after the high speed train trip from Brussels to Paris and an impromptu hotel-room dinner enjoyed with his ex-(not-quite)-girlfriend's mini-dissertation opened on his lap, he fell into a fitful sleep filled with dreams of a prior call-room encounter confused with museum exhibit-room time-traveling escapades transpiring 'in the buff'. In the morning, bleary eyed from a not-so-restful sleep, Thierry had taken a taxi in early morning traffic to *Pitié-Salpêtrière* and found himself following the pretty brunette administrative assistant down the hallway, his heart thrumming wildly in his throat. She led him through the half-open door to the last office on the right, to an exciting but uncertain professional and personal destiny.

CHAPTER TWO

The door closed behind him with a finality that clearly stated there was no going back now; but when he saw her he thought: *why would I ever want to?*

Of course he had searched her hospital profile—the marketing persona created by the health-systems public relations team consisting of a photographic image of her top-half clothed in a crisp white lab coat, accompanied by an impressive bio that thoroughly described her achievements and expertise; but the PR piece hardly did justice to the real-life woman standing up from her desk chair to greet him. Fifteen years had passed but she didn't look a day older. She was something *so* much more than beautiful, now even more than then: her face a chiseled sculpture of classic lines and her body's gently-exaggerated curves nothing less than idyllic. Her hair was still a wind-blown field of Nordic winter-wheat, and her eyes as crystal-blue as a clear, crisp glacier-fed lake. His heart cried: *I have missed you so* as she made her way around the desk, hesitating for just a moment before taking the few steps necessary to bring them face-to-face.

She met his eyes, and he—hers. "Hello, Thierry," she said softly, waiting for him to make the next move. Her hands were folded in front of her, a perfect invitation for him to take them in his...which he did, since this form of greeting represented a fitting display of just the right amount of subdued affection.

"You look well," she commented, pressing her palms fondly in his. Her smile was warm and sincere, but also tentative...as if she wasn't quite sure if he held a grudge for what had happened between them years ago, and if so to what extent.

"You too, Gennie," he replied, which was really an understatement, since she looked nothing less than phenomenal.

"We should talk...about 'us'," she stated quietly, disengaging their hands gently as if discussing their 'broken' past required breaking the bond of touch between them as well. "I was so confused, back then..." she began to explain, looking away. He needed to put her at ease or else the awkwardness would sabotage everything professional and personal between them for the rest of the day...and potentially well beyond.

"I agree, for sure; but how about we save it for over dinner—business first, then pleasure? There's a nice restaurant at my hotel—my treat, of course."

Her demeanor eased to less tense, almost immediately. "Oh, that would be lovely! Shall we call it a 'date', then?"

"That goes without saying! It will be *so* very nice to catch up with you, Gennie."

As he noticed her breathe a visible sigh of relief, he knew that his warm and genuine offer, completely devoid of resentment or anger, had produced its desired effect. Apprehensions allayed, she offered him a seat and positioned herself directly across from him—her shapely legs crossed. A few minutes later, after ringing for beverages, she expertly balanced a cup of *café au lait* on her

28

delightfully-exposed thigh, while Thierry assumed the same pose seated in a matching upholstered chair, but sipping a black double espresso instead.

"I can't tell you how pleased I am that you agreed to this consultation, Thierry. She's been here since early March, and despite state-of-the-art psychiatric management for schizophrenia, she still firmly believes that her delusions are true."

The psychiatric patient in question had been discovered by a security guard in the famous *Musée d'Orsay* art gallery after hours about four months ago, having set off the alarms by violently removing Courbet's erotic masterpiece *The Origin of the World* from its wall-display and physically accosting it before collapsing on the floor— delirious and semi-conscious, in what appeared to be a classic psychotic break. Leading up to her bizarre emotional outburst, she had presumably hidden somewhere with stealthy premeditation prior to the museum's hour of closing—perhaps holed-up in a utility closet waiting for the opportune moment in the middle of the night to execute her bizarre and mentally-unstable plan. She had been rushed by ambulance through a driving pre-spring rain to the nearest medical facility, followed by her prompt transfer to *Pitié-Salpêtrière* where Gennie had been waiting expectantly to accept the perplexing case.

When her delirium and amnesia eventually cleared, the patient swore up and down that her name was Susanne Bruante, asserting that her twenty-first century identity had been stolen by an imposter—Nicole Bruante: her great-great-great grandmother, of all people, who had been inadvertently transported from 1876 to the year 2011 by hallucinogen and genetically-induced time-travel. 'Susanne' alleged that Nicole had inherited a specific double mutation-pairing in an X-linked gene coding for a hormone called chronotonin, whereas Gennie's patient had inherited only one. *Both* mutations were apparently required to open a *Time-Tunnel*, rendering herself: a single-mutation carrier, incapable of doing so. However, by latching onto someone with two instead of one DNA alterations, Susanne had managed to subvert (or be subverted to) the time-traveling process not once, but twice.

The first time the 'hijacking' was intentional when, in 2011, Susanne had schemed to have Nicole open up a *Virtual-Hole* leading from 'here to there' that Susanne subsequently appropriated, passing through alone after pushing her relative aside at the last moment. The second time, occurring just a few months earlier in the here-and-now, had been *unintentional*, when Susanne had been tricked into riding along as a passenger with *another* conniving relative named Noëlle (abbreviated 'Elle') Bruante: her great-great-great-*great* grandmother. *This* time the journey had occurred from 'there to here' rather than from 'here to there'—a very tall-tale representing Susanne's ludicrous explanation for a delusion-shrouded arrival in present day Paris in the early morning hours of 1 March, 2021. Thierry literally couldn't wait to hear the entire far-fetched story culminating with the details of exactly how Susanne had been hoodwinked by Nicole Bruante's mother—straight from the horse's mouth, when his interview with the woman he believed to be suffering from a unique triple-malady would shortly begin.

Susanne had quoted a bizarre set of time-travel 'rules' that supposedly predicted her return to the same present-day *Time-Shell* (as she referred to it) from which she had previously exited in 2011, but at a parallel point in the forward march of time: exactly nine years, eight months and two weeks later. Applying this axiom to her make-believe journey accounted for just short of a full decade of time's passing, both there (1886 to 1896) and here (2011 to 2021)—an entirely crazy postulate that only someone crazy could create; so naturally she was duly committed and remained under a 'house arrest' of sorts in the mental facility where she was still being treated. Her confinement had been justified in part because she had no confirmable identity and thus could not be released to any responsible party's care, but also due to an unspoken concern that she might be a danger to herself or others.

Thierry had been told that not only had their soon-to-be-mutual patient 'confessed' to murder of a relative by poisoning (according to her bizarre time-traveler's pretension), but that she had also demonstrated real-life non-fictional violent tendencies illustrated in her act of defiling and damaging a priceless national treasure. She had zealously created a torn and crescent-shaped defect in *The Origin of the World* canvas with her fist and boot-heels in the exact location of the anonymous model's explicitly depicted genitals, almost as if she had been fulfilling a personal vendetta against the erotic *poseur*; and if she had not pleaded innocent on the basis of insanity for the desecration of a priceless piece of artwork, Susanne would have faced criminal charges and potentially even prison-time rather than indefinite treatment in a psychiatric facility.

Exactly this had happened to a man named Andrew Shannon, who had been sentenced to six years in prison after he walked into the National Gallery of Ireland in Dublin in 2012 and punched a hole in *Argenteuil Basin* by Claude Monet (1874)— a painting worth £8 million. In Susanne's case, her violent outburst and the resulting adulteration of not only Courbet's erotic masterpiece but also three Degas nude sculptures that had been chipped and cracked when overturned, had become the focal point of an international repair project led by a team of acclaimed art restorers.

"As you know, our working diagnosis at first was paranoid schizophrenia—the inherent variety favored over drug-induced, since her 'tox-screen' was negative." It was well known that certain hallucinogenic drugs, most notably PCP, could not only cause acute psychosis when ingested in excess, but could also bring about permanent chemical changes in the brain with repeated use that occasionally led to the equivalent of chronic schizophrenia. If Susanne's blood and urine toxicology testing had failed to detect any of these illicit substances on the day in question, that *suggested* but didn't prove a constitutional malady. Thierry knew as well as Gennie did that one negative test did not necessarily mean that Susanne was not a 'user', and that the psychiatric consequences of ingesting mind-altering pharmaceuticals related more to the 'build-up' of these chemicals in the brain rather than from acute intoxication. "But when her delusions persisted despite a variety of medications appropriate for this diagnosis," Gennie continued, "it became quite clear that we were focusing on the incorrect disorder."

"Are you medicating her now?"

Gennie responded by shaking her drop-dead gorgeous head 'no' while placing her now empty cup on a small circular coffee table positioned slightly off-center between them, drawing attention to carefully manicured nails on long and delicate fingers. Thierry carefully suppressed his elation when he noticed that she wasn't wearing an engagement or wedding ring, leading him to hope that she *hadn't* married Marc; or if she had, the union had ended in separation or divorce. "We ultimately discontinued all of her anti-psychotics since they made no difference whatsoever in her mentation, which seems normal now except for some interesting and often abrupt fluctuations in temperament, demeanor and mood. She claims to have been the nude model for a variety of artists, including—can you believe it—my great-great-great grandfather, Jules Joseph Lefebvre."

"That's an uncanny coincidence."

"No kidding. You see, she also claims to be a direct descendant of Gustave Courbet. He and my great-great-great grandfather were artistic rivals:

33

something very akin to enemies; so, the delusional happenstances just keep coming."

"But there's no way she could have known that *you* would end up being her treating psychiatrist!"

Gennie shrugged. "Who knows. I'm a prominent name in the Parisian medical community, so it's not inconceivable that a repressed desire for my help led her to subliminally plan the psychotic break in a way that would ensure my involvement. It would have been easy enough for her to call the hospital operator posing as one of my patients to inquire about the on-call schedule. But regardless, she describes other unlikely *and* unethical brushes with artistic greatness centered around alleged family members that only serve to further illustrate the depth and scope of her mental disorder."

"For instance?"

"For one, she affirms that she had an incestuous sexual relationship with her great-great grandfather: Martial Caillebotte, and posed for him as the model for an ultra-erotic set of photographs that she calls the 'bodyscape' series. She says she became his insincere lover, manipulating him with seduction into unwittingly betraying his very own brother, Gustave Caillebotte: whom she actually admits, in her fantasy, to *killing* with lethal-if-ingested film-developer painted onto the back of his collectible, 'lick-able' postage-stamps. Her goal in all this, allegedly, was to gain early access to a hefty inheritance. These boasts are only figments of her imagination, of course; but they show she has no sense of right or wrong."

34

Thierry seconded Gennie's diagnostic thoughts. "These are hallmarks of a sociopath, for sure. There's no question in my mind that she has *that* particular personality disorder...as well as others."

Gennie's interest was definitely piqued—his intention of course, since *this* was a woman that he was almost desperate to impress, this time around more than before. "Go on," the most beautiful woman in the world implored; and he was ever so anxious to oblige.

CHAPTER THREE

Thierry was an MD, PhD physician-scientist: one of those rare individuals who had spent years of training in the laboratory, classrooms and hospitals; beginning his studies at *Pierre and Marie Curie Université* and then completing a neurology residency and clinical psychology fellowship back-to-back at *L'Hôpital Européen Georges Pompidou*, in Paris. His PhD thesis concentrated on a certain neural peptide that he had painstakingly identified and named *mnemosyne* after the Greek goddess of memory, since the substance appeared to play a crucial role in a variety of memory tasks in humans and other animal species. Thierry's discovery spawned a flurry of worldwide research focused on this peptide, eventually providing incontrovertible evidence that it was integral to the recall of ancestral migration maps stored in the 'memory center' of birds, butterflies, and salmon.

Meanwhile, the French-born and educated Thierry, as junior faculty at *L'Université de Paris*, had become the world's most respected authority in mnemosyne-related neurological and neuropsychiatric disease causation in humans, proving that the blood-level of this neurotransmitter had a direct correlative relationship to memory capabilities. In his best-known clinical experiments, he had documented nearly undetectable levels of mnemosyne in patients with Alzheimer's disease, other dementia disorders, and amnesia syndromes, in contrast to easily measurable levels in healthy volunteers with intact memory.

His groundbreaking research, occurring over a decade ago immediately after he had taken a joint position in Brussels at the Neuroscience Institute of *L'Université Libre de Bruxelles (ULB)* and the affiliated *Brugman Université Hopital Bruxelles-Queen Astrid*, had resulted in the development of a genetically-engineered synthetic mnemosyne analogue that the scientific community hailed as the pharmaceutical of the century. *Mnemositide* (the name coined by Thierry, of course, as its main molecular 'inventor') was a long-acting intramuscular injection that was recently approved to use in patients with Alzheimer's-related memory loss. Although not a cure for the disease but rather a variably effective abrogation-treatment depending on the severity of a patient's infliction, mnemositide nevertheless represented a significant breakthrough in the symptom management of dementia which was predicted to earn Thierry the Nobel Prize in Medicine as a result of his work in its development.

Thierry rose rapidly in the scientific and medical communities, maintaining and running a robust scientific research laboratory while at the same time expanding his prominence in the realm of psychological inflictions. It was in this capacity as a renowned researcher and as the chairman of the division of Neuropsychology at *Brugman* that he had made some astounding breakthroughs just recently in the relationship of *excess* mnemosyne to certain personality disorders. It was specifically because of some of this related and well-publicized research that Gennie had reached out to him for an opinion.

"Go on," she urged.

Thierry placed his now-empty cup right next to hers on the coffee table stationed between them. "Have you seen any evidence at all during your psychotherapy sessions of other distinct personalities that are not 'Susanne'?"

"Not in the classic 'multiple personality disorder' sense, by any means; but as we discussed on the phone, we *have* noticed some subtle changes in her behavior and comportment from time-to-time that could qualify. That's when it dawned on me that maybe you could help."

It was somewhat problematic invoking a disorder when the specific component *defining* the diagnosis—i.e. the indisputable presence of multiple defined personalities each emerging and submerging periodically within one individual—was absent; but the temperament changes that Gennie had described to him could very well represent repressed personalities attempting unsuccessfully to make their appearance. In addition, Susanne's recounting of her exploits to Gennie seemed to invoke uncanny insight into the other 'characters' in her complex delusion, which could qualify as 'personality mining', for lack of a better term; and suggested to Thierry that they might be dealing with a rare variant of Dissociative Identity Disorder blended with others, with some heavy psychotic overlay. He would know more shortly, after talking to the 'research subject' directly.

38

"After reviewing the medical chart as well as your thorough case summary, I believe we may be dealing with an unusual case of multiple personalities where either the weaker entities are being subdued and muted by the dominant identity that she calls Susanne Bruante; or else the patient's identity is so confused that elements of numerous personalities are being intermittently expressed and repressed simultaneously within a single ego. It would be interesting to measure and analyze her blood levels of mnemosyne."

Gennie got up, sauntered over to her desk giving Thierry the opportunity to discreetly admire her perfect derriere, and picked up some papers. She turned around, walking back while displaying the sheaf in one hand like she was presenting evidence. "This scientific study that you published earlier this year in *Neuropsychiatry* is fascinating." She sat down again, while pulling at the short hem of her skirt in an unsuccessful attempt to hide exposed skin, flipping through the journal article on top of her partly-bared lap.

Her leggy-assets were very much on display, whether sitting or standing, in a short but professional skirt that hiked up pleasantly to mid-thigh while seated, becoming as much of a distraction now as they had been fifteen years ago—equaling or exceeding the magnetic pull of her azure eyes, flaxen hair and sultry lips. "How did you conceive your hypothesis that mnemosyne blood-levels would be *higher* in patients with dissociative identity disorder than in normal control

39

subjects?" she asked. "It's far from intuitive that this would be the case, at least to me."

He grinned. "Do you know much about 'past life regression' hypnosis?"

"A little. Some people have very vivid experiences during the procedure that they interpret as reincarnation recollections."

"Correct. But are they really remembering past lives?"

She shrugged. "Anything's possible but that conclusion doesn't make scientific sense to me."

"Actually, I think it makes *perfect* scientific sense. What if those experiences induced during hypnosis are true *ancestral* memories?"

"Meaning…?"

"Meaning that their ancestor's memories are encoded in their inherited DNA, just as they are in *all* of us…except that most people are unable to readily access these stored recollections. In dreams or in particularly susceptible hypnosis subjects, these recalled experiences are released from the subconscious brain during past life regression hypnosis by elaboration of excessive amounts of mnemosyne in the hippocampus."

"You'll have to explain that to me in more detail, Thierry. I'm not a neurologist, *or* a molecular geneticist."

"It's actually quite simple. Geographic maps in birds and other migratory species are encoded in 'germline' DNA, meaning that sperm and egg cells contain the information in a genetic package that's passed on to their offspring during the process of reproduction. That's how those animals know exactly where to fly in the wintertime or swim in the spring, and precisely how to get there."

"So what you're saying is that mnemosyne releases ancient memories in patients who successfully undergo past life regression hypnosis, just like it does in migratory animals?" Her mind was quick, sharp and engaging—as attractive to an intellectual like Thierry as her spot-on perfect body.

"Exactly. We've measured levels of the peptide before and after a hypnosis session, discovering that the amount of mnemosyne more than doubles when a patient is 'under' and then normalized again about five hours after awakening. This data infers that mnemosyne plays a vital role in the generation of past-life experiences—which I have postulated are, in-reality, stored memories in inherited DNA passed on to them by their forefathers and foremothers, unlocked by the peptide."

"So how does that relate to dissociative identity disorder? I don't see the connection."

"It occurred to me that if mnemosyne could induce ancestral memories during hypnotic past life regression therapy, then maybe it was doing the same thing in patients with DID. My idea, you see, is that inherited recollections unlocked by mnemosyne in these psychiatric patients may have led to the creation of their various personalities. So, to test this hypothesis I gathered blood samples from patients with varying severities of the syndrome; and sure enough, there was a linear relationship between the number of distinct personalities and the serum concentration of the neurotransmitter. Even patients with only *one* alter-ego had two to three-fold higher levels of mnemosyne than the controls." He pointed a finger in the general direction of the journal article balanced on her smooth and inviting thighs. "You've read all about this discovery and that's why you asked for my consultation."

She nodded, causing some strands of blonde hair to fall partly over her face, gaining his undivided attention and requiring hers. "Very interesting," she commented while at the same time sweeping the sunburst of yellow back with both hands to secure it in a ponytail with a decorative elastic-band that she had retrieved from an ornamental pottery bowel on the table—her method entirely innocent but unintentionally provocative. "But your 'ancestral memory' theory hasn't been publicized yet, in *either* group of patients."

"That's correct, because it's extremely difficult to prove that the hypnotic experiences in past-life regression therapy patients, *or* the various personalities in people with dissociative identity disorder, correspond to actual ancestors. I'm working on it, though. I have some graduate students assigned to a few particularly interesting past-life regression cases, trying to pair their hypnotic experiences with verified historical events and people. This is no easy task, as you can well imagine, mainly because most of us don't have the recollections of *notable* relatives stored in our memory banks. My ancestors for instance were quite mundane—not even *close* to famous or infamous in a historical sense."

"That's fascinating. Have you made any efforts to validate memories in patients with multiple personality disorder yet?"

He smiled. "No, although I have high hopes that Susanne might be my first case-in-point...although I believe her 'version' of DID is unique and highly unusual."

She paused for a moment and he could see her connecting the dots. "So are you postulating that if she *does* have dissociative identity disorder, that one of her alter-egos could be a real ancestor named Nicole Bruante?"

"Of course; or, Gustave Courbet, Martial Caillebotte, Edmond Bruante, Elle Bruante...or any of the various cast of characters that your medical report mentions." There was no question in Thierry's mind that this psychologically-fabricated time-travel 'story' represented extremely fertile material for ancestral-memory mining. "*All* of these people could be distorted versions of actual relatives pieced together from snippets of ancestral memories, hiding in the vast ocean of her memory-cell psyche," he explained. "And the beautiful thing is that unlike you and me, her memories just happen to involve *famous* people and events that could potentially be verified. The lives of the nineteenth century French artists that she claims to have known *personally* in her confabulations have been well documented, giving us a rare opportunity to pair a patient's memories with historical facts, if my theory pans out."

"She would be an intensely interesting subject for you to study."

43

"That would be an understatement." Yes, she *would* prove to be a most interesting research subject indeed, especially given her potential links by way of heritage and memory-association to the likes of Courbet, the Caillebotte brothers, and the models for their artwork who concurrently or subsequently became their love-interests.

"I gather, then, that you would have no issue with a transfer to your facility in Brussels to facilitate your research?"

"Are you that anxious to get rid of her?"

She laughed lightly. "Actually, yes—mainly because we've hit a brick wall with our therapeutic efforts these past four months and I don't think we'll ever break through." She gazed over at him with a playful glint in her eye. "Plus there would be an added benefit to her transfer."

"Which would be...?

"That you and I would have a professional excuse to keep in touch—permanently, this time."

To his delight, something electric stirred between them, very much akin to their residency-day chemistry. "I see." His pause was intentional as a way to emphasize his understanding of their dueling, tantalizing sub-text. "I therefore propose that we get on with the initial interviews as soon as possible—strictly in the name of collegiality, of course!"

Her half-smile indicated that she was on the same page. "For the sake of collegiality then, I'd say it's high-time for you to meet her."

CHAPTER FOUR

Gennie admired Thierry Duvalier out of the corner of her eye as they walked on a pathway that wound its way through the well-maintained medical campus grounds leading from the clinic and office space to the locked psychiatric ward, surrounded by the blooms of early-summer flowers. She had been nothing less than stupid to let him go, fifteen years ago—with his eyes a hazel pool swimming with hypnotic swirls of brilliant green, and his hair an ambrosial chocolate-brown; but how was she to know that her relationship with Marc would go sour…not right away, but years later.

She had loved Marc, in the safe and controlled kind of way that high-school sweethearts fall into—their lovemaking satisfyingly efficient but lacking the passion of the early days, until they both drifted apart without realizing that they had done so. Who could blame him, really, for stepping out on her…because after all, she had done the same to him with Thierry after a fashion, except that she hadn't gone all the way. Marc had—repeatedly it seemed, until a pregnant lover made his infidelity impossible to ignore. Thank God they hadn't married; or even worse, produced a child or two from their seventeen years spent together.

Their break-up had been a relief, expressed by a pent-up sampling of countless 'other' men and a serious relationship or two; but through it all, she had never completely forgotten Thierry, whose quiet patience with her internal struggle all those years ago had made its mark on her as much or more than his stunning good looks, his breathtaking mind, and his unselfish prowess in bed. The latter she had only partially sampled, stopping short of the point of no return—but only after he had brought her deftly into the realm of ecstasy. She hoped that he would allow her make things right between them, first emotionally and then perhaps physically, even though so much time had passed. She would have to tread delicately with a man who likely felt rejected—the injury compounded by a decade-and-a-half of radio-silence from the penitent perpetrator.

Of course she had followed his career—the prominent physician-psychologist nothing less than famous in medical-science circles not only for his professional achievements, but also for his tall, olive-skinned, dark-haired, and green-eyed good looks. It was rare to find a man like Thierry—and still single, to boot, if her gossipy sources could be trusted.

"So what do we know about her true identity?" he asked—the question nearly startling her out of her introspective reverie.

"Well, one thing for sure is that our Susanne Bruante is *not* the 'real McCoy'," she replied, focusing on the professional matter at hand in an attempt to conceal her excitement that he actually seemed quite open to a personal reconciliation. She slowed her pace so that she could have more time with him, strolling as if they were enjoying a romantic constitutional—meandering through a garden on a prearranged first-of-July, 'first' date. "You may already know that the woman in question and her husband died last winter in an automobile accident—and there is no evidence whatsoever that the deceased was the imposter that 'our' Susanne charges."

"By imposter you mean the distant relative from the nineteenth century named Nicole Bruante?"

"Exactly. You see, Susanne Bruante was appointed the Director of Acquisitions and Special Exhibits at *Musée D'Orsay* in 2008. By 2011, she had been considered a rising-star in her profession; so it was a big surprise to everyone when she gave it all up by marrying Dr. John Noland: an American theoretical physicist, moving with him to Chicago after a very brief romance—albeit rekindled, since they had been lovers in college. Rather than continuing along her expected career-trajectory in the States, she had devoted herself instead to raising their only child: Noëlle, who had been born a short nine months later. 'Our' Susanne, on hearing this, immediately accused her alleged time-traveling great-great-great grandmother: Nicole, of assuming her identity. She was initially indignant but that emotion didn't last very long. After all, our Susanne claimed to have assumed *Nicole's* identity in the nineteenth century, at least initially; so she quickly came to terms with the same arrangement but in mirror-image, in the twenty-first."

"That makes sense, in a mixed-up mentally-deranged sort of way," Thierry commented.

"You'll be interested to hear, however," she continued soberly, "that we enlisted the assistance of the University's genomics department, and discovered a definite genetic connection between the two Susannes."

"What DNA source did they use?"

"A strand of Susanne Bruante's hair from a brush provided by John Noland's sister: Diane, who is now their daughter Noëlle's designated custodian since both of the poor girl's parents are deceased. There's a definite familial concordance; but this is no surprise given the physical resemblance, shown in photographic comparison, between the 'real' Susanne and the 'fake' one."

"Which family members are relevant to your missing-persons research so far?"

It seemed that Thierry hoped to gain some clues regarding Susanne Doe's identity from her present-day family tree, so she offered what limited information she had. "Well, there's the daughter and her aunt in Chicago that I already mentioned; but Noëlle is only nine years old, which essentially eliminates her usefulness as a resource—and the aunt isn't much help, either."

"Why not?"

"She's never traveled outside of the U.S.; and being an in-law living in far-off America, she has no knowledge of the real Susanne's French relatives."

"Okay, so that's a double strike-out. Who else?"

"There's an illegitimate half-sister to the real Susanne: coincidentally named Nicole, believe it or not. She was completely estranged from the family due to some sort of scandal surrounding her birth. The circumstances had been swept under the rug for so many years, and the poor woman so decisively cut-off from the Bruante 'clique', that literally *none* of the handful of remaining, snobby relatives have any clue about what happened. I suspect she was the pregnant-product of an extra-marital fling, although this sort of ostracism seems kind of extreme to be caused by something this mundane." She shrugged. "Maybe she's the love-child resulting from a Bruante *wife* stepping out on her husband, rather than vice-versa. Now *that* little twist might have caused some particularly hard feelings."

"Surely, *this* Nicole should be able to provide some insight?"

Gennie shook her head. "No such luck.

"How so?"

"Because like icing on the cake of a family's cursed-fortunes, she suffered first for years from an incapacitating mental illness of some sort, and then died of breast cancer later—sometime in 2011 or 2012, I think."

"So *she's* another 'dead'-end, you're saying?"

"Very funny."

"Sorry."

His sheepish look mimicked what she fondly recalled seeing on his face from time-to-time on resident hospital rounds, when he would enlist some gallows-humor to lighten the burdensome levity of dealing with patients inflicted with often-terrible acute and chronic illnesses. She smiled in response to the moment *and* the memory. "Moving right along," she hurried on, "there's a drug-addict cousin named Claudine Bignon who has adopted the world's oldest profession, living right here in the city. She never knew or met the real Susanne, though, and has no interest whatsoever in helping us determine our patient's identity."

"Why is she so unwilling to help?"

"Because both she and her alcoholic father were disowned years ago by her deceased grandmother: Joelle. That leads us to the last of the living Bruantes: a great uncle named Henri in his mid 70's, still living in his home in *Saint Germaine des Pres*."

"This lead sounds promising! Is he cooperative?"

"As much as a man who requires 24-hour in-home care due to his diagnosis of Alzheimer's dementia *can* be. He's being treated with mnemositide, by the way."

"What a shame. I hope my brainchild is helping, though."

"I'm sure it is, but not enough for the police to get any useful information out of him." She sighed heavily. "As you can see, information-gathering has been a real challenge due to an alliteration of d's."

"How do you mean?"

Now it was *her* turn to offer a witty quip. "Let's see." She started counting them out one-by-one with raised fingers. "Death, distance, drunkenness, drugs, disinterest, disinheritance and dementia."

"Cute." He smiled and she suppressed a very strong urge to kiss him. "Could she be the estranged child, niece or grandchild of one of these *d*'s?"

"Possible; yet if she was a relative of one of these Bruantes, then why in the world didn't any of them ever file a missing-persons report? On top of that, our Susanne's fingerprints and photograph don't match to anyone in recent criminal or abduction databases."

"Her true identity notwithstanding, the familial link between the two Susannes may represent a key to unlocking the intricacies of her mental disorder. Is it possible they knew each other?"

Gennie shrugged. "Who knows. Unfortunately, the sane 'half' of a potential 'whole' relationship isn't alive to tell us."

"What was their age difference?"

"Why do you ask"

"Because romantic competition between cousins, let's say, of a similar age could have caused enough emotional trauma in our Susanne to incite a psychotic break. How old was the real Susanne last year when she died?"

"Forty-five according to her birth certificate; although honestly from the photos, she looked ten years younger, or more—*easily.*"

"By your visual estimate, how old is *our* Susanne?"

"Mid-twenties at the oldest, although she claims to be in her mid-forties. She explains away the actual age-to-physical-appearance discrepancy by invoking the far-fetched theory that time in the past has far different physical properties than it does in the present, to someone displaced there from a future *Time-Shell.* She asserts that she didn't feel the ravages of time because her body was 'tuned in' to the present, which conferred an illogical reverse acceleration to the chronological situation. In other words, she is utterly convinced that her decade-long

51

experience in nineteenth-century Bohemian Paris actually made her ten years *younger*."

"Don't you agree that this is classic 'magical thinking' quite typical for a patient with paranoid schizophrenia?"

"Absolutely; and this psychotic contention is extremely deep-seated. She'll tell you all about her wacky theory if you ask—or even if you don't. You see, her self-esteem seems to hinge on the appeal of her outward appearance, which she constantly references whenever the opportunity arises."

"Well, her age-specific self-awareness is totally unreliable since it's biased by her dominant DID-personality's mentally-distorted perceptions. As you know, patients with multiple personality disorder often assume the personae of children or elderly individuals who aren't even *close* to their actual age."

"True."

"Regardless of their actual ages, a sexual competition angle is a possibility—either on its own or combined with some type of emotional or physical abuse." He stopped walking and turned towards her, his irresistibly-handsome, dark-complected face intense with concentration and only inches from hers. She felt her *own* face flush slightly as a reaction to being so close to him again, after so many years; and once again, she had to resist the urge to kiss him; but then she suddenly thought: *why not?*

On an impulse she leaned forward slightly (either against her better judgment or perfectly in-line with it) and pressed her lips tenderly,

lovingly...*longingly* on his in an emotional plea for
forgiveness and a second chance.

53

CHAPTER FIVE

It was a high stakes gamble; but one that to her relief paid off. The kiss went on and on, making it clear that her risky throw of the dice had landed on her lucky number. "Oh, Gennie," he murmured, looking into her eyes with moist, hazel-green affinity. "I was hoping for this."

"About what happened between us, years ago…" she began again; but he interrupted her with another kiss that prevented her from embarking on a not-so-simple apology offered at an admittedly inopportune time.

He stopped and drew her closer. "You were in a tough spot, back then," he spoke softly, his words whispering softly in her ear—sounding just as understanding now as they had then. "A commitment should never be taken lightly."

"I know, but…"

"It won't help to dwell on the past, you know." He was kind…*so* kind; and also *one* of a kind. How she wanted him—now…later…and for the rest of her life. "Let's focus on the future instead. Agreed?"

"Agreed," she acceded, especially since their future together was very much on her mind; "although I insist we talk some more about this tonight, over dinner."

"I'll be all ears." *And mouth, tongue, and lips*…she hoped! He took her hand in his, and asked: "Is this okay?" referring to the gesture as they kept on walking. *It's more than okay*, she thought, responding non-verbally by squeezing his palm firmly in hers. They moved through the courtyard-garden silently for a few seconds, nearly basking in their mutual rediscovery of each other, until he took the lead in resuming their professional discussion where they had left off.

"You know as well as I do that patients with DID often develop the syndrome as a consequence of severe psychological trauma," he stated, "which I happen to be studying as a mnemosyne release trigger. It's conceivable that some kind of associated emotional crisis triggered within her a barrage of mnemosyne-induced ancestral memory snippets from a variety of distant relatives— *including* Gustave Courbet, Nicole Bruante, Elle Bruante, Charlotte Berthier, and the Caillebotte brothers. She then proceeded to subconsciously process these recollections in the only way that made logical sense to her psyche, which was to organize them into personalities."

"That would correspond to the accepted thinking on the post-traumatic psychological inception of dissociative identity disorder, *minus* the ancestral memory piece of course."

"Except I think her mental coping mechanism went a step beyond the simple creation of multiple personalities. You're aware, I'm sure, that DID manifests itself in various ways from patient to patient. I won't be able to confirm this until after I've had the chance to evaluate her with hypnotherapy, but I think she has formulated her ancestral memories not only into a confused patchwork of personalities, but also into a very vivid and delusional personal story-line that she interprets as real experiences when they are actually imagined, albeit based on inherited recollections. I've even coined a medical name for her syndrome pending its confirmation."

"Which is…?"

"Confabulatory Identity Confusion, or CIC. I consider it an overlap syndrome combining elements of both personality and schizoaffective disorders."

It took her a moment to process what he had just explained. "This certainly makes sense, and would place her intricate and complicated narrative in a much more understandable psychiatric context. We had been viewing it as a complex schizoid hallucination, which it obviously is *not*, since the anti-psychotics didn't cause them to dissipate. As I said earlier, she still believes those events really happened to her." He nodded affirmation, so she drew the next logical conclusion. "So I'm assuming your hypothesis is that her unique variant of DID that you call CIC was triggered by mnemosyne?"

"Yes, of course. It's a very potent memory inducer, and I'm convinced it's the cause not only of *her* psychic confusion, but of multiple personality disorder in general."

"You're talking about a universal etiology?" If true, this discovery would be *huge*, and would totally change the medical perspective on DID and related treatment research.

"I am. My thinking is that mnemosyne accounts for most cases of DID except that in Susanne, the syndrome is especially potent…most likely due to

56

excessive production of this brain peptide resulting in a severely mixed-up hodgepodge of DNA recollections originating from multiple personalities in her family tree."

He picked up their pace, to her distinct chagrin. "If overelaboration of mnemosyne is the driving factor causing and perpetuating her convoluted CIC personality disorder, then reducing blood levels should solve the problem—correct?"

"Theoretically speaking, yes."

"Is there a way to do this?"

"Maybe. It's a fascinating research question that I'm just beginning to study."

He wrinkled his brow and lowered his voice as if they were co-protagonists in the opening chapters of a would-be medical thriller. "Let's just say that manufacturing a mnemosyne-like peptide by manipulating gene transcription in bacteria and using it in 'replacement' therapy for Alzheimer's patients was hard enough; but developing a drug that shuts down mnemosyne production just enough to normalize levels without eliminating them altogether and causing dementia in the process? Well, *that* task is easier said than done."

"I can well imagine."

"Having said that however, we *have* identified a promising pharmaceutical candidate in a remarkably short period of time that we have only just started testing in humans. It's an oral drug that doesn't affect mnemosyne blood levels at all, but blocks the mnemosyne receptors on memory brain cells instead."

"I get it," Gennie interjected. "One wouldn't expect dementia if the degree of receptor blockade is partial rather than total…correct?"

He smiled. "You definitely missed your calling, Dr. Lefebvre. You would have been a fabulous laboratory-scientist." They had now reached the inpatient facility and entered one-after-the-other, with Thierry following her in gentlemanly fashion after holding the door open with an extended arm.

"Gennie," he said when they were standing inside the front-hallway, "I need to know before I meet her if you have stumbled upon any elements of truth to her story about the museum and 'Nicole Bruante', from ten years ago. It could ultimately help in a strategy of mental health recovery, which will involve bringing to the surface her other alter-egos—if my theory about her diagnosis is correct."

"Oddly, yes; although nothing about the news story confirms her alleged identity as Susanne Bruante, especially since the case quickly turned 'cold'. You see, a night guard and his presumed male lover were found naked in the special exhibit gallery—murdered directly in front of *The Origin of the World*. The security officer's skull had been bludgeoned, and his partner had sustained a bizarre, unexplainable crush-injury. A naked woman resembling the real Susanne Bruante was captured on video-tape, but she escaped and was never found. Her DNA, retrieved from blood and secretions containing skin cells at the scene, ruled out the Director of Acquisitions and Special Exhibits as her identity."

58

"If the police have been involved in trying to establish 'our' Susanne's identity, then I'm sure they've compared her DNA to the mystery woman's archived specimens, *and* the Director of Acquisition's samples that were obtained, I'm sure, by the police during the 2011 case-investigation?"

"Unfortunately, no. The stored biologic materials processed by the evidence lab and all of the paper records were all misplaced during renovations and relocation of 'the 36'; and electronic files on slews of cold cases were lost around the same time, during a major server migration snafu that took place during the move."

"How about the detectives involved in the investigation?"

"The chief inspector: a guy named Deschamps, retired and moved to the south of France—but promptly died of a massive heart attack just a few months later. This kind of thing ironically happens to some people, when they no longer have their career to preempt their health-issues, I guess."

"That's why I'm never retiring."

"Me, neither. As physicians, we need to live up to the stereotype."

"Which is?"

"Staying in practice *well* into our eighties...at least fifteen years beyond the point where we should have given it all up."

"Ah, the 'old country doctor' syndrome."

"Or the 'out-of-date quack-doctor' syndrome, is more like it!"

"How about the 'lead' detective in the case?"

"The primary officer was a woman named Michelle Crossier, who resigned from the investigation as soon as it became clear that 'cold' was the only temperature she would ever generate from the slew of collected dead-end clues. She didn't survive a diagnosis of rapidly progressing, unremitting multiple sclerosis, dying just over twenty-four months after the initial diagnosis was made—six years ago."

"Hmm, that's truly unfortunate. This case seems to be plagued with premature fatalities and difficult-to-treat medical disorders."

"Unusually so," Gennie confirmed.

"Let's revisit the crime-scene for a moment, then, so I can get 'Susanne's' story straight in my mind, before meeting her. She claims, of course, that the nude museum visitor was her long-since deceased great-great-great grandmother: Nicole Bruante. Does she attest to being related in any way to the dead security guard, or to his presumed male lover?"

"'No' to the night-guard; but 'yes' to the other naked dead guy. She says he was Nicole's lover: René Caillebotte, brother to both the famous Impressionist artist Gustave Caillebotte, and the notable photographer Martial Caillebotte. Recall that she thinks Martial was her great-great grandfather, and that she seduced him when she went back through time to the past."

"I remember."

"Well, she asserts that Nicole and René were propelled through Courbet's erotic painting *The Origin of the World*, hanging at the foot of her bed, because of Nicole's double-chronotonin gene mutation—activated by hallucinogens...*and* sexual arousal."

"Kinky." He smirked, and she did too. "Is there any evidence that this science fiction related to altered genes and *Time-Tunnels* is based in fact?"

"Kind of. One of my residents uncovered a transcript published in various international newspapers in the spring of 2011 of a question-and-answer press conference with Dr. John Noland: the 'real' Susanne Bruante's husband; along with some corresponding news coverage of his rudimentary time-travel experiments with rodents. It appears though that the journalistic-hype quickly died down when no further progress was made in the field, perhaps related to restrictions placed on Dr. Noland's research instigated by some uproar generated by animal rights activists."

"Would you agree then that the combination of Dr. Noland's curious scientific area of specialty, the 'real' Susanne's romance with John Noland that ended happily in marriage, and the incident at the museum could have all somehow molded *our* Susanne's confabulated narrative?" Thierry inquired.

"Perhaps; but only if she participated in these events, either directly or indirectly. The problem is that we have no way of confirming her involvement without first solving the puzzle of her true identity." She led him through the security doors, drawing him aside with one arm and pointing to an entryway at the end of the hallway with the other. "She's waiting for you in there, Thierry. I have to warn you, though—she's gorgeous, flirtatious, and highly manipulative; plus, she has definitely done her research on you."

"Promiscuous, exploitative and grandiose behavior is a common feature of personality disorders that I've encountered before."

"But in Susanne, these pathological character traits are magnified many-fold. Just be careful."

"I will. Don't worry Gennie—I can handle her."

She hoped that he could.

CHAPTER SIX

As Thierry stood in the doorway having just been spellbound by a pair of rediscovered, once-again familiar crystal-blue eyes, an unfamiliar set of intense hazel ones—more brown than green, in contrast to his own—looked him up and down in their own game of discovery.

"I wasn't supposed to end up here," 'Susanne' declared flatly, getting right to the point and skipping the usual introductory formalities. He was taken aback not only by her forwardness but also by her admittedly striking physical appearance, which he instantly recognized as an asset that Gennie's patient had used before to her seductively-successful advantage. Thankfully, he had been duly warned.

"Yet 'here' you are," he replied mildly, unsure if she had meant the 'here and now' of 2021 versus the physical confines of *Pitié-Salpêtrière*, although practically speaking, it didn't much matter. The important point was that Susanne felt imprisoned—and unfairly so, which could help greatly in Thierry's attempt to gather information if she thought he possessed the key to her release.

He tried to establish his negotiating dominance by taking a seat at the head of the rectangular table immediately to her right rather than directly across the table from her, but realized a moment too late that he had grossly miscalculated. Why? Because in this choice he had found himself sitting in uncomfortably close proximity to the remarkably stunning woman who claimed to have been a nude artist's model and bed-partner for the likes of the acclaimed Impressionist painter Auguste Renoir among others, as well as the 'father' of artistic photography: Martial Caillebotte—at least in the delusional fantasy-world that he felt certain she had created as a way to organize a virtual rainstorm of ancestral memories.

"I know you've read my medical file, and discussed the details of my 'ailment' already with the charming Dr. Lefebvre," she continued, once again leading the conversation rather than meekly following; "but I've read all about *you*, too. Never mind your professional credentials. I'm much more interested in the mystery of Thierry Duvalier the *person*: single, never married except to his career; a medical genius and an internationally-desired bachelor, with either no personal life, or one that's concealed by an odd penchant for privacy. Which one is it, Dr. Duvalier?" Her provocative and determined stare-down reminded him of a tigress sizing up her prey before the pounce-to-kill. But little did she know that he had his professional weapons to defend himself.

"We're not here to talk about me." This was the standard psychiatric line used to deflect an inquiry like this one, usually followed by a question directed to the patient; but before he could continue with the first item on his evaluation checklist, she was back in attack-mode and going for the jugular.

"*You* may not be here for that kind of conversation, but that doesn't mean that *I'm* not!" She repositioned herself, angling the chair towards him while crossing her legs, partially visible in a knee-length skirt, screaming an unspoken *I dare you*. There was no way in the world that he ever would, for a variety of reasons but primarily because he was the doctor and she was the patient, which meant that any plunge into the realm of the physical was strictly taboo. Not only that, but Thierry was much too experienced to fall for Susanne's variety of insincere flirtation, designed to throw him off balance and achieve whatever ulterior motive was brewing in her manipulative mind. Yes, Susanne *was* gorgeous (Gennie had chosen the perfect adjective), and the type of woman who without question routinely used her good looks as enticing bait; but although she might be accustomed to catching the proverbial fish, she wasn't about to hook *this* one.

"I'm sure you would," he replied, "so what if I make you a deal?" He had to diffuse her physical advances so that he could assess her mental condition, as well as set the stage for the type of non-confrontational interview, akin to a friendly conversation, that he had in mind. His intention was to do this while simultaneously making her believe that he was as pliable as any of her previous conquests. "If you let *me* question *you* for a little while, then I'll allow *you* to question *me*."

"That's an interesting proposition." She smiled, her lips full and perfect and her teeth whiter than sin. "Are you suggesting a sort of 'truth or dare' arrangement?"

"In a way." This was exactly how he meant for her to view it. "I dare you to be truthful, and I promise the same in return."

"That's fair..." (she winked) "...and potentially entertaining."

He'd just have to deal with her version of entertaining when the time came; but for now, it was *his* serve, not hers. "So how about we start playing?" When she nodded her assent, he asked: "Would you mind elaborating on how you ended up in *Musée d'Orsay* and what you recall about the preceding events leading to your discovery there?" He hoped that focusing on the climax of her mental crisis might give him some clues about the precipitating cause.

She leaned over, her face now so close to his that he worried she might try to kiss him. "I was tricked." The pitch of her voice was distinctly more soprano than the sultry alto of a moment before. Could this be another personality fragment clamoring for a voice? "She dragged me with her into the time portal in the painting as an unwilling passenger."

The words were Susanne's, but Thierry distinctly thought he could hear the double meaning tapped out in Morse code by another woman inside who *herself* was an unwilling passenger of sorts, subdued by or incorporated within the domineering personality that called itself Susanne Bruante. He studied her face, and believed he recognized in her expression that other woman, if only for a fleeting moment. "But in the end, she got what she deserved." Susanne was back and the fleeting alter-

66

ego was gone, but it was just as well. To try and draw out that other personality would take more time than he had today, and would require a level of trust that he would have to gain slowly. This involved procedure would have to wait for the planned transfer to Belgium.

"And the 'she' you refer to is Noëlle Bruante: your   great-great-great-great grandmother...correct?" A rather complete picture of the circumstances had been painted for him in Gennie's summary; but his hope was that Susanne would color in the fine details these next few hours...*if* he could gain her confidence, that is. He was hoping to make her comfortable enough that she would open up to him with the full narrative describing her nineteenth-century delusion.

"Of course."

Her tone was audibly defensive which meant that he needed to try harder to relax her state of mind. "I know we're starting at the end of your story instead of the beginning; but don't worry, Susanne—I want to hear it *all*, starting from day one. If you're agreeable, we can spend all day together, right here, discussing your experience. You see, I'm intrigued..." (he paused for effect) "...and honestly, uncommitted to any conclusion so far." He hoped that his professional sincerity, which did in fact dictate an unbiased examination of the facts before forming a firm diagnostic opinion, would give her the impression that he could still be convinced that her time-travels actually occurred.

Her eyes widened slightly. "So you *believe* me?"

"Now let's be fair—I'll have to hear the entire story before I make that judgement. But I promise you, my mind is open." There was a lot of truth in this assertion—because his theory about her required almost as much faith in the scientifically-incredible as accepting her self-deceptive fable at face-value.

"Alright," she relented; "I'm game...*especially* if it means I can spend some 'quality time' in close quarters arguing my case with a 'hottie' like you." To say that 'flirtatious Susanne' had returned would have been grossly inaccurate...because she had never left.

Pleased with his tactical success so far, he took out his notepad and a pen from his briefcase and placed them on the table between them. The digital-recorder would come next—but not quite yet in case the concept of a taped interview this soon in their doctor-patient relationship might have the effect of spooking her. "So, Elle is responsible for your current situation?"

"Correct," she confirmed, placing her hands in front of her less than an inch from his own; tapping her fingers on the table in a clear ploy to distract his note-taking. This move was a blatant invitation for contact, which he would pretend not to notice on the pretext that at the moment he was hyper-focused on his professional task. "The name is a shortened version of Noëlle." Her demeanor remained calm and controlled—not at all like it had been on that night Dr. Lefebvre had admitted her, when she had to be tied down with four-point restraints to prevent self-injury... per description.

"I've been told. The problem is that no one has been able to find anyone possessing *either* given name combined with the surname 'Bruante' in their search of recent Parisian birth records. I'm sure you can understand why your psychiatric team has concluded that she must be a psychological fabrication."

He said this in a mild and non-confrontational tone, while knowing full-well that Susanne would likely take offense to this intentional psychological provocation and jump vehemently to her own defense. He was banking on his theory that Elle, whom he postulated did *indeed* exist as a very real person in the distant past, was the sum of ancestral memory fragments in Susanne's head that had coalesced into a distinct hallucinatory identity.

"That's ridiculous." Her face flushed red with the precise degree of indignation that Thierry had hoped to instigate. "She's no figment of mine or anyone else's imagination. I assure you that she exists all right, but just not *here*. I've told them repeatedly that they need only search the correct century to find her." Yes, that was exactly what he and his medical team intended to do, as a way to validate his inherited memory hypothesis. "I've already told them what I'm very certain happened to her," she added.

"That she was transported back in time as soon as she arrived with you, because she landed too close to the painting…correct?"

"Exactly. I was thrown clear, but she wasn't as fortunate."

"You contend that she 'bounced back' to turn of the century Paris?" He was interested in hearing her explanation of this impossibility first hand.

"It's not a contention, but a fact."

It was true that a heavy glass showcase containing some Degas sculptures situated two yards or so immediately in front of the notorious painting had been overturned, with the presumed destructive mechanism being intentional psychotic rage rather than the impact of a speeding time-traveler's body—giving the international repair team three additional pieces of priceless artwork upon which to focus their attention. "The display-case interrupted her trajectory," Susanne went on, "leaving her within the *Time-Tunnel's* sphere of influence. You see, the concentration of absinthe and laudanum coursing through her system was still high enough when we arrived to continue interacting with her gene mutation to keep the *Virtual-Hole* open. The same thing happened to John's mice, when they were kept in a confined space too close to the *Common-Object*."

Thierry had no idea if her comments on the 'science' of time travel reflected Dr. Noland's actual aborted experiments ten years ago versus delusional fantasy, although he suspected the latter. "Why, then, hasn't Elle returned here, to this time and place? You told Dr. Lefebvre's team that she was desperate to be reunited with her daughter: Nicole."

"It should be obvious to a man of your intellect...*Thierry*." She stopped talking, watching silently for his reaction to her use of his given name—uttered in a power-play of sorts: the kind between patient and doctor that happened all too often in the mental health field. But he was used to this and knew exactly what to do, looking her straight in the eyes and responding in kind, with his *own* pregnant pause. And then he simply waited...for what? For the gestation to fully ripen, of course.

CHAPTER SEVEN

His options were to: correct her by throwing a 'Dr. Duvalier to you' in her face; ignore the premature familiarity; or acknowledge the 'Thierry' with a 'Susanne'—giving her clear-cut permission with reciprocity. In this case, the last choice would buy him the most credit in future doctor-patient negotiations, he decided.

"Intellect aside, *Susanne*," he replied, breaking the silence while emphasizing her name, "it just seems logical to a practical-thinker like myself that Elle would have tried to come back by now. If she has the correct gene mutation, why wouldn't she?"

Susanne looked away—down and to the left rather than right, which curiously seemed to indicate that she truly believed what she was about to say (if there was any truth, that is, to identifying a liar based on the direction of their gaze). "First of all, remember that I unwittingly eliminated her mode of transportation to get back here by snuffing out one of the two 'ends'." Her voice was laced with a hint of condescension. "If I hadn't behaved so irrationally, I'm certain she would have travelled back through the same painting, open for business on both sides of the *Time-Tunnel*, to search-out and find Nicole over here. In that case, I have no doubt whatsoever that she'd be in the States right now at this very minute, happily getting to know her granddaughter: the *other* Noëlle."

Susanne certainly knew her alleged family history, which served to bolster her claim that she actually *was* someone in the Bruante bloodline—but *who*? This was still the question that begged an answer. But beyond her talent for accurately identifying various relatives: living and dead, Thierry had to admire Susanne's logical thinking, which she applied unflappably to an extremely illogical story-line. "So the painting is some sort of a conduit?"

"Of *course*. It's not just oil-on-canvas, you know. It's a *Time-Tunnel*, with specific end-points located on either side when activated by the right individual with the correct double-gene mutation. I'd gladly swap locations, as I'm sure she would too." She shook her head regretfully. "What a cruel twist of fate that in my fit of rage, I destroyed a sure way back-and-forth from this 'time-space' location to the other." A devious smile crossed her face. "But there are plenty of other 'vehicles' available to hot-wire, for those of us with ingenuity and some of our *own* theories about manipulating chronotonin gene mutations to draw upon."

"Meaning?"

"Let's just say that artistically-speaking, the late nineteenth-century presents a gold-mine of opportunity for certain genetically-aberrant individuals."

Despite the roundabout language, Thierry knew immediately what she meant because he had thoroughly studied Gennie's case summary. Susanne clearly believed that if she located another piece of artwork that matched her delusional specifications, she would be able to use it to return to the past...*despite* the fact that she allegedly

73

harbored one rather than two X-linked chronotonin mutations. Thierry knew full well that according to the rules determined by her confabulated time-traveler's 'science', a solitary gene-alteration dictated safe passage through a *Time-Tunnel* but would *not* allow her to create one. This blunted talent contrasted with the sharp and seasoned 'open sesame' ability apparently reserved for 'dual' mutation carriers…as he had just discussed with Gennie, a short while ago. God only knows what kind of twisted psychotic logic Susanne was applying to her fantastical molecular make-up to scheme and plan a made-up return.

"But at least that deceptive liar got exactly what she deserved," Susanne sneered with unconcealed vitriol; "and I guarantee you, she's never coming back."

"How so? If *you've* conceived of a potential way back, then why not her?'"

"I'll put it plainly. Quite frankly, the woman doesn't possess the intellectual know-how *or* the bravery to make it happen, if she's even alive."

Susanne's cold and unsympathetic portrayal of these imaginary circumstances would have been jarring, if she wasn't plagued with a mental illness that was often characterized by this exact variety of emotional harshness. Plus, if Thierry's hypothesis was correct, the patient he was in the midst of evaluating was not necessarily the 'true' Susanne in an identity sense. In many individuals with multiple personality disorder, the most 'malignant' personality often took over as the controlling entity—which meant that the 'real' person occupying the utterly stunning body sitting right next to him might very well be the vulnerable prisoner that he had glimpsed from just a moment before, submerged and drowning under the unrelenting dominant mental force that pushed down tirelessly on her from above.

Obviously, she truly believed her far-fetched story so treading carefully was an uncontestable requirement. If he wanted to gain her trust, then he needed to try not to antagonize her with overt disbelief. "Well, at least you don't have to worry about her interference now, in this time and place. That's good—isn't it, *Susanne*?"

The short-interval repeat of 'first-name basis' had its desired effect. "Yes it is, *Thierry*…" she replied, acknowledging the intimacy implied by the use of given names—her 'bedroom eyes' locking into his in what could only be described by this classic cliché, "…but now I'm stuck here." She waved a hand in the air dramatically, which did little to clarify what she meant by 'here'. Once again, Thierry couldn't be entirely sure she was referencing *Pitié-Salpêtrière*: her physical location, versus 2021: the year.

"Is 'here' really that bad, though?" His plan was to tease out as much information about the 'where' and the 'when' as a way to solve the riddle of the 'who' and the 'what'.

"Don't be ridiculous. Let me ask you a question. How old do you think I am?"

He had to laugh quietly to himself, since Gennie had predicted this particular tangent. "I don't know—twenty-three or twenty-four, perhaps?" This was actually his honest estimate minus a few years at the most to stroke her barefaced vanity.

"Well, I have news for you. I'm forty-seven."

Well, to put it bluntly—this was simply impossible; because just as Gennie had estimated, the young woman sitting next to him couldn't be any older than mid-to-late twenties, at the very most. It was bizarre...no—*fascinating*. Somehow, this intriguing victim of a rare psychiatric ailment whom Thierry hoped would provide the necessary data for a groundbreaking medical theory had psychologically aligned herself via some kind of traumatic life experience with either a single relative, or more likely a blended ancestral memory-based persona whom Susanne believed to be forty-seven at this juncture in her concocted familial timeline.

Was it coincidence that the real Susanne Bruante would have been forty-seven, had she not been killed in a car accident? Probably not, since the woman sitting next to him seemed to truly believe that she *was* the very-same woman. As the interview unfolded to reveal the inner workings of this riveting patient's intricately disordered thinking, Thierry felt more and more convinced that this victim of happenstance and biologic predisposition who called herself Susanne Bruante was inflicted with the unique variant of DID that he referred to as CIC.

Who *was* this baffling woman though, really? Could she perhaps be a sequestered Bruante love-child alienated by illegitimacy; an estranged niece hidden away after some kind of embarrassing family scandal; or a second or third cousin of ill-repute, so far removed from the main bloodline that no one would think to recognize the connection? Answering this question, he knew, would require complex psychological procedures that he was anxious to implement after her transfer to Brussels: namely, deep-dive hypnotherapy and past life regression analysis. It just so happened that he was particularly proficient in both of these methods of probing the psyche.

"I suppose you simply have youthful genes, then," he said in response to her age-confusion; "because you look at least two decades younger, if not more." Showering her with flattery was one way to keep her guard down.

"Thank you," she narcissistically beamed, "but no—it has nothing to do with genetics at all. I'll tell you a secret," she confided in a low voice. "A person's physical and chemical properties are altered when they travel through a *Virtual-Hole* such that time moves forward outwardly; but *inside* the body, time doesn't follow the expected rules."

"How do you mean?"

"I mean that aging flows *backward* rather than *forward* for someone displaced from the future into a past *Time-Shell*. I literally gained just short of ten years of age, rather than losing them."

"So, let me get this straight. You were thirty-seven when you left *here* in 2011 and arrived *there* in 1886…" He paused momentarily, which gave her the opportunity to interrupt and finish his train of thought.

"And now I'm physiologically twenty-seven although technically, my age is actually *forty*-seven if you add on the ten years that I lived in the past." She laughed a little bit hysterically, it seemed. "Thank God I traveled *back* in time rather than to the future; because if my theory holds true, the passage of time probably works in reverse for someone passing through a *Virtual-Hole* going in the *other* direction. Who knows? I might have looked a little bit shy of sixty right now instead of twenty-something if I had jumped *ahead* of 2011 rather than behind."

He dared not mention that 'Nicole', posing as 'Susanne', had reportedly travelled *ahead* in just such a fantastical fashion, but did not seem to age prematurely during her nine years living in Chicago before her untimely death—disproving Susanne's fanciful theory. "I see." He thought that giving brief, non-opinionated responses seemed the best way at this point to avoid confrontation.

"Do you *really* see? Because if you do, you'd understand that my being trapped in this place means that I can't get on with my life—*unless* you can help me with a 'prison break'." Her bedroom eyes were gone and in their place he saw the calm and methodical gaze of a seasoned hostage negotiator.

"Well, in actuality I *was* thinking of breaking you out of here, very shortly." Thierry would use her analogy to conveniently reveal his professional intentions. "I think I can cure you," he declared, "but to do so I will have to move you from this hospital to mine, in Brussels."

Her first reaction was visibly irritated, followed by an abrupt softening in the lines of her utterly ravishing face as she appeared to be weighing the positives and the negatives of a change in her medical surroundings. Or was he actually seeing the outward evidence of an internal identity conflict?

"But how can you 'cure' someone who isn't ill?"

Suddenly, the intonation of her voice had changed, once again, from alto to subtlety soprano; and her comportment had perceptibly transformed from arrogantly cocksure to soft and vulnerable. Who was trying to emerge out of the confusion of this woman's subconscious?

"I realize this is difficult for you to comprehend since you don't feel physically sick, but my theory is that you have…" (he paused, picking his words carefully) "...a 'disorder' stemming from over-production of a brain peptide called mnemosyne. Abnormal regulation of this peptide often leads to personality…*disturbances*."

Next, he braced himself for a testy reaction to his side-step: a fancy-footwork of medical double-speak intended to dance around her true diagnosis of 'crazy'. So was he waltzing with Dr. Jekyll, who would mildly follow Thierry's lead; or doing the jitterbug with an ill-tempered and fast-footed Mr. Hyde for a partner? In a second or two, he would know.

CHAPTER EIGHT

"What, exactly, do you mean by 'disturbances'?" Dr. Jekyll asked, as mild as a kitten.

The innocent way she gazed at him was actually entirely devoid of the feline predatory challenge from just a moment before, leading him to conclude without a doubt that someone other than Susanne was now speaking. "Mixing up one's identity with those of others," he clarified patiently, while at the same time writing some notes on his pad describing the truly fascinating transformation.

"You are obviously trying to be sensitive to my feelings, which clearly means that you've mistaken me for the fragile type," Mr. Hyde stated harshly. Abruptly, the tigress was back with a roar, in an interesting but disconcerting 'see-saw' of emotional extremes. "You promised the truth, so why don't you just put it out there, Professor. You're talking about multiple personality disorder—correct?"

"Yes, although the official diagnostic term is dissociative identity disorder; and I believe you have a variant called CIC." He didn't offer the unabbreviated name, since the words 'confabulatory', 'identity' and 'confusion' had negative connotations that could derail the figurative train of progress that he had made so far.

At the moment, she seemed thankfully uninterested in spelling out a definition of CIC, focusing instead on the DID label. "You're chatting with the only person that *I'm* aware of, residing in this delicious body."

Although this type of grandiose and exaggerated self-admiration was normally seen in patients with narcissistic personality disorder, he was not surprised at all to observe this behavior in his newest patient with DID. Why? Because it was extremely common for individuals with one personality disorder to exhibit character traits drawn from the other nine or ten sub-types in a mix-and-match fashion, since the line dividing one from the other was indistinct rather than sharply defined. "A 'party of one' hardly qualifies me as the world's next Sybil!" she added.

She was of course referring to the most famous psychiatric patient with multiple personality disorder: Shirley Ardell Mason, whose case was documented under the fictitious name of Sybil Isabel Dorsett to protect Mason's true identity and privacy. "There are variations of this syndrome that don't meet the usual diagnostic criteria, and you might be someone like that. In order to confirm this hypothesis though, I would have to run some tests and examine you thoroughly in intensive and ongoing psychotherapy…in Brussels."

"Why not here?"

Now was not the time to provide the necessary informed consent for participation in his first-in-human trial of a promising mnemosyne brain-receptor blocking agent that he had mentioned to Gennie just moments before. Rather than tell her 'I might have a medication available to help you that only has the letters and numbers *AXP34125* for a

81

name so far, but it can only be administered in a controlled research setting in my facility,' he decided to take an off-handed and humorously dismissive approach in order to avoid scaring her off. "Because you asked for a file baked into a cake smuggled into your prison-cell, and that's exactly what I brought."

She laughed while twirling a strand of auburn hair in her fingers in the most provocative way imaginable, looking off over his shoulder as she seemed to be contemplating the merits of an escape. "Alright, I'll come," she finally declared, as if she had any choice in the matter, "but only if I get special treatment from you personally, on a daily basis."

This was a dangerous game to play, but he would have to ante-up to keep her engaged. "That's a guarantee. I promise you'll be my one and only priority."

"I'll hold you to it." She folded her arms across her chest and under her breasts, which had the effect of bolstering her cleavage upward into the open 'V' of her chemise. He rolled his eyes internally at this blatant sexual machination that she mistakenly viewed as her ace in the hole. "Now it's my turn to ask a few questions."

"Go right ahead." It was only fair, since she had answered a handful of his with minimal or no resistance.

"Do you like women, or men, or both?"

He had to admit that he hadn't expected this unfiltered line of questioning, right out of the starting box. "I…"

"Come now. It's a simple question, and you promised the truth."

"Fair enough." He put on his best poker-face, playing his cards just as she was playing hers. "Women," he replied nonchalantly, crossing his own arms on his chest in mimicking defense.

"Are you seeing someone?" She uncrossed her arms and placed them on the table, leaning on her elbows with her face cupped in both hands. The tight-angled, narrow positioning of her limbs pressed against the outside-border of both breasts caused them to jut forward, drawing even more attention to her generous décolletage which was literally squeezed to overflowing between the equivalent of two enabling vices, in a cartoon-like pose that was honestly laughable. Despite his professional contact with countless of patients with personality disorders over the years, Thierry had never encountered this type of extreme and exaggerated promiscuity in any other clinical case or research subject to-date. Again, Gennie's description of Susanne was right on target.

"Not at the moment." He decided to keep his answers brief which he hoped would semi-discourage her boldness.

"Describe your fantasy woman."

He wasn't at all prepared for the 'long essay' and already had plans to turn the test in early without completing that part. "How do you mean?" he stalled.

She rolled her eyes in feigned exasperation, obviously enjoying his discomfiture. "What turns you on, Doctor? *Surely* you remember your female

83

anatomy and reproductive biology from medical school!? I'm certain you scored an A+ in both classes."

She actually seemed to expect him to start listing off this-or-that body part along with explicit commentary on his carnal preferences, which was a notion that left him flabbergasted. "I can see I'll need to lead you by the hand on this one," she interjected into the silence of his speechlessness, "so how about we start with the tamest physical feature imaginable: hair color."

She must have noticed his relieved expression, which gave her the opportunity to rub his face in the upcoming line of questioning that she was already planning with the comment: "Don't worry, we'll get to more exciting physical attributes in a moment." She highlighting her meaning by a quick glance downward at her own protruding Double-D's which caused him to roll his eyes internally.

"Are you partial to blondes, redheads or brunettes?" she went on to ask.

"I'd have to say brunettes." He bargained that it would work to his advantage to choose *her* color as a self-serving white-lie.

"Like me?"

"Oh yes; you could *definitely* say that."

His artificially-enthusiastic response elicited an emboldened triumph in her eyes, which meant that her 'spin-the-bottle'-style questioning would soon reach new evocative heights. Sensing that the game was about to change, he decided to scramble out of the hot-seat to safety. "I think the timer's run out on this round of 'Jeopardy', though," he stated—his

84

doctor's authority stepping in to orchestrate a major re-direct.

She pouted and grumbled: "Just when it was getting interesting."

"Don't worry, Susanne…" (he winked for effect) "…we'll have *plenty* of time to thoroughly explore my most intimate 'preferences', when you arrive in Belgium." She opened her mouth to say something; but he rushed ahead to prevent whatever commentary she intended. "I have an idea," he said quickly. "How about you tell me your entire story starting from the very beginning?"

Her brooding dissatisfaction turned to elation in the blink of an eye. "Oh, yes!" she blurted out.

Just as Thierry had hoped, the narcissist-portion of Susanne's multi-faceted personality disorder couldn't resist the prospect of talking about herself for hours on end to a captive audience. He would play, then, on her hunger for attention and the accolades that she expected to glean from the tale-telling. "We can start from the moment of your arrival," he suggested, "and you can pick the most exciting moments from your decade-long adventure in the late 1800's to tell me about."

She nearly beamed with self-aggrandizement. "That sounds lovely! There's *so* much to tell…about me, and all the others."

His thoughts froze. 'All the *others*'? What in the world did she mean by *that*? Had she inadvertently let it slip that multiple personalities coexisted in her disturbed mind? She must have noticed the stunned look on his face, and laughed.

85

"No, Professor—you haven't hit the multiple-personality jackpot. I'm referring to Elle, and Edmond, and Martial—you know, my *relatives*." But then she looked down, her expression pensive and abruptly disquieted. "But before we start, I should tell you that every so often, I *can* imagine, quite vividly, what's going on in certain people's heads."

"Are you saying you can read minds?" This kind of fantastical thinking was more consistent with schizophrenia than DID, although the entity that he called CIC could in some ways be considered an 'overlap' syndrome incorporating both disorders, just as he had pointed out to Gennie earlier that day.

"Not really. It's more like viewing an event that happened to them before, like a video-clip of the experience—but only if we're related. It must be some kind of a psychic interaction between our similar genes or something." Susanne had inadvertently gotten it 'right'—hitting the nail squarely on the head by invoking the power of familial DNA located deep within her psyche as the cause of her unique 'talent'. "I wouldn't pretend to understand the mechanism plus I'm really not interested at all in how it works—I just know that it does…but unpredictably." She sighed dramatically. "It's a curse as well as a blessing."

He acknowledged her delusional reasoning with a knowing nod, since her claim to have paranormal talents specifically related to bygone recollections was yet *another* affirmation that she was likely inflicted with the psychiatric malady in question. "I can well imagine that seeing those images might be upsetting to you."

"To the contrary. It's loads of fun to 'color in' my story with theirs. You'll see!"

He had no doubt he would—and very shortly. *Now* was the time, he concluded; so he pulled out a mini-digital recorder from his briefcase nonchalantly and asked: "Do you mind if I record this?"

"Not at all," she replied vivaciously. "Let's make an audiobook!"

Thierry smiled at her attempt at comic relief and at his own perfect timing. Quite pleased with himself, he placed the recorder on the table-corner between them, and pressed the 'on' button. "Shall we get started, then?" His tone had changed from playful and amicably-coercive to all-business. "At the beginning, please."

PART TWO
*loosely based on the previously released
and now out-of-print novel*
THE VALE OF YEARS

*When to the sessions of sweet silent
thought
I summon up **REMEMBRANCE OF THINGS
PAST**,
I sigh the lack of many a thing I sought,
And with old woes new wail my dear time's
waste*

William Shakespeare
Sonnet 30

CHAPTER NINE

"I'll say right off the bat that Dr. John Noland was right about everything...except for one tiny detail. Never mind that it was the one that really mattered."

She paused for a few seconds to let this theatrical opening sink in, and then kept on going. "Sure, he was right about the science of chronotonin; because just as he had hypothesized, my physically-identical great-great-great grandmother's double gene-mutation successfully opened the connection between two *Time-Shells*. He also correctly predicted that my single chronotonin mutation would create a protective halo around me, ensuring that I would make it safely to the past unhurt should I ever 'unexpectedly' find myself being sucked into a *Virtual-Hole*. Little did he know that I would intentionally go it alone—executing a stunning 'hijack' of Nicole's *Virtual-Hole* by pushing her out of the way and passing through it all by 'my lonesome'. Despite the surprise substitution, I'm sure John was ecstatic; because as I'm sure you've gathered, he was head-over-heels in love with her." She rolled her eyes dramatically.

Thierry nodded his understanding, keeping up so far with the outlandish narration, which Susanne continued. "He was also right about the *Time-Tunnel* opening to nineteenth-century France with *The Origin of the World* stationed on both ends of the portal; *and* he was spot-on when he pin-pointed the time of arrival, which occurred exactly as he theorized at precisely 2:09 AM on June sixteenth—because time *does* run in perfect parallel between synchronized *Time-Shells*, in exact accordance with his theory of *Chronologic Symmetry*. His *Rule of Recollection* also held true, because I discovered later that I really *had* landed, as planned, in Nicole's 'native' *Time-Shell*: the one where she and René Caillebotte had been doing the 'dirty deed' together when they were dragged against their will by the painting into the future."

Her manic story-telling had been picking up speed down a few roads at once. "What was the 'tiny detail' that Dr. Noland was wrong about, then?" Thierry asked, attempting to redirect her tangent and clear up his confusion—both at once.

"It was the *year* of my entry-point. I was supposed to land in 1876, but I arrived instead exactly ten years later: in 1886...to the second. Thank God that major miscalculation didn't end up killing the 'someone' that I had traveled so far to save."

"And who, may I ask, was that?"

"Nicole's son and my great-great grandfather: Edmond Bruante. But don't get the wrong idea—my decision to take her place was hardly altruistic. I wanted to save *myself*, too." He raised his eyebrows in response, while she continued. "Come now; *surely* you see! Nicole's translocation into the future put *all* of Edmond's descendants at risk. If the nine-year old in question had died that day on Sunday the eighteenth of June in 1876 because Nicole wasn't there to save him—trampled to death instead of his mother, then all of his future ancestors, including myself, would never have been born.

"This was the main reason we decided to send Nicole back two days in advance of the accident, armed with her own obituary tucked away in a pocket in case some kind of time-traveler's amnesia caused her to carry-through with a heroic do-over of her motherly self-sacrifice. This creative solution was conceived, as you may well guess, in sheer panic by our totally love-struck scientific 'consultant', who couldn't bear the thought of Nicole dying—as she had in her dream-premonition, or memory...or *whatever* it represented in John's endless theorizing. I figured that I could prevent the accident as well as *she* could but without killing myself in the process; but the unexpected substitution must have acted like a wrench being tossed into the 'Noland virtual time-machine', sending me to the wrong year in Nicole's native *Time-Shell*. So, I'll grudgingly take a small part of the credit for the major blunder."

"*You* were the wrench?"

"Of course. I'm no scientist; but if you ask me, John's fancy-formula just didn't add up when, at the last minute, I became the 'x' substituted for Nicole's 'y' leading to a mathematical outcome that was a full decade off. Add to this the unequal conditions surrounding the *Time-Transfers*: one compared to the other..."

"Meaning?"

"I'll put it bluntly. Nicole and her partner were having drug-enhanced sex on a cot in the corner of her attic room in 1876 when the *Virtual-Hole* opened up in the painting hanging at the foot of her bed, more-or-less as a direct response to Nicole's altered-state combined with her physical ecstasy. Contrast *these* circumstances to the asexual, fully clothed and *totally* contrived situation that night in *Musée d'Orsay*, in 2011. Honestly, it was a miracle the *Time-Tunnel* didn't pull apart altogether given the less-than-identical scenarios, especially when the intended lead-lady was suddenly replaced with an unrehearsed 'understudy' at the last, critical moment of opening night."

The confabulation was complex and surprisingly well-formulated. "My best layman's guess," she continued intensely, "is that the straight-lined *Time-Tunnel* attachment between our two *Time-Shells* pivoted abruptly forward on the 'far-side' of the connection due to the complicating factors I just described, with Nicole's native *Time-Shell* stuck on the far-end, like a marshmallow on a stick. I believe that Nicole's *Shell-of-Origination*, or 'native' *Time-Shell*: the marshmallow, hurtled like a sling-shot forward in time, screeching to a halt a decade later, displaced from 1876 to 1886 in the blink of an eye. I don't think that same displacement would have happened, if Nicole had ultimately gone through instead of me; but who knows…and who cares, really? Because it all worked out in the end, at least for a while…just short of ten years, to be exact."

"So you displaced Nicole that night in the museum after she opened the portal and got sucked into the *Virtual-Hole*…" Thierry offered, knowing full-well that this was the story she had offered her medical team.

"...just as I had planned," she finished. "I lost consciousness but then woke up lying face-down on a wooden plank floor, disoriented and slightly injured, having only sustained some minor cuts, scrapes and bruises. I eventually recognized that I had arrived in some kind of storeroom—large enough, fortunately, that when I had been ejected out of *The Origin of the World* I hadn't crashed into the opposite wall. The open-legged masterpiece was leaning against the wall—one of only several positioned like this. The remaining seventy or eighty were stacked in piles—all of them *Common-Objects* that thankfully I would not be able to 'activate' and open up into *Time-Tunnels* because I only had one rather than two sex-linked chronotonin gene mutations."

As she rambled on with pressured excitement, Thierry was amazed by her consistency. Her delusion was incredibly intricate and intellectually sophisticated. "I realized almost immediately that this must be the 'secret room' underneath the stairs at Gustave Caillebotte's country estate: *Petit Gennevilliers*, where his hidden collection of erotic masterpieces had been stashed for more than a century, before being discovered during major renovations of the Impressionist-era mansion initiated by my own relatives in 2011."

"Your great-grandmother was a Caillebotte...correct?"

"Yes: Genevieve. She was Martial's daughter. It was actually this knowledge of my own family history that helped me to identify the 'where' of my time-traveler's landing followed quickly by the 'when'."

"The 'when' being 1886?"

"Approximately, by my calculations. I knew right away that if I was standing in a secret storeroom at *Petit-Gennevilliers* surrounded by a cache of erotic paintings that included about a dozen-or-so Courbets, sold to the house's owner: Gustave Caillebotte (my great-great-great uncle) by Nicole Bruante (my great-great-great grandmother), immediately before her displacement to the future, that it couldn't *possibly* be any earlier than 1881."

"Why?"

"Because this was the year Gustave used his portion of the family inheritance to buy the property located on the banks of the Seine near Argenteuil. He lived there part time at first, until eventually taking up permanent residence in 1888, focusing most of his attention on landscaping the sprawling grounds as his main hobby. I found out soon enough that I had in fact arrived *exactly* ten years, to the milli-second, later than planned—in the early morning hours of the sixteenth of June, in 1886."

"Fascinating," Thierry commented sincerely. This was quite a story. "So, what did you do next?"

"I ventured out, of course…through a half-door into a dark hallway that skirted around a staircase heading up to the first of several upper-floors. Everything was quiet, which I took to mean that despite my noisy arrival, the household was still asleep—which was fortunate, to say the least, because I would find it a little bit difficult to explain how I had gained entry to a private residence in the dead of night. I tiptoed to the front door and stole quietly out, into a well-kept front garden, leading to my conclusion that it must be closer to 1888 than 1881 since my great-great-great uncle's landscaping hobby had taken on a life of its own as a hobby by the time that he was residing full time at *Petit Gennevilliers*. In other words, the fastidious and organized plantings gave the later-rather-than-earlier 'date' away.

"I decided that it would be best to conceal myself for the rest of the night and then emerge the next morning—posing as a relative who had just returned from a long journey, which would be a perfectly honest representation of my identity and situation. I didn't know yet at that point whether I would claim to be the 'missing' Nicole Bruante herself, who had disappeared mysteriously a decade earlier; or a cousin from the distant south, who just happened to look like the other woman's identical twin, even down to the smallest freckle…except for one." She smiled deviously and then asked: "Aren't you curious?"

Honestly, he was afraid to inquire but duty called. "Do you have a birthmark or something, that Nicole doesn't have?"

"It's the other way around. It was located on her uppermost inner right thigh, in a very delicate location, if you catch my drift. I can show you where, right here and now, if you want." She giggled deviously at the tongue-in-cheek offer, but didn't wait for his answer. "I don't have one, but Nicole does. Its absence, when eventually discovered, ultimately clued Elle in to my little white lie about being her daughter; and the revelation that I *wasn't* led to nothing but trouble for me. But that part doesn't happen until later so you'll just have to wait to hear all about it."

He tried to limit eye-contact so as not to distract her with too much personal interaction, which he hoped would encourage her to stay on-task. "Go on then," he said without meeting her gaze, but concentrating instead on the notepad in front of him and some scribbled nonsensical comments at the top. After all, this was all being recorded, so there was really no point to taking comprehensive notes, in the moment. "I'm listening."

"I spied a not-so-distant tree," she continued, "positioned 'just-so' on the inside of the gated property-line, not even three yards from a stone wall quite near to the driveway of packed-dirt. I made my way to the far side, wedging myself between the trunk at my head and some field-stones at my feet, in such a way that even after sunrise my body would be concealed by a screen of wood and rock to anyone that happened to look my way. I cradled the arch of my shoulders into the curve of a giant root and curled myself into a living blanket of tall grass, and fell asleep.

"I wasn't used to 'roughing' it but due to what I'll refer to as 'time-traveler's lag' (which by the way is *much* worse than jet-lag), I slept soundly enough. I woke up shivering in the morning air since I was scantily clothed. You see, Thierry, I was wearing a *very* sexy dress that showed *beaucoup* skin," she explained, rubbing the tip of her index finger provocatively on her bare forearm to illustrate the concept, "which ended up being the perfect formula for seductive-success when used on the security guard at the museum—just a few hours, or centuries, before...*you* pick the time-perspective."

She tilted her head and analyzed his expression, hoping for a reaction to the concept of a sparsely-clothed Susanne using her nudity to snare the guard. "If this upsets you, there's no need for it because I didn't sleep with him; but I'll come clean." She actually *winked*. "I *was* compelled to use that kind of extreme measure on a *different* security guard, just a week or so before. It was only sex, though...and meant nothing. It would be *very* different with us."

Now was not the time to discourage her 'romantic' aspirations, however insincere. "Oh, I'm sure," he conceded mildly. "But you were just about to tell me about day two. What happened next?"

"Aren't we impatient!"

He certainly was; because the story, and the pathology behind it, was a full-fledged page-turner.

CHAPTER TEN

"So as I was saying: there I stood on the edge of my family's nineteenth century country estate, brushing off the straw from my shivering body, and combing the wild disarray out of my hair with my fingers. A nebulous plan had started to form in my mind that I would have to 'tweak' depending on 'who' I ran into first...and 'when', exactly, I had landed."

"By 'when' I assume you mean the year?"

"Not exactly. I was more concerned about the specific *Time-Shell* I had landed in, rather than the year itself. You see, if I had been flung like a slingshot ten years fast-forward into the *same Time-Shell* that Nicole and René had exited against their wills in 1876—the *same 'Shell'* that John Noland liked to refer to as Nicole's 'native' one—then those two individuals were simply 'missing' and I would be free to safely pose as the *actual* Nicole. However, if I found myself in any *other 'Shell'*, Nicole and René were 'history'—dead and buried a decade earlier. It wouldn't do, in that case, for me to play imposter to a corpse. Get it?"

"Got it."

"It's interesting, though, to think about the *historical* repercussions of Nicole and René's 'time-transfer', in a chronologic sense." It was fascinating that Susanne would actually wax poetic on the foundation of a complete fabrication. "My 'take' was—*and* is—that it didn't really matter whether the pair of them were rendered 'absent' due to

98

premature death or untimely time-transfer, because the end result is the same. 'Gone' is 'gone'…with their double-subtraction, as it were, occurring in *Shell*-after-*Shell*-after-*Shell*—a repetitive event guaranteeing the preservation of past events leading to a future that would not be altered by deviation; because there *was* no deviation. They were both missing, irrespective of the mechanism."

"It sounds perfectly logical to me." And it did, in a crazy way.

"Anyway, my identity relied on determining if I had been transferred to Nicole's native *Time-Shell*; and Elle's immediate reaction when she saw me walking up the driveway told me, without question, that I had."

Of all the unlikely happenstances, this seemed nothing less than extraordinarily dubious. "Do you mean to tell me that *Elle*: Nicole's mother and your great-great-great-great grandmother, was the first person you encountered on Gustave Caillebotte's property?"

"Indeed. She was living there, part-time…under an assumed identity."

"Who was she pretending to be?"

"Charlotte Berthier: a mystery live-in mistress well documented in histories detailing the life of Gustave Caillebotte. Her name was purported to be entirely contrived—but as it turns out, it was a partially-true personal designation. You see, Noëlle Bruante's maiden name just happened to be 'Berthier', and her middle name 'Charlotte'. The Berthier family lived in a town called Louveciennes, located directly west of Paris a full day's carriage ride away." She shook her head, as if the coincidence was just as hard for her to believe as it was for Thierry. "Who in the world would have guessed that one of my relatives was actually the 'beard' intended to protect the secretly-gay artist's masculine reputation, rather than Anne Marie Hagan? *No-one*, unless they happened to be a snooping time-traveler like myself."

Thierry's knowledge of the Impressionist era's colorful artistic personalities could be measured in a thimble; so he would need further clarification. "Who was this 'Anne Marie Hagan' that you just mentioned?"

"A prostitute that Gustave had taken in years before, and the person considered by most experts to be the most likely candidate for the Charlotte Berthier 'alias'. They say that Gustave made her change her name for propriety's sake. She inherited Caillebotte's entire estate and fortune after he died."

"Was she actually a prostitute?"

"Oh, yes; and she was, in fact, convinced to change her name...but *not* by Gustave, contrary to legend. You see, Martial: Gustave's brother, became infatuated with her after he saw her posing naked for one of only two paintings by Caillebotte depicting the unclothed female body, titled *Nude on a Couch*. Gustave started the piece in 1876 but didn't finish it until years later—in 1880, when it was finally displayed. Martial's lust for his brother's 'beard' and nude model culminated in a proposal of marriage, but with the requirement that she call herself 'Marie Minoret' to disguise her true identity."

She looked across the table and met his eyes, almost defiantly. "*Nude on a Couch* was a provocative-enough painting; but Gustave's *other* oil-on-canvas female nude was called *Naked Woman Lying on a Couch*. It drew significant erotic attention many years earlier because Caillebotte used a *much* more stunning garmentless model: a woman whose body and mine are as near identical as one can get."

"Nicole Bruante?"

"The very same. She posed for it in 1873 when she was about twenty-five years old, gaining the attention of two very randy Caillebotte brothers—*both* of them being sibling-roommates with Gustave at the time—in the doing. René's affections were quiet, polite and reserved—eventually winning Nicole over. Martial, in contrast, was like a bull in a China shop; so quite understandably, Nicole wouldn't give him the time of day. That's why, when *I* came onto the scene pretending to be Nicole...well, let's just say that Martial was like putty in my hands."

"But he was married!"

"Since when did that ever stop a Frenchman?"

He nodded his acknowledgment of that cliché and then asked: "So, why was Elle living part-time with Gustave as a 'beard' at *Petit Gennevilliers*?"

"To protect her son, Edmond Bruante: Gustave's bisexual lover."

Now *this* revelation took the concept of 'unbelievable' to new heights. "Alright," Thierry said in a convinced tone of voice while at the same time thinking that Susanne's multifaceted

101

constellation of mental illnesses had not only generated an impressively intricate fiction but had also caused her to meander off track once again, in typical ADD fashion. "But let's get back to your story," he said, refocusing her. "You emerged from behind the tree and stone gate; walked down the dirt carriage-path leading to the front entrance to *Petit Gennevilliers*; and met up with Nicole's mother?"

"Yes. She was watering some flowers on the front porch. She looked up when she saw me and her jaw dropped in disbelief when she 'recognized' her missing daughter."

"I can well imagine, if 'you' had disappeared a decade earlier."

"Or died in a carriage accident while in the process of saving Edmond. Recall that I didn't know at that moment whether or not I had arrived in Nicole's native *Time-Shell*. It's true though that the first words that came out of her mouth gave up my 'timely' location."

"Which were?"

"Something amounting to 'where have you been?' rather than 'how could this be possible, since you died years ago?' There were too many tears interspersed between the hugs and kisses for me to make it out clearly, except that she clearly didn't react like she was greeting the ghost of her daughter."

"So you ran with it?"

"Of course I did! From that moment forward, I became her long-lost Nicole, having slipped away to the south of France ten years previously with the love of my life: René Caillebotte. What a shame he died tragically while on an ocean journey, traveling alone from Marseille to Marrakesh—or so I lied. Unfortunately, they never recovered the body...I fibbed." She grinned deceitfully at the fabrication, which was unsettling in its blunt disregard for the man's true fate: whether it was death by way of cardiac arrhythmia as history theorized, or instead by the unlikely crushing-force inside a delusional *Time-Tunnel*. Thierry found himself shivering in reaction to her staggering theoretical insensitivity.

"What happened next?"

"Plenty; but how much or how little do you want to hear? Ten years is a long time, Thierry."

She had a point. At this rate, it would take her a few weeks to tell her complete 'tale'; and truth-be-told, the specific details of her confabulation were less important than the general concepts at this point. "How about you tell me your story with a 'character-specific' focus?" he suggested. This stream-lined approach would save time, while giving Thierry crucial insight into Susanne's psychological pathology along with a sampling of her ancestral memories. These genetic recollections could be more thoroughly explored, eventually, by way of deep-dive hypnosis after Susanne's transfer to Brussels.

She gazed at him quizzically. "What do you mean?"

"As you say, describing a full decade of experiences chronologically isn't very expedient; so why not select a handful of relatives and your interactions with them, to tell me about? I just need a representative taste of your adventures, rather than the entire meal...right now." She nodded comprehension, so he added: "How about starting with Elle? After all, she was the first person with whom you interacted in your displaced environment."

"*And* the last."

"So you can begin *and* end with her. In between, you can choose anyone else you deem as the most relevant to your story—maybe Edmond, and Gustave..."

"And Martial...we can't leave out Martial. He was pivotal to my plan."

"Of course. It's up to you." He said this because he knew that she needed to think she maintained control.

"Okay...*Elle*, then." She said the name like she was spitting it, accompanied by a mixed expression of loathing, condescension, and brooding. "You know of course that 'Elle', in French, means 'she', or 'her'," Susanne said. "Noëlle would often explain that the shortened name had been wittily-conceived by her father when she was five or six years old; and the clever (or should I say instead: stupid) nickname stuck. 'She'—or should I say 'Elle'..." (Susanne rolled her eyes and smirked as she pointed out the double-meaning) "...was constantly quoting him, word-for-word; so many times that it became nothing less than nauseating to hear. 'Noëlle minus the '*No*',' Susanne quipped in a voice a full octave lower than her own, intended no-doubt as a comical imitation of her male-relative, 'turns my pretty little daughter into a feminine pronoun.'"

104

An unmistakably wistful look flickered briefly on Susanne's face, which Thierry interpreted as the unintentional emergence of true sentiment stemming from what he guessed might be an actual DNA-encoded aural memory, belonging either to her great-great-great-great grandmother or her great-great-great-great-great grandfather...*or*, potentially *both*. In other words, she was literally *hearing* the spoken words in her stored genetic recollection-bank.

"Anyway, we'll skip over the maudlin details of our initial mother-'would-be'-daughter reunion, which I already described in any case as nothing less than blubbering, at least where one of the two involved parties was concerned. You're probably more interested anyway in the nitty-gritty of how I managed to supplant Elle in Gustave's household."

"You actually took her place?"

"Yep. It was really quite easy, to be honest; but I'll admit there were a few crucial factors working to my advantage. Shall I list them?"

CHAPTER ELEVEN

Thierry nodded—fully prepared for some nonsensical 'plot-twists' in Susanne's admittedly entertaining narrative, which simply couldn't be taken at face-value. Of course Susanne's concocted trip to the past was a total fabrication: a mélange of distorted memories attributed to a patchwork of relatives, conceived by a person harboring a complex constellation of mental illnesses. He expected nothing less than a completely dubious and farfetched storyline, which he would need to view as an example of neuropsychiatric pathology rather than a true description, obviously, of the woman's time-travel experiences. It would be nothing less than fascinating, though, to examine her fairytale with his medical magnifying-glass.

"Let's start first with appearances. You are aware, I presume, that Nicole and I look identical?"

"Yes. Dr. Lefebvre mentioned it."

"Well, the same could be said of mother and daughter. I'm not exaggerating when I say that Nicole and Elle could have passed for identical twins; which means that for the second time in less than a month, I found myself staring at a mirror image in that garden when I happened upon Noëlle Bruante."

Susanne was proposing, of course, that if 'a' equals 'b' and 'b' equals 'c', then 'a' by default *also* equals 'c': a premise that was mathematically sound but could rarely be applied to physical features in humans unless paternal twins were involved. Of course it was not unheard of in families for a child to share some or even *most* features with a parent; but an exact replica? Susanne's contention that mother, daughter, and great-great-great-(great) granddaughter were perfectly interchangeable was 'exhibit A' in Thierry's argument that Susanne's far-fetched story was the pure product of a delusional mind piecing together confused and exaggerated fragments of ancestral memories. "So, are you saying that because you looked exactly like Elle, that you were able to replace her at *Petit Gennevilliers?*"

"That was one reason. Another was that Elle and I were closer in age than you'd think. You see, she birthed Nicole when she was only 14 years old. This means that she was barely into her forties when Nicole disappeared in 1876; and only fifty-odd-years old or so when I made my appearance in 1886."

"But you were only in your thirties when you made the time-transfer to the nineteenth century!" (…or so this woman who looked to be in her early twenties claimed).

"True; but the gene for youthful appearances runs strong in the Bruante blood-line. Elle could have *easily* passed for someone in her early thirties when I met her that day—no problem at all; just as *I* can pass for twenty-something, even though I'm well into my forties now." Here was 'exhibit B', presented almost in direct response to his own skeptical thoughts from just a few seconds before— served as if on a silver platter by 'opposing counsel' labeled unabashedly with the words 'utterly unlikely' for judge and jury both to examine. Sure, there were some people who looked younger than their actual age; but two decades? This was simply too much.

"So," she continued with a conceited smile, "here was a woman who looked just like me, not only in appearance but in age. Add to this the fact that she didn't really *want* to be there under an assumed identity anyway, and you've got the magic formula for a quiet and secret exchange."

"Are you saying that no one knew about the 'switch'?"

"Gustave and Edmond knew, of course; and eventually Martial too, since making him believe at first that I was the 'real' Nicole: a woman he had lusted after years before, was an essential part of my evolving plan to use seduction to make him an unwitting accomplice to his own brother's pre-arranged death."

Her nonchalance in discussing the ultimate act of foul-play was jarring. Gennie was 'dead-on' in her assertion that Susanne had no sense of right or wrong whatsoever, pegging her as a sociopath as clearly as if she was the very definition in a textbook describing personality disorders. "But they were the only three," she went on. "Even Pierre Renoir: the famous painter—a married man who spent an inordinate amount of time at *Petit Gennevilliers* supposedly visiting with his artsy 'buddy' Gustave but who was really coming over to get some sugar 'on the side'—had no clue about my true 'assumed' identity as anyone other than Noëlle 'Charlotte Berthier' Bruante. Not that he ever did much talking during his quickies in the dark with *either* Charlotte, anyway; so the truth remained buried in the murky silence of night-blindness."

Thierry nodded, perhaps a bit unconvincingly, but Susanne didn't seem to notice. "Were there any issues with your mother-and-daughter exchange?" he asked quickly, as a distraction to cover up his disbelief.

"Not at all. In fact, I'd say the substitution was seamless, allowing the good *grandmère* Berthier-Bruante to go back to her widow's residence in the city full-time and resume a close-to-normal life, while still coming and going at the country estate now and again to visit her daughter and grandson—carefully, mind you, so that no one would see us side-by-side and put two-and-two together."

"She must have been ecstatic to see 'Nicole' after ten years; and as such, I'm sure she tried to rekindle a relationship with 'you'…right?"

"At first. I put her off though, as kindly as possible—giving the excuse that I had to make up for lost time with Edmond; and having his grandmother hanging around and interfering wouldn't help in that arena."

"Did she understand that?"

"Sure. She wanted me to re-familiarize myself with my son—you know, get to know him. She was big-hearted, that way."

"Which leads to the obvious question…which is: how did you explain why Nicole—or should I say 'you'—never tried to contact her, *or* your little boy, over the span of a full decade?"

"I told her that I was head-over-heals in love with René, and that the emotion caused me to throw my common-sense completely out the window. That kind of thing happens, you know."

"But, to the point of totally abandoning her son?"

"That was easy. I told her I had been pregnant with René's baby and that the pregnancy consumed my full attention. Since I knew Edmond was in good hands with his grandmother, it was easy to leave my old life behind and concentrate on my new one conveniently located in Louveciennes: Elle's very-own pre-marital home-town." She feigned a grief-stricken countenance. "Unfortunately, the pregnancy ended in a miscarriage. This led to a full-blown nervous breakdown which made me useless to anyone, for years."

"I guess that makes sense." It did, in a way…to the point of being incredibly clever, in fact.

"Anyway, there's not much more to tell about Elle for the next few years of my residence in the nineteenth century…until she barged in on me with Martial during an intimate moment one day." Thierry raised his eyebrows. "That's right; and from her fortuitously-placed vantage-point on the abruptly opened door-threshold, she had a full view of my privates 'laid-bare'."

She chuckled at the double-meaning. "You see, my preference, regardless of the century, is *always* for cleanly-shaved—a custom which clearly showed off the absence of Elle's daughter's beauty-mark in-between my legs." She looked across at him slyly. "I referenced it before, located on Nicole's right

110

extreme inner-thigh, but not on mine—so close to the 'lip' of erotic that the tip of someone's tongue could lick them both at once." She slowly ran her *own* tongue over her upper lip, letting it linger there pornographically, by way of illustration.

Thierry replied with a voiceless nod, trying to avoid a prolonged discussion focused on the mental image of Nicole's, *and* Susanne's, blush-provokingly exposed genitalia.

"Needless to say," she barreled on, "the game was up after that; so I had to make up a totally different story to appease my indignant relative. I had to swat off questions like: 'Who are you, really?' and 'What have you done with my daughter?' It went on and on until I finally 'leveled' with her…or so she thought."

"What did you tell her?"

"It's what she told *me* first, that resulted in some quick thinking on my part. She gave me the idea of *really* posing as a 'Berthier' when she herself suggested it."

"How so?"

"She made the off-handed comment that I was a dead-ringer (as were she and Nicole, for that matter) for her deceased great aunt, Vivienne Berthier—which caused me to pounce on my 'true' identity as a member of that family-line."

Susanne was offering the ludicrous *fourth* claim of perfectly-replicated physical appearance, which to Thierry represented nothing more than another example of a confused fragment of memory-imagination. He smiled knowingly to himself as Susanne, oblivious to his skepticism, continued.

"I told her I was one of Vivienne's grand-nieces: the grand-daughter of one of her many brothers. I had correctly banked on the nineteenth-century Catholic practice of having a multitude of children, which rapidly expands a theoretical family tree to literally *hundreds* of members in the span of a few generations. There was no way on earth that Elle could easily track me, without seeking out and questioning a very large number of distant relatives. My lie went off without a hitch. It turns out that great-aunt Vivienne had no less than ten siblings with each of them having close the same number of children and a mind-boggling number of grandchildren...so I was golden."

"What name did you give?"

"You won't believe this; but I gambled on a 'sure thing' and just stayed with the alias."

"Do you mean Charlotte?"

"Of course. I figured that since it was Elle's middle name, it had to run in the family; and with so many Berthier family-members milling around out there, it wouldn't be at all unlikely that a child would have the same given-name as, let's say, a great-great grandmother. Anyway, it made it easier for everyone involved since I had been living under that assumed name for those people looking 'in' from the outside for a full three years anyway."

"Didn't this all look particularly contrived to Elle?"

She shrugged. "Some coincidences are just meant to be, you know—which is exactly what I told her." Talk about far-fetched! This little twist took the cake, for sure. "You have to admit that

112

given my time constraints," Susanne went on, "it was, on the whole, a beautiful piece of fiction. Not only that, but the way the alias had fallen right into my lap was nothing short of incredible."

The look on her face turned decidedly thoughtful. "Thinking more about it, taking the name 'Charlotte Berthier' as my very own was a sure sign that I was really and *truly* meant to be there, belonging in the nineteenth-century instead of the twenty-first—my inevitable and intended destination, all along. Why else would that name surface as an historical identity just begging for me to claim it as my own? In every other *Time-Shell*, Charlotte Berthier was an alias for Edmond's mother: Noëlle Charlotte Berthier Bruante; but in Nicole's 'native' *Time-Shell* where I had landed, *I* had become the fateful stand-in. Pretty crazy, isn't it?"

Crazy was the right term, for sure. "Unbelievable...*truly*," Thierry said, hiding his 'tongue-in-cheek' so she wouldn't notice the sarcasm.

"So in the span of a few seconds, I had no less than brilliantly come up with a perfectly logical accounting of where I had come from and who I really was. Next, I had to do some quick thinking to explain what had happened to the missing-in-action Nicole."

Her lengthy pause, during which she took a leisurely drink of water after pouring it into a glass from a pitcher on the table, meant that she was must be waiting for a prompt. "So what, may I ask, had 'happened' to Nicole?"

"Her story, I'm afraid, ended tragically—just as it had over here with the *real* Nicole, masquerading as me." She drew her index finger across the front of her neck in the universal pantomime for 'dead'. "I had to stick with my previous contention that Elle's daughter had been living near Louveciennes with René Caillebotte, her lover, until after his unfortunate 'boating accident' that took his life. After his death, Nicole, in dire financial straits, of course, went back to her original vocation 'plus', taking a job as a nude model…and *more*, if you catch my drift."

Thierry gave a quick nod to indicate that her 'drift' had been 'caught'. "She posed and fornicated for money," Susanne forged ahead with shocking indelicacy, "at a 'revival' of an Impressionist painting commune in a small town near Louveciennes called Pontoise. The original artistic community has its basis in fact, which I of course knew from being an Impressionist art-history scholar; but *this* one was a total fabrication of my ceaselessly creative mind."

"Care to elaborate?"

"Gladly. You see, there was a band of artists which included Claude Monet and Alfred Sisley, led by Camille Pissarro in the 1860's and located in Louveciennes, that focused exclusively on the landscape venue of painting. That group officially disbanded in 1870 when Pissarro, an open left-wing anarchist, fled to London to escape the right-wing extremism of the Paris Commune government in France. When Pissarro eventually returned, he and his family settled in the village of Pontoise,

114

immediately adjacent to Louveciennes, where he continued to paint the French countryside. He never painted nudes; but claiming that his painting club had regrouped with this very different artistic concentration: namely, the naked female body rather than trees, rocks and hillsides, came to me as a brainstorm since it would provide Elle's nude-model daughter a perfectly logical reason to stay down there."

"Ingenious."

"Indeed.

"And how, may I ask, did you 'meet' Nicole?" Thierry thought he knew what she would say; and sure enough, he was right.

"I was another nude model at the commune-revival, of course; and it was pure coincidence that we happened to be related. It makes sense though; because there were literally *hundreds* of Berthiers living in that region."

"It all adds up…" he said; although thinking to himself: *…in a bizarre, difficult-to-believe, chock-full-of-coincidences kind of way*. "So let me guess—you eliminated the loose-end named Nicole by saying she was killed by one of her artist-clients?"

"Nothing that morbid. I said she contracted a venereal disease from her lucrative erotic sideline…a rip-roaring pelvic infection that got into her bloodstream, causing her to die of sepsis. What a stroke of bad fortune."

"Elle must have been devastated."

"Of course she was; but grief wasn't her dominant emotion—*anger* was…directed at *me*. Not only was she livid that I hadn't told her Nicole was dead, but she was also incensed that I had had the gall to play imposter as I had for so many years. Believe me, it took a while to smooth things over; but even then, to say that it was chilly between us would be an understatement."

"I can well imagine she resented you."

"And more. She held her grudge until she had a chance to get her revenge. But that comes later. In that moment, I did some fast-talking—explaining to Elle that I had befriended Nicole in the execution of our mutual nude 'calling', as we posed for *and* seduced the same cadre of artists...oftentimes together. We were very close...*so* close, in fact, that on her deathbed she pleaded with me to seek out and look after Edmond. I learned all kinds of helpful details about her family in those final hours when I made my promise, which made it easy to step into Nicole's shoes...and watch over Edmond, in the doing. I claimed that I did it all out of love for Nicole—a *noble* deed, if you will."

"So she *bought* that?"

"Not entirely; but just enough to get her off my back. It was really brilliant of me to kill-off Nicole permanently though, mainly because having her out of the picture meant that Elle wouldn't feel compelled to track her down. You would agree that the last thing I needed was a nosy relative snooping around in Louveciennes or Pontoise, searching for her estranged daughter in a wild goose chase ending in my big lie: revealed. *My* goose would have been *really* cooked if Elle had learned in her fruitless travels that my fable about a drowned lover, a tragic miscarriage, the resulting nervous breakdown, two nude models doubling as harlots, and a fabricated painting commune was nothing but cock-and-bull."

"Wow," was all Thierry could manage to say— but this one word *did* seem to sum it all up. In an instant, he felt mentally exhausted from the sheer complexity of her delusion; which is why the knock on the conference room door came at a most opportune time.

He looked at his watch as the door opened, noting that it was later than he thought— high-time for lunch. An orderly brought in a small tray of food, enough for one; placed it on the table in front of Thierry; and lifted his chin in Susanne's direction. "Let's go, Ms. Bruante; you'll be eating lunch as usual with your fellow-patients, in the community dining hall."

"I'd rather stay here with my new friend."

"Sorry, ma'am; that's a 'no-go'." The attendant meant business. "Come with me, right now."

Susanne stood up, grudgingly complying; and left Thierry to his sandwich and some time alone to organize his thoughts— moving to the seat *opposite* Susanne at the table, rather than right next to her, in preparation for an afternoon session that he expected would be as tangled and elaborate as the morning one...or even more.

CHAPTER TWELVE

It was about an hour later when Susanne slipped back into her chair at the table, directly across from him this time as he had expressly designed. "Are you scared to sit next to me, now?" she jeered. "I don't bite, you know."

"I can see you much better this way," he said, while restarting the mini-digital recorder. "Face-to-face, without straining my neck." She looked back at him across the 'void', with a dubious expression on her face. "Seriously," he reacted. "I've got some C-spine issues."

"Whatever," she shrugged. "Edmond is next, if you're still taking notes to supplement the taping," she commented, resuming her story conversationally without skipping a beat. "The first thing you need to know about him, Thierry, is that he had inherited the Bruante inclination for modeling in the 'buff'."

"That's interesting. Wasn't it unusual in those days for a man to pose like that?"

"Not just unusual, but virtually *unheard* of…mainly because painting the nude male body in those days was considered unnatural and obscene. This homophobic viewpoint reflected the ruling prejudice of those times, really." Now her tone of voice was almost scholarly, as if she were a noted sociologist giving a lecture to a classroom of graduate students instead of a seriously ill psychiatric patient baring her delusional and psychotic soul as a prelude to experimental therapy.

Whoever Susanne 'Doe' actually was, formal or self-taught education had definitely sharpened her already-gifted intellect. In other words, she was no dummy.

"Being gay like Gustave, or bisexual like Edmond, was actually much more widespread in the nineteenth century than one would think," her discourse continued. "Outward appearances did not accurately reflect what went on behind closed doors, because propriety ruled that time-period with an iron fist. Believe me, I *know* because I personally lived in that sub-culture for ten years and saw plenty of mixed-gender action involving a plethora of so-called 'deviant' sexual practices, enjoyed privately but simply not 'advertised' publicly. Admitting a preference for the same sex, or both, would have resulted in social isolation or even blatant ostracism back then, especially for public figures such as artists."

"So, Edmond leaned *both* ways?"

"Absolutely. He was the very definition of bisexual: an equal-opportunity lover if I ever saw one. He was the 'real deal' from a sexually-egalitarian standpoint—just as happy in bed with the pretty live-in maid at *Petit Genevilliers* named Isabelle as he was with the estate-owner himself. He eventually married her, you know...after Gustave's untimely passing."

"The maid?"

"Yep. They even had children together, including their oldest son: Marcel Bruante, who was destined to become my great-grandfather." She looked soberly at him from the other side of the

119

table. "You of course wouldn't know because you've never 'time-traveled'; but can you imagine seeing your family-tree actually come to life right before your eyes? It's bizarre—that's for damn sure! As a case in point, I knew full well that the Bruante and Caillebotte bloodlines would eventually be co-mingled with Marcel's arranged marriage to Martial Caillebotte's daughter and heir: Genevieve; but this is someone else's story, not mine—thanks to Elle. She yanked me out of our family history before I could make another decade my own."

Thierry jotted down a few notes mainly related to this woman's impressive knowledge of a very specific family-line, which by all appearances seemed to take the form of first-hand. She *had* to be a Bruante, a Courbet or a Caillebotte; and the story she was telling *had* to be based on ancestral memories. It was high time to refocus her train of thought though, so he asked: "How did Gustave feel about sharing his lover?"

"He accepted the arrangement. It seems he was simply grateful to be 'out of the closet' within the private inner-circle of his own household; and as long as he was 'getting some' behind closed doors, he gave Edmond permission to be heterosexually-promiscuous. View it as the modern-day equivalent of an open relationship. Knowing this background, I'm sure you can see why having Charlotte Berthier as a 'beard' was imperative to preserving Gustave's outward reputation in the face of his secret lifestyle."

"For sure." As in everything she had told him so far, the story was highly believable, even if peppered here and there with elements of the truly 'incredible'. The foundation was based, he felt certain, on the memories of her relatives; while the personal touches were distorted embellishments painted in by her altered psychological state. "How did Edmond and Gustave meet?" he asked, ever-intent on moving the interview along so that they would finish before sundown...because after all, he had an important 'date' to keep at his hotel restaurant, at eight o'clock sharp.

"Through a mutual artist-friend named Francois Salle. He was a little-known painter with only one notable piece of historical consequence, depicting a male model posing nude from the waist up for an auditorium full of medical students. Salle worked laboriously on that painting for five years, beginning in 1883 and completing the masculine focal-point in about six months—*long* before the peripheral details were finished in 1888 prior to its first showing. It was called *The Anatomy Class at the École des Beaux Arts;* and I'll give you one chance to guess the identity of the half-stripped, *and* strapping, guy who posed as the center-piece."

"Edmond Bruante, undoubtedly."

"Bingo. Gustave was in the midst of a casual affair with Francois, who also happened to be gay; and stopped by during one of the modeling-sessions. Gustave's attentions, from that moment onward, were totally fixated on the buffed and *in*-the-buff Edmond. Gustave took him in, and actually painted Edmond's firm, naked *derrière* in an extremely controversial piece called *Man at His Bath*, first shown in 1884. As we discussed already, painting a naked male subject was completely taboo in those days, and nearly gave away Gustave's homosexual tastes. He heeded society's warnings however, and stopped painting masculine nudes after that—cold turkey.

"But by then, Edmond had moved into *Petit Genevilliers* full-time, with his grandmother tagging along as a pretend mistress to the estate's master; with the end result being that Gustave's appetite for that particular brand of 'erotic' was being satisfied in his very own bedroom, eliminating the need for an artistic surrogate. The 'beard' of outward heterosexual appearances was duly passed on to be worn by *me*, of course: Edmond's 'mother' and perfect physical replica of Elle Bruante, when I arrived two years later in 1886."

Thierry would bet his last dollar that Susanne's 'recollection' of stepping into Noëlle Bruante's shoes as another person entirely simply represented a psychotic perversion of Elle's *actual* memories. Thierry's strong suspicion was that Noëlle Bruante, in 'history', had actually taken on the Charlotte Berthier alias not only to protect her grandson's reputation, but also in all likelihood to underhandedly procure the Caillebotte fortune in the process. Elle Bruante was presumably the *true* perpetrator of whatever foul-play transpired at *Petit Genevilliers* during the ten years beginning in 1886, detailed in a most sinister narrative that Thierry had no doubt would unfold quickly during the course of today's afternoon story-telling—based, he was quite sure, on ancestral memories.

Susanne sighed. "Edmond was handsome to a viral extreme, and he knew it. The combination of self-absorbed egocentricity and a particularly dull intellect helped my cause immensely, though. He devoted his full attention to his own sexual enjoyment with Gustave alternating with Isabelle; and because of his pre-occupation with his own carnal pleasures, he didn't have the attention-span or the brains to figure out my *real* intentions for Gustave or his inheritance."

"Which were…?"

"To take the money and run, to coin a phrase…*after* Gustave was dead and buried. Let me map out the lay of the so-called 'inheritance-land' first, though—as seen from history's perspective: outward-looking-in; followed by *my* viewpoint: inward-looking-out. The intriguing thing is that really, the two frames-of-reference correspond with each other, except for some minor details regarding identity."

"I'm listening."

"We've already discussed Charlotte Berthier's historical persona as an alias for Anne Marie Hagan: a low-born prostitute who became Gustave's 'pretend' mistress to cover up his homosexual inclinations. No one knows for sure why she changed her name, although rumor has it that Gustave insisted she do so in order to conceal her previous profession and protect her reputation…*and* his. Gustave left his entire estate and fortune to Charlotte. She was listed as the sole

123

heir in his Will, even though they were never even married. This odd bequeathal was viewed suspiciously by historians since Gustave died suddenly, under circumstances that were vaguely suspect for foul play.

"Whether or not I'm in the picture, it turns out that Charlotte Berthier was *not* an alias for Anne Marie Hagan at all, but for Noëlle Charlotte Berthier Bruante instead. Anne Marie Hagan was in fact a prostitute who lived with Gustave for a while, as I've said; and in a little while I'll expand on the details of how she was actually wooed by Martial Caillebotte, and convinced by her future husband to assume the made-up name of Marie Minoret prior to marrying him. This name-change occurred for the exact-same 'sake of appearances' reason that had been applied to history's explanation of the Anne Marie Hagan-to-Charlotte Berthier name-switch. Are you following me?"

"I think so. What you're saying is that in history, Gustave's first and only 'beard' was a prostitute called Anne Marie Hagan whose name was changed to Charlotte Berthier to protect the painter's reputation; whereas in 'reality', Gustave's 'beard' was romanced away by his brother Martial, who insisted she change her name to Marie Minoret prior to marrying him in order to preserve the artistic *photographer's* reputation. Charlotte Berthier, in actuality, was the pseudonym for Gustave's second and final 'beard': Noëlle Bruante, his gay lover Edmond's grandmother."

"Exactly! You're a fast learner, Professor! So, from a financial perspective, Gustave's fortune had been designated in Charlotte Berthier's behalf, under the agreement that she would represent a pass-through entity for the money to flow right through her, down to her grandson, Edmond Bruante: Gustave's secret romantic partner. This arrangement, as seen from the outside, gave Gustave heterosexual legitimacy, since his fortune was legally and publicly designated to a common-law wife of sorts. It couldn't have been more perfect…in history, that is.

"Now it's time for some ethical speculation. Did Elle *truly* had Edmond's best interest in mind by agreeing to be the temporary custodian for a 'cache' of cash? Maybe, or maybe not. Her plan could have very well been to siphon some of it off for herself; but that's neither here nor there— relevant to every *other Time-Shell*, for sure, but *not* to the one in which I found myself. In Nicole's 'native' *Time-Shell*, Elle fatefully agreed to give me her alias, at a time when she was convinced I was her daughter. She was naively pliable, in the days before learning that I wasn't Nicole at all, but a Berthier-cousin instead. In the moment, I can only assume that she trusted me to function as a diligent inheritance-conduit 'stand-in', perhaps sharing the money with her in some kind of a 'devoted-daughter-rewards-grateful-mother' type of nonverbal contract, before eventually passing it on to Edmond. Blood is thicker than water, she may have conjectured. Well, she was wrong on all counts.

"You see, I wanted the money for myself, sooner rather than later since Gustave seemed to be depleting his cash at an alarming rate attributed to his hobbies: yacht building, stamp collecting, gardening, and collecting paintings. In the end, after I spent what I wanted and passed away peaceful and rich—well, *that's* when my 'son' would get the left-overs and pass it on down the line to all of our future ancestors (including myself) in the twenty-first century. It couldn't be more perfect. I would have my cake in the eighteen-hundreds, and eat it too in the far-distant future where I had come from to begin with…and where I would eventually be born-again into 'family money' and raised in *another* century, when Nicole's native *Time-Shell* advanced ahead."

She pursed her lips, thoughtfully. "The Bruante-Caillebotte 'money trail' would meander, in this fashion, through the decades and centuries, continuing long after my death but paradoxically, well *before* my birth." The look on her face was speculative. "In fact, who's to say we aren't dealing with an endless *loop* of francs and 'Susannes'?"

"Meaning?"

She shrugged. "All it would take is for 'another' Nicole from 'another' *Time-Shell* to repeat the accidental *Time-Transfer*, and voila: I might find my 'future' self 're-living' that Deja-vu-day in 2011 at Musée d'Orsay, traveling back in time myself once again, so that the process would start over from the beginning." A dark shadow passed over her face. "But Elle ruined it all by forcing a 'reset' with my unwelcome displacement. Coming back here short-circuited my plan to become rich as well as infamous. I underestimated her, for sure;

126

and have tossed and turned, lying awake at night…ever since she tricked me into coming back here, thinking: 'what if'?"

"What if…*what*?"

"What if I had locked that door while Martial and I were going at it, for instance? If I had only taken that precaution, Elle would have never seen the spread-legged absence of her daughter's erotically-placed birthmark between my legs, cueing her in to my identity as '*not*' her darling Nicole. That's just one example. Another has to do with that damned museum badge, which I should have destroyed rather than keeping it as a memento. If it no longer existed, I wouldn't have been able to show it off to Martial that night; it would have never ended up in the wrong hands; and, most importantly, it wouldn't have become the pivotal bargaining-chip in Elle's underhanded scheme."

Thierry raised his eyebrows, repeating: "Bargaining chip?"

She responded: "Yes—in exchange for *The Origin of the World*." She shook her head regretfully. "I could *kick* myself for agreeing; but at the time, it seemed that I really had no other choice. The painting had been stored safely out of the way in the secret room under the stairway with all of the other erotic masterpieces that Gustave had purchased directly from Nicole in 1876 before she 'left'—perfectly incapable of doing any damage. Elle wanted it back in exchange for my ID badge, and I naively complied."

"Why did she want the painting?"

"The reason she gave was to have it in her possession in order to protect her daughter's reputation by keeping it private—but this was only a ploy. Be assured—you'll hear all of the details of her double-cross soon enough. I'll cover that in the climax to my page-turner."

"Fair enough."

She stared intently at the table, darkly self-absorbed. "The piece that was already in her possession that she was holding for Edmond, called *Waking Nude Preparing to Rise*, just wouldn't do for the *true* purpose she was planning. I'm certain she understood that although it might very well be used as a portal to the future, it wouldn't necessarily lead to the correct point in time...*or* to the right *Time-Shell*. A painting like that could still be very useful however, given the right circumstances and manipulated by the proper hands."

She seemed to be lost in contemplation, perhaps weighing the merits and demerits of this *other* piece of artwork that Thierry was not familiar with. He was worried that her reflective trance might deepen if he didn't say something to break the 'spell', so he asked: "Could you tell me something about that other painting? I've never heard of it."

"You wouldn't have." Her gaze shot up to meet his, no longer inward-looking. "It's a private, family piece: an unsigned Courbet nude, featuring Nicole of course; his very last painting, nearly finished and just lacking some minor finishing touches, including his signature. He literally had to drop his paintbrush, fleeing from governmental creditors who had come in the dead of night to arrest him. He spent his final years in self-imposed exile you know, in Switzerland." Thierry nodded her on, and she continued. "Nicole 'gifted' it to her son Edmond, setting it apart and holding it back from the other pieces she sold to Gustave Caillebotte. Elle remained the custodian of the painting for her grandson even after he came of age, since he was much too self-consumed to bother himself with it at all."

She looked him straight in the eyes. "Furthermore, Nicole had concealed a letter for Edmond in the backing which revealed her identity as the anonymous nude model for virtually *all* of Courbet's erotic pieces. Edmond never found that letter, though; but my Uncle Henri, an art restorer, *did*—stumbling on it 135 years later in 2011, when he was working on the piece in his home workshop. Discovering that document provided proof for my 'model singularity' theory, and made me famous for a brief moment before my boss at *Musée d'Orsay* stole my glory."

Now she was *really* going off script. "Shall we get back to Edmond?" Thierry prompted.

"Oh, yes; of course. We're just about finished with him anyway, since he's really an ancillary character in all this. The point is that Elle had the painting, which she planned to pass on to him later, perhaps when he settled down with his 'conventional' family later on—a hope that Elle harbored secretly if not overtly, from the very moment that Edmond began periodically bedding Isabelle. That painting, at this very moment in the past, is probably still in Elle's apartment hanging next to *The Origin of the World*, side-by-side...*if* Elle survived the journey back to participate in that sort of interior decorating.

"Did you interact much with Edmond at *Petit Genevilliers*?"

"At first. He was curious about me, as you would expect an abandoned child to be; and I accommodated his interest...for a while. He was nine years old when his mother disappeared—old enough to remember the sting of disappointment when Nicole didn't show up on the designated day and time at Place Pigalle, that fourth Sunday in June, 1876."

"So he obviously didn't run out in front of the horse and carriage that day."

"Thank God, no! John's worry that the act itself was destined to occur regardless of whether he saw 'me', or someone that looked like 'me', waving him on from across the square was, in the end, utter nonsense. Nicole or her 'stand-in' didn't have to be there to save Edmond because the rescuer's absence *itself* actually prevented the accident from ever occurring. Of course we had no way of knowing this for sure; but there he was: living proof that Nicole's return trip, or mine for that matter, wasn't needed after all...although for both of us, it seems that our 'wants' far exceeded our 'needs' anyway, so things had really worked out for the best."

"I'm not sure I know what you mean by that."

"Well, I can only assume Nicole was *more* than content staying back in the future: *her* 'want'— judging from a husband and child in present-day

130

Chicago as a measure of being 'lucky in love'. And me? Well, I was happy as a clam living in the past: *my* 'want'…so it was a win-win. But in order to fully execute my 'wants' in the way I desired, I really needed to get Edmond out of my hair; so I told him, in fairly short order, that I didn't want to cramp his style—giving him my 'permission' to focus his emotional energies elsewhere."

"Did he listen to you and 'back-off'?"

"Believe me, he had no difficulty following that instruction, since he was extremely self-centered and basically didn't care a wit about anything aside from his own pleasure, anyway. Remind you of someone?" she asked, in a rare moment of self-awareness. Susanne didn't wait for Thierry to reply, sliding right into a surprisingly-sophisticated musing intended to explain the biological basis for certain affinities she shared with her great-great grandfather. "Thinking about it, I've concluded that gene-inheritance is a very powerful force in molding someone's personality. There's a reason for the saying: 'you can't fight genetics'; because there's quite a bit of 'Edmond Bruante' in me, at least as it relates to everything 'sensual'. Thank heavens I didn't inherit his lack of intellect, though. My 'smarts' were passed down from my great-great-great grandfather Courbet, I think. Now *he* was a deep-thinker—very analytical in both his approach to art in general, and in his advanced reasoning surrounding the use of the 'erotic' as an expression of the human condition, in particular."

"Yes; there's no question in my mind that 'nature' overrides 'nurture' in most cases."

131

"Well, the originator of my inherent, lascivious DNA was soon out of my way, so I was perfectly free to pursue my *own* 'natural' desires—such as erotic modeling, and allowing the men who depicted my nude body artistically to express themselves 'in' the real thing rather than just 'on' a painting canvas. Life at that very moment was truly beautiful, and I should tell you that I really miss it."

She paused at length, quite sadly it seemed—which Thierry interpreted as a cue to change the subject under discussion before nostalgia darkened into despondency, potentially interfering with the continuation of her story. "Is Martial next?" he asked, trying to sound upbeat.

"You read my mind," she replied, taking a long draft from the glass of water in front of her as a way to compose herself, prior to adding: "...except that Martial can't be discussed in isolation. I'll have to sprinkle in quite a bit of 'Marie Minoret' here and there as well. The wife clinging to the cheating husband will make for a richer and more interesting tale, wouldn't you say?"

The question, obviously rhetorical, didn't really need an answer; so he nodded, just barely, and she was off again.

CHAPTER THIRTEEN

"I explained before that Anne Marie Hagan was a 'lady of the evening', who met Gustave while walking the streets—approaching him with her usual proposition as he left a painting exhibition in the heart of Paris. Little did the girl, barely eighteen, realize that the random solicitation would change her life forever. He purchased her 'services' alright—just not what she was selling...and *not* for just one night.

"He took her home, you see—cleaning away the dirt and desperation to reveal a beautiful woman who gladly gave up a profession that had been forced on her by necessity, in exchange for room, board, and every luxury a counterfeit live-in mistress could enjoy. And as part of the deception, thoroughly enhancing her credibility as a 'beard', she posed as the nude model for a piece that took years for Caillebotte to complete titled *Nude on a Couch*. It wasn't displayed until 1880, when it served to effectively dispel the rumors that Gustave was gay since, after all, it depicted his sensuous live-in partner in the implied act of self-stimulation."

"I see," Thierry commented, as mildly as possible.

"Gustave positioned her suggestively on the sofa," she continued, as if she had actually been there, experiencing the entire posing—which perhaps she had in a way, in the form of ancestral memories. Susanne spoke with trance-like

133

assurance, derived (Thierry surmised) from her recollections of DNA-engrained 'Minoret' genetics—because after all, Marie was a direct blood relative: the mother of Genevieve Caillebotte, who was in-turn Susanne's great-grandmother. "My great-great grandmother rested on her back with her left arm draped suggestively over her forehead," Susanne 'recalled', "her eyes closed in the contradiction of private ecstasy made public. He instructed her to place her right hand on the opposite breast and commanded her, artist-to-model, to stimulate her nipple with her index finger. Sexy…right?"

Thierry nodded but not too vigorously. "She dutifully complied," Susanne explained, "placing it directly on the swirling pink erogenous zone in question causing it to tighten in response—clearly depicted in the completed nude masterpiece. On his pointed instruction, she rested her straightened left leg along the outer length of the sofa while the right one she bent at the knee and reclined it against the cushioned-back, spreading her legs apart ever so slightly. Incidentally, Martial was introduced to her while she was engaged in this not-so-subtle display of her genitalia, which he could admire simply by walking around to the end of the couch, to take a peek…which is exactly what he did, the very first day he made her acquaintance. Believe me, she didn't mind. She was sexually deprived living with Gustave, and offered an open-legged invitation that Martial greeted with his own anatomical salutation, if you catch my meaning."

Thierry nodded, again—but maintained an impassive expression. "I should explain that Gustave and his two brothers shared everything," she went on, "a precedent that began when their father left them a fortune when he passed away in 1874. Martial Caillebotte Sr. had inherited the family's exceptionally lucrative military textile business, making millions on top of his *own* father's millions during various European conflicts, ending with the Franco-Prussian War. He also brought home an enviable salary as a judge at the Seine Department's *Tribunal de Commerce*, likely supplementing his income by taking bribes on the side. When their father died, the brothers moved their mother into the modern day equivalent of a nursing home and sold both the family home on *Rue de Miromesnil* in Paris *and* the sprawling country estate in Yerres; but until the properties were sold and the proceeds split, the brothers took up joint residence together for many years in an apartment on *Boulevard Haussman*.

"Gustave, René and Martial Jr. had each inherited millions of francs when their mother finally passed away; and René, as you know, died in 1876—with the 'mechanism' differing, of course, in Nicole's native *Time-Shell* compared to all the others but leading to the same end-result. Gustave and Martial split their brother's portion of the family wealth, which made them both very wealthy indeed; but they still continued to live together out of convenience for many years, until Gustave relocated to Petit Genevilliers…and Martial got married."

135

"To Anne Marie?"

"You bet. Since he and Gustave were living together when the reformed prostitute moved in too, the younger heterosexual-brother had ample opportunity to admire and lust after his homosexual-brother's 'beard', *especially* when she was modeling in such a provocative state of undress for *Nude on a Couch*—right there on their living room sofa, day after day after day.

"It wasn't long before Martial 'proposed' a physical relationship with the statuesque, sensuous redhead; but on one condition, conceived jointly between Gustave and Martial. For the sake of Caillebotte propriety, Anne Marie would change her name—a ploy meant to disguise and erase her sordid past. She would drop the 'Anne', keep the 'Marie', and change her last name from 'Hagan' to 'Minoret': an intentional misspelling of the word 'minaret': a word with Eastern origins that meant a slender tower with a balcony used to call people to prayer, which seemed fitting for the slim, tall and beautiful woman that Martial had quickly come to 'worship' with a romantic adoration much akin to religious zeal.

"The timing of the whole thing couldn't have been more perfect. Gustave completed the painting of Marie in 1880. In 1881, Martial moved out and took Marie with him, while Gustave started staying part-time at the country estate he had purchased and christened *Petit Genevilliers*. Marie and Martial lived as common-law spouses until she became pregnant with their son Jean in 1887, which prompted them to marry. Jean was born in 1888;

and their daughter, Genevieve—my very own great-grandmother—came into this world in 1889. You see, Genevieve eventually married Edmond's son, Marcel—blending the Courbet, Bruante, Hagan-'Minoret' and Caillebotte blood-lines."

"This is quite a story." Thierry's observation was true on more than one level. Her knowledge of art and family history, if true, simply had to reflect a submersion in the subjects that could only come from a rich education in these matters—and/or, he surmised, actual *memories* of the events she was relating.

"Now we arrive at my fortuitous insertion into this saccharine love-story. I took Elle's place posing as Nicole at *Petit Genevilliers* in 1886 and of course, my sexy good-looks *far* surpassed Marie's; so it was truly a cinch to seduce Martial: a sucker for a roll in the hay…or two, or three. I was fully prepared to step in as his mistress, and into the unfilled role of ultra-erotic model for his explicit photo shoot concept—shortly before Marie stepped up her game, using pregnancy as a legal snare which by no means put a halt to Martial's extra-marital activities with 'yours truly'."

Now Thierry noted to himself that the story seemed to be evolving into some sort of art-history soap-opera, featuring Susanne as the sensational main character. "Martial approached me shortly after we 'met' for the first time on one of his frequent visits to *Petit Gennevilliers*," she was saying, "to pose nude for a radical concept of artistic nude photography that he had conceived. Of course, he thought I was Nicole since Elle

137

introduced me with that identity, believing at the time herself that I was her long-lost daughter. This was the second time Martial had tried to sweet-talk 'Nicole' into being a model for this very same concept—the first being years earlier, when my sexy lookalike had posed for Gustave's *Naked Woman Lying on a Couch* in 1873, showing off her stuff to the three Caillebotte roommate-brothers, lying deliciously nude on their living room sofa while being painted by the oldest of the trio.

"Martial's concept was to push the boundaries of propriety by using a stunning, uninhibited model who was willing to 'bare it all' in the name of erotic art. Of course, snapshots of naked woman had been done before, but with lurid intentions and sold to a pornographically-inclined black-market audience. This low-brow genre was *not* his intention. He planned to use shadows and light to accentuate the most intimate perspectives of skin and flesh imaginable. Of course, I fit the bill; and, you can well imagine that I jumped at the chance to show off my naked, fully-exposed, and irresistible body-parts…especially when, to my distinct surprise, I heard his planned title for the photographic series. I had actually already *seen* them—in the future turned queerly on its tail, existing in the here-and-now as my 'personal' past…in 2011."

"What were they called?"

"The 'bodyscapes': unsigned and attributed to Martial Caillebotte only because they had been found in his brother's mansion. I had only just recently assembled the cadre of shockingly-explicit erotic nude photographs of the same name uncovered at Gustave's estate for my *Musée d'Orsay* 'singular model' exhibit—the pieces discovered in the hidden room under the stairs, where Martial and I had apparently concealed them after inception. Naturally I put two and two together, realizing immediately that these photos had, in fact, been created by the youngest Caillebotte brother...using me, *not* Nicole, as the model. *Now* I knew why the female subject of the series lacked that tell-tale birthmark in an unmentionable place. Nicole had noticed, too, leading to her total confusion in seeing those pieces in 2011, that she suspected did not depict her."

"Because it *wasn't* her," Thierry chimed in helpfully, staying engaged as a way to encourage her ongoing cooperation. It seemed to be working.

"Correct. It was *me*—shaved to smooth perfection and beautifully 'unmarked', in contrast to Nicole's bushy, congenitally-marred equivalent." She smiled luridly, visibly reveling in her sensational description of something so deliciously indecent. "Nicole had rejected Martial's modeling proposal *and* his romantic overtures in 1873, in favor of his brother René's advances (albeit delayed three years)," she went on; "so in a way, Martial felt as if he had been given a second chance when he miraculously discovered his dead brother's former lover living at *Petit Gennevilliers*.

"So, you agreed to be his erotic model?" Thierry asked in a question that was really more of a statement.

"I was only too happy to comply, not only as a way to fulfill my destiny in that role, but also to snare a key player in a plan that even then, early on in my displaced residence in another time, had started to materialize."

"Which was?"

"To get my hands on Gustave's money as soon as possible, of course. We haven't gotten there yet; but be patient...we will."

"I'm the definition of patience," he responded lightly; and he truly needed to be, now and over the next few months, since the road to Susanne's therapeutic recovery would take that much time...or more. "I'm waiting—patient as can be."

CHAPTER FOURTEEN

"Patience always pays off," Susanne quipped. "Anyway, getting back to Martial. He was, by that time, one of the most noted photographers in Europe. Granted, that wasn't saying much since the field was still in its infancy, so we're only speaking about a handful of artists exploring that venue at the time. Nevertheless, Martial was quite keen on maintaining his reputation in part because his status as the 'premiere' photographer of his day countered the insecurity he felt when compared, creatively and otherwise, to his far more famous and better-looking older brother, who received all the accolades as the more traditional artist acclaimed for his oil-on-canvas creations.

"To say that competition existed between the two siblings would be an understatement, which meant that Martial was motivated in-part by his jealousy of Gustave to protect his good-name, and remain anonymous as the architect of what he knew would be viewed as the most scandalous albeit groundbreaking photographic series in history. You see, he knew that nudity, captured on photographic film, was distinctly different from nudity painted onto a canvas."

"How so?"

"Because the image of a subject the camera produces is identical to the subject itself. You can't discriminate between them. On the other hand, a painting, no matter how realistic it appears, is still just a painting: some brushstrokes on a canvas, a creation of the artist's mind; *not* an actual imprint of a person's visual likeness transferred directly by a light-box onto photographic paper. Martial was fully aware of Félix-Jacques Moulin's fate."

"Who was he?"

"A talented Montmartre photographer who had produced hundreds of nude in-color daguerreotypes of young women. His works had been considered 'obscene' and eventually confiscated, leading to a brief imprisonment that had put an end to his production of erotic photographs. Martial did not want to risk similar consequences with his photographic project. That's why he decided to keep his ultra-explicit bodyscape series of me unsigned."

"That makes sense."

She nodded wistfully. "The photo shoot was a pivotal experience, leading to our first sexual encounter—unforgettable for him, and memorable for me only in the sense that it represented the finger that pushed the first domino of my evolving plan against the second, initiating the fateful rippling sequence." Once again, she seemed to withdraw inward, as if re-living the past. "Imagine how exhilarated I felt as the camera lens focused on my exquisite, naked body while Martial's lusty gaze examined the same awe-inspiring, singular nudity from his 'peep show' vantage-point under the camera-blanket." Modest, she was not. "I can still hear him commenting from underneath, his voice muffled, that even though the shots were turning out remarkably well, the mainstream artistic community would never accept them as the masterpieces they really were, during his lifetime. I took this opportunity as a perfect opening.

"'Are you familiar with Courbet's *The Origin of the World*?' I remember asking Martial as he emerged from under the canvas drape, red-in-the-face due to arousal as much as from his need for air.

"'Yes,' he managed to reply despite the overheating. 'It was banned from exposition due to the explicit nature of the subject matter. Why?'"

Now, Susanne seemed completely lost in the recalled-moment of her back-and-forth conversation with the now-famous Impressionist photographer; and Thierry dared not interrupt her word-by-word recitation. "'Have you seen it?' I questioned him.

"'No, but I have heard it described.'

"'I' was the model,' I proudly declared, referring to Nicole as myself, '*and*, I know precisely where it is.'"

Not unexpectedly, he was stunned to hear my duet of surprising revelations. "'*You* were the model? And you *know* where that painting ended up?'

"'A big fat 'yes' to both. I actually *have* the masterpiece, indirectly, in my possession.'

"'What? In your possession?' I remember that at that moment he reminded me distinctly of a parrot with his inane repetition...*and* his looks, truth be told—starting and ending with his beaky nose, lanky wing-like arms, and pear-like body-shape."

Susanne giggled lightly at her comparison, her laugh sounding mildly hysterical to Thierry, before she hurried on with her dialogue. 'Gustave has it,' I

143

clarified, 'but it's as good as mine, eventually—hidden in a secret room located under the stairs at *Petit Gennevilliers*. Didn't your brother tell you? 'I' sold him a dozen-or-so of my ex-lover: Courbet's, erotic paintings ten years ago—right before René and 'I' eloped. I'll show it to you sometime, along with all of Gustave's other naughty collectibles.'

"He nodded enthusiastically, but I could still read the uncertainty in his eyes. He didn't quite follow where my conversation was leading; but he didn't have to wait more than another second to find out. 'It took real courage, you know,' I explained, 'for my Jean to paint that view of 'me', up close and personal; which brings us to my idea.' He stared back at me blankly like an imbecile. It seemed that I had to spell everything out for this idiot. 'What if we do the same thing with your camera and my private parts, right here and now? Do you have the nerve to photograph me like that? Because I'm certainly game!'

"He replied by stuttering: 'Well, uh...I, uh...'

"'Don't be such a coward,' I scoffed. 'Look, I'll make it easy for you.'" Susanne paused to assess Thierry's reaction to her X-rated recounting, which by intention had been limited so far to a few meager eyebrow-raises. The last thing he wanted to do was embolden her aggressive and unfiltered flirtation: executed by way of lascivious storytelling. "So, do you know what I did?" She didn't wait for Thierry to reply. "I'll *tell* you what I did—I simply assumed the same shocking pose Nicole had embraced for *The Origin of the World*; and in reaction, Martial's

144

eyes looked like they would pop right out of their sockets.

"He went back into hiding beneath the curtain, snapping one sinful shot after the other— until he finally made his triumphant appearance from under the light-blanket a few minutes later when the most audacious pictures-on-film in the history of nineteenth century art-photography were finally complete. *That's* when I closed my opened legs; stood up; sauntered over to him, as naked as the day I was born; and pressed my nude body invitingly onto his fully-clothed one, kissing him long and deep.

"I had been unapproachable eye-candy just a minute ago; but *now* I had given him the chance to 'eat' it. Never in a million years would he refuse— my own great-great grandfather, no less; and wouldn't you know—all I had to do was lay a hand on the tense bulge in his crotch, and he was incestuously mine, forever."

She seemed to literally *feed* on the shocking and sensational—although of course, Thierry's theory was that it had actually been *Elle* seducing Martial rather than Susanne, meaning that there wouldn't have been anything even *remotely* Oedipal about their love-affair; but now was not the time to question the patient's befuddled memory-based recounting. "So, now we get to what came next," she continued. "Do you want to hear *all* of the gory details?"

"That's really not necessary," Thierry replied. "I have a healthy imagination." He was deftly walking the tightrope between encouraging and

145

discouraging her implicit sexual advances, aimed at her listener by way of a blow-by-blow description of her past 'imagined'—or rather, 'recalled'—erotic exploits.

"As do I," she teased, glancing through the table it seemed—her exaggerated gaze focused in the general direction of his lap, under the tabletop and safely out of sight. "All I'll say, then, is that he was out of his clothes and on the floor with me in one heartbeat; and by the second or third, he had prematurely finished. Some men simply have *no* self-control," she scoffed; "but in his defense, his revolver had been cocked and the trigger half-way pulled for several hours by then, while he was engaged in the prolonged tease of some very tantalizing visual foreplay."

"And your intention in all this?"

"Was to use my female talents to become his adulterous mistress, and gain control over his every move and action. In actuality, I would be much more accurate in describing my goal as utterly dominating—which in the end I achieved, becoming very much his dominatrix. My seduction complete, he did whatever I told him from that moment forward; and all I had to do was dangle 'hard-core' in front of him as a motivator. He was an easy mark who never bothered to ask any questions, as long as he got his 'sugar'. You see, I meant to enlist him as an accomplice (knowing or unknowing, I wasn't quite sure at the time) in my plot to inherit Gustave's estate sooner rather than later.

"His brother was a literal *spendthrift*, throwing away 'my' money on ludicrous, eccentric, and overpriced hobbies like stamps, yachts, paintings, exotic plants, and his live-in boy-toy. His fortune (or whatever was left of it after Gustave's pricey diversions had taken their toll) was dog-eared, after his death, for this *latter* guilty-pleasure: his clandestine 'partner' Edmond, but designated in his Will to my alias of Charlotte Berthier as the first stop of two on the inheritance train. 'I' would function as a pass-through entity for a hefty wealth that to my horror was being depleted faster than sand pouring through the widening channel of an hour-glass. I had to stop the hemorrhage, you see; and I had a plan. You'll hear all about it momentarily—when we get to the end of Martial's drawn-out tale and move on shortly to Gustave's shortened-one."

She smiled deviously, which made Thierry's blood curl; but somehow he seemed able to maintain his game-face, despite Susanne's Machiavellian sub-plot. "After that first taste, Martial's trips to Petit Genevilliers became more and more frequent, under the pretext of brotherly visitation. History got it wrong, for sure, because he *definitely* wasn't coming out there twice a week to meet exclusively with his sibling semi-nemesis. The dominant emotions that Martial held for Gustave were envy, resentment, and low-boiling but carefully concealed animosity—*not* love; and for the older brother towards the younger: bland and uncaring indifference. All of Martial's trips to the country estate, you see, began and ended in his great-great granddaughter's bed—although he wasn't cognizant of our common bloodline."

Thierry's head literally swam as his senses were bombarded with Susanne's blatant unconcern with basic human ethics. Even though he knew the theoretically-incestuous nature of Susanne's relationship with her great-great grandfather was a fantasy—born from identity confusion imprinted on the ancestral memories of two totally unrelated people: i.e. Elle and Martial Caillebotte—it was still particularly disturbing to hear her nonchalant description of a societal taboo.

"In contrast to everyone's impression," she was saying, "Martial's house-calls weren't spent, exclusively, in a living room armchair discussing art-theory with *another* frequent visitor to *Petit Gennevilliers*: Auguste Pierre Renoir; *or* sitting at a table in the game room, keeping Gustave company pasting stamps. Admittedly, though, he devoted a goodly amount of time to that second distraction, and thankfully so; because as it turns out, keeping Martial involved in that mundane hobby, working side by side with his brother, became the hinge upon which the door to my future, and fortune, swung."

"Stamp collecting?"

"Uh-huh. I'll tell you all about it—right now."

148

CHAPTER FIFTEEN

"Stamp collecting is an antiquated leisure-interest by modern standards, but in those days it was quite the thing…along with coins, postcards, preserved butterflies, and other boring collectible amusements reserved for the wealthy elite. The brothers shared an impressive, and famous, stamp collection. I actively encouraged their continued collaboration in that shared avocation, especially after I had conceived my plan that truly depended on their continued reciprocal interest in philately."

"Now *that's* a term I can honestly say I've never heard."

"You and me both until I found myself in the nineteenth century, where stamp collecting was all the rage, with philatelists as common *then* as a car on the highway is *now*. But I digress. Marie caught on quickly to Martial's cheating; and where she failed in preventing our bi-weekly rendezvous, she succeeded in sinking her territorial 'talons' deeper into his malleable flesh by getting pregnant—not once, but twice."

She shook her head, a look of smug annoyance painted on her face. "One thing for sure is that there was no love lost between the alias known as Charlotte Berthier and the other one called Marie Minoret; but the reason was that I was sleeping with her husband, *not* because Gustave had named 'me' rather than Martial as the sole inheritor of his estate and fortune—my assumed identity serving as a 'rest-stop' on his designated-fortune's circuitous journey to its true intended heir: Edmond Bruante. As I explained before, Martial and his family didn't even *remotely* need Gustave's money—because they had plenty of their own.

"Now that you know that background, we should jump ahead to the night that changed everything—and *not* in a good way, believe me, for *any* of the involved parties; but especially me."

"Are you referring to Elle barging in on the both of you?"

"No—I described that prelude-to-disaster already, occurring shortly before. My worry was that if Elle was given the chance to share my 'true' identity as 'not' Nicole with Martial, it would lessen my control over him by diluting our trust. I needed to get to him first so he could hear it from *me*, rather than from a resentful, grieving mother who might distort the situation to my disadvantage."

"That's understandable."

"Right; except my desire to 'beat her to the punch' made me hasty, and created a sense of urgency that definitely contributed to my lack of judgement. That doomful night, Martial had been pasting and organizing stamps with Gustave as an 'alibi' until well past midnight—the lateness of the hour serving as a valid excuse to 'sleep over' in his usual guest room situated just down the hall from my unlocked living quarters. My 'apartment' took up a full third of the second level floor-plan of the four-story mansion—complete with a sitting room, dressing alcove, and bedroom all to myself (except when I had a gentleman caller...or two, or three: a circumstance occurring most days of the week, truth be told).

"He came to my suites at about one in the morning as we had previously arranged, rapping lightly with his knuckles on the unlocked door. "*Entré*," I called out softly, sitting on the couch fully dressed—at least for now.

Martial shut the door behind him with barely a sound, making his way across the carpeted floor with a bottle in one hand and two brandy-snifters in the other, gripped with two fingers wrapped around crisscrossed stems. His behavior was normal, so I was pretty sure Elle hadn't poisoned the water...yet. He placed the two empty glasses on the coffee table in front of us wearing a wide grin, and started to pour. 'You can fill mine all the way,' I told him, deciding in advance that getting him totally wasted would make him a more pliable listener; and getting *me* plastered would make the sex with him afterwards a tad more palatable.

"'Are you sure? This absinthe is pretty powerful stuff,' he explained, 'distilled by Abram-Louis Pernod himself in Couvet, but laced with laudanum and other goodies by a friend of mine that has the right contacts.' I smiled knowingly, since Nicole had sampled something similar many years before, perhaps doctored by the same 'friend' with the same 'contacts' known to both Caillebotte brothers: the deceased and the living, alike. 'The 'extras' enhance the psychedelic experience,' he added—*and more*, I thought, *if the someone sampling the mixture had two rather than one chronotonin mutations.*

151

"I decided that now was the time, and he had given me the perfect opening. 'I know someone who wasn't exactly tolerant of the *exact* same stuff.' That comment was akin to the first piece of clothing to come off in a tantalizing strip-tease. Having removed the one, it was inevitable that all the others would come off in a jiffy.

"'It depends a lot on the purity,' he answered, unaware of my hidden meaning. 'The wormwood concentration is the key to its potency—the higher the better, in my opinion; but I've known some people who get freaked out by the experience.'

"'I'm sure the laudanum doesn't help those who have a tendency to 'over-react',' I said, intending to play the tease using double-entendre for a few minutes more. The second piece of figurative clothing was off, and I was left in my mental skivvies.

"He nodded agreement and then asked: 'What happened to her?'

"'Let's just say she had an 'other-worldly' experience,' I responded, smirking internally at the dual-meaning while showing him one metaphorical breast.

"'But isn't that kind of the point?' he asked.

"I laughed out loud, and he stared back at me blankly, discerning nothing at all funny in his question. I found it hilarious, though—because after all, it *was* the point; but the nature of that 'other-worldly' experience ranged from imagined to literal, depending on the presence or absence of a very specific hallucinogen-sensitive chronotonin gene mutation, numbering either one or two. For me as a single-carrier, any 'trip' resulting from psychoactive agent ingestion would naturally always take place exclusively in my mind; but for my related alter-ego: an individual who harbored a double-dose of that same gene mutation, drinking super-charged absinthe had transported her physically to another 'world' that she presently called home.

"'It's complicated,' I replied vaguely, visibly piquing his interest with my brush-off. 'I'll tell you all about it, someday.' In actuality, I fully intended to tell him that night.

"He poured me a glass, filling it almost to overflowing. 'How about telling me now?' he predictably nudged. His gaze studied mine and vice versa, almost like dueling challenges. 'Your secret is safe with me,' he added.

"'Perhaps,' I mused, sipping the deliciously burning liquid gingerly at first, feeling it trickle down my throat and expand into my body, eventually insinuating into my being like truth serum, drop by drop and flame by flame, the full glass exploding inside me with the heat of subconscious and ultimate revelation. *Tell him, tell him, tell him*, the thujone and opium seemed to chant while I gave him an allegorical eyeful of full-frontal—both breasts out. The persuasive elixir reverted to catcalls, demanding: *Take it all off*; echoing like a catcall in my altered brain. So I did. 'The person I'm referring to is Nicole.'

"'You mean...you?'

"'No—I mean Nicole. You see, I'm not 'her'. I'm...' I was about to say 'I'm really Charlotte

153

Berthier,' but didn't—because at that very moment, something very odd happened."

"What?" Thierry found himself asking eagerly, inadvertently drawn into Susanne's mesmerizing story-telling quite a bit more than he had expected.

"The psychedelics had somehow disembodied my sense of self; and suddenly, I could actually *see* the woman named Susanne Bruante, drinking a second glass of bitter sweetness 'down there', as perceived from a unique vantage point somewhere above the room, on the ceiling or roof perhaps. The mind-blowing concoction had caused me to hover over the transpiring scene as an objective spectator. It seemed perfectly normal, to be an observer like this—and great entertainment, too.

"Let's see what Susanne will say now, shall we? the watcher cooed; and almost in direct response, I heard myself blurt out: 'My name is Susanne Bruante. I only have one gene mutation; Nicole has two.' I had just wiggled lasciviously out of my fanciful panties and stood there stripped to emblematic nude, basking glorious in the light of the naked truth.

"'Huh?' Martial squinted at me dully, not comprehending. 'Can you repeat that?'

"'Nicole,' I said, 'has two DNA alterations. It interacted with the narcotic-laced absinthe during sex with René, back in 1876, and sent them *both* forward in time. I have the same gene mutation, but only one, not two.' The bemused look on Martial's face egged on my blathering; and I found myself prancing around the stage—showing off the unthinkable to a rowdy and audibly-appreciative

154

audience. 'The hallucinogens did something scientific to her magnetic field,' I chattered on. 'I can't really explain it, because I don't fully understand. You would have to ask John—*he's* the expert.'

"'I'm afraid you've lost me,' he said quietly— much calmer, I remember thinking, than he should have been in the face of just learning that I wasn't who I claimed to be; that the actual Nicole and his brother had disappeared as the result of a science-fiction like interaction between narcotics and a time-altering gene mutation; and that he had been sleeping, all along, with a Nicole look-a-like rather than the real thing.

"'Look, it's not important,' I hurried on. 'All you need to know is that Nicole and René ended up in the future; and now *I'm* here instead of her, in the past.' I saw myself, down below, lean over and touch him confidentially on the knee. 'I'm not really Nicole Bruante, *or* Charlotte Berthier,' I whispered. 'My name is Susanne Bruante, and I can prove it.' Then I did the inconceivable. I got up from my seat next to him on the couch, walked into the adjacent bedroom, and retrieved the little piece of plastic from inside my jewelry box sitting on the dresser. If this didn't convince him, then *nothing* would.

"*Is this really such a good idea?* I heard my out-of-body onlooker ask. Definitely not; but at the time, common sense disguised as the on-the-ceiling 'me' had absolutely no say in the matter. 'Take a look at this,' I heard myself say, making my way back to the couch but sitting this time in Martial's lap rather than right next to him. I held up my

155

Musée d'Orsay ID badge that I had recovered years ago from the front pocket of the blouse I had been wearing that day I journeyed through the *Time-Tunnel*, discovering it after the fact as I was throwing away the tattered garment. I had slipped it in without thinking, right after using it to activate the parking garage entry-sensor that night at the museum, rather than tossing it back in my purse—a deviation from my usual routine; but who could blame me? After all, there was nothing at all 'usual' or 'routine' about that trip that I had taken a few years earlier.

"His eyes widened in disbelief as he took the rectangular keepsake from me, analyzing it intensely. I definitely had his attention now, judging from the shocked expression on his face. 'That picture was taken in the future,' I said. 'Do you see the name: 'Susanne Bruante' underneath?'

"He nodded as if in a trance, seeming to have difficulty processing the incongruity; but who wouldn't? For the moment he was speechless; but *I* wasn't. The wormwood and poppy-seed extract had turned me into a reckless chatterbox who seemed determined to leave no secret unsaid. 'I hitched a ride—or took somebody else's place, to be more exact...' I prattled on '...through a *Virtual-Hole*; and *voila*...I ended up here. Don't you see the date printed on the bottom, right there, under my name?' I pointed with an index finger in the general direction of the badge, my accuracy degraded by the intoxication.

"As I watched Martial examine the exceptionally convincing piece of evidence, the

156

fragments of my personality abruptly decided to rejoin into one entity, finally; and I found myself back in my body again, seeing things now with enhanced but still-detached clarity, almost as if reuniting my scattered senses had given the experience an ultra-sharp focus. The letters and numbers stood out in fluorescent 3D fashion, it seemed; and since he was still numbly quiet, I read the date for him. "The tenth of March, 2008. That's when I was hired as Assistant Director of Acquisitions and Special Exhibits at the museum.'

"'But that's impossible!' he burst out, much like a slow-boiling kettle whose whistle had finally reached the sounding-point.

"'Obviously not, because here I am,' I declared, hearing my words come out slightly slurred from the mounting inebriation. Now the room was starting to spin, and there were two Martials, not one. I giggled, watching both of them rub their fingers against the synthetic laminate. 'What kind of material is this?' their double-voices echoed.

"'It's called plastic,' I said. 'It won't be invented for another decade and a half or so.'

"'The image of you printed on it is so clear! Is it a colored-in daguerreotype?'

"'No, it's called a digital image, taken by a camera built right into a laptop computer. You'd be surprised how quickly technology advances, come the turn of the twentieth century.'

"There was only one Martial again, but the head that he was shaking seemed at least triple its normal size. 'This can't be real.'

157

"I leaned forward and kissed him, long and deep—somehow exhilarated by the divulgement. 'Real enough for you?' I asked huskily, feeling more intoxicated than ever before, and reveling in the hyper-sexuality that came with it.

"'Mmm, yes,' he reacted, just as I knew he would; and that was that. My secret was out, and so was the ID badge: 'out' of sight, 'out' of mind, in fact."

By now, Thierry was completely enthralled. "If Martial came to believe you were from the future after seeing your badge, did he ever find out that you and he were related?"

"Of course not. He had no way of knowing his toddler-daughter would eventually marry Edmond Bruante's son: Marcel, my great-grandfather—and in so doing become my great-grandmother Genevieve. He, unlike me, was not privy to events that hadn't yet happened. It's a good thing, too. I'm sure he would have had major reservations, unlike me, about having a sexual relationship with his transposed yet-to-be-born great-great-granddaughter. So before I knew it, my *literal* dress was off, we were naked on the floor, and I had forgotten all about my irrelevant ID badge.

"But 'irrelevant' it certainly wasn't—quite the opposite, in fact. Underestimating the importance of a relic I had saved purely as a nostalgic afterthought really explains my nonchalance about the damn thing, and why I had allowed it to go missing without even realizing it was gone. I simply didn't *care* about it, which was the essential, fatal error that later destroyed my perfect life in the past.

"Sure, there were other contributing factors, like literally being consumed by the drugs and the psychedelic sex, culminating in the ultimate distraction building hot and wet between my legs. By the time we climaxed together—his ending quickly, but mine going on and on and on—the covertly crucial item had completely 'slipped' my mind, giving Martial the opportunity to 'slip' it into his pocket when he gathered his clothes to leave.

"Did I think about it even *once* after showing it off so foolishly? Maybe fleetingly, truly believing that in my confused delirium I had actually returned it back to its hiding place in that box on my dresser without even remembering I had done so. After all, I was accustomed to memory lapses after drinking too much; so why wouldn't absinthe laced with laudanum, *so* much stronger than alcohol, be any different?

"But honestly, an idea came suddenly to me that night, which totally supplanted every other thought. Once this brainstorm came to mind it became an all-consuming distraction, pushing everything else aside so that frankly, I could care less about a useless piece of plastic from a past life. The 'lightbulb-moment' coincided with the bitter taste of that kiss with Martial just a few minutes before, which settled in my mouth and sparked my plan. Do you remember what Martial had been doing right before he crept down the hallway and knocked on my door?"

"Sure," Thierry responded. "He had been with Gustave, working on their mutual stamp collection."

159

"Exactly. Now, it's a fact that in those days, philatelists routinely licked their new mints rather than using stamp-paste to adhere them into their inventory books; and the Caillebotte brothers were no exception. Martial's tongue was literally *plastered* with the sour taste of the backing-glue that he had licked for hours and hours prior to showing up in my bedroom suite to 'make-out'. That acrid smooch set me off—mentally, that is. If only I could find a fast-acting poison to paint onto the back of some stamps, the inheritance would be mine almost instantaneously. Martial worked with chemicals every day, in his developing dark-room. All it took was some carefully worded questions, and I had my answer."

"Which was?" he managed to prompt, shocked by the cruelty that Susanne spoke of so matter-of-factly.

"Well, as it turns out, less than one tablespoon of a newly introduced developing-powder called monomethyl-p-aminophenol hemisulfate: more commonly known as *Metol* and easily dissolved in water, is rapidly fatal when ingested." Thierry's cold shiver turned immediately to a core of ice as he listened to evil-incarnate. "And now, working through a certain clueless cuckold-photographer, I knew just where to find it."

CHAPTER SIXTEEN

"Metol is a film emulsifying powder used in black and white photography invented in 1891, widely used in the late nineteenth and early twentieth century by both amateur and commercial photographers. When I asked Martial what would happen to someone who ingested it, he looked at me strangely for a moment but then seemed to internally dispel any suspicious thoughts after I explained: 'You need to be careful, my dear—you *are* careful, aren't you? Because I wouldn't want anything to happen to my lovey-dovey.'

"'Oh, of course I'm careful.'

"'Do you wear gloves when you work with dangerous chemicals like that?'

"'Always.'

"'And keep your fingers away from your mouth?'

"He nodded like an obedient child being questioned by his mother, assuring me that he took every precaution; and then proceeded to inform me, as naïve and as clueless as they come, that even a small amount leads to asphyxiation."

Thierry knew from his study of medicinal chemistry that phenols lead to the formation of met-hemoglobin in the bloodstream: a 'poisoned' form of hemoglobin that cannot bind oxygen within red blood cells. The disorder leads to rapid death by oxygen depletion of critical organs, like the heart and brain. This woman—*or* someone else named Elle, whose memories Thierry surmised she was 'mining'—was nothing less than ethically barren. Cold-blooded murder perpetrated on a benefactor, whether real or imagined...relative or *no* relative, could only be conceived in the mind of a sociopath—pure and simple.

"By January of 1894, it seemed as if I had strung Martial along forever as his 'faithful' mistress," she sped forward. "For seven-and-a-half long and painful years I had to sneak around, giving the impression that Martial was my only bed-partner (which, believe me, couldn't be farther from the truth); waiting more-and-more impatiently to learn how he might serve me best in my scheming. I have to admit that I had nearly lost hope that he would ever be helpful.

"At first, I thought that the phenomenal sex and my promise to marry him if he would only divorce Marie would have made him putty in my hands. This theoretical union would have made him wealthier than sin, if my inheritance as Gustave's heir was added to his own pile of gold. But I soon learned that Martial was indifferent to money because he had plenty of his own, so greed for more wouldn't lure him into a new set of wedding vows; and then there were the children, functioning as two immovable obstructions in my pointed-path. I'm afraid that Marie's calculated and sequential pregnancies terminally confounded the marriage angle."

"Would you have actually married him, if he was willing?"

"That's hard to say. In all honesty I'd rather walk down the aisle with a monkey than hand-in-hand with Martial Caillebotte; but a gal's gotta do what a gal's gotta do. Nothing lasts forever, anyway. Husbands drop dead unexpectedly all the time and my guess..." (her black-widow's lips curled deviously) "...is that good 'ol Martial wouldn't have lasted more than a couple of years at the most as my certified significant-other."

Thierry was nothing less than floored by her satanic machinations; but she didn't give him any time to process her musings as she moved right along. "It was also true that he was used to having his cake and eating it too—an attitude that I'll admit I encouraged, by taking him into my bed so regularly without placing conditions on the easy 'lay'. But it was really his infuriating sense of sibling loyalty: a sentiment that ran deep, overriding the simmering animosity that I told you about before, that had put an end to my hopes that Martial would be a knowing accomplice in Gustave's mode-of-exit from this planet.

"So out of necessity I started thinking of ways to use my clout to involve him as an *unknowing* accomplice, and had just about thrown in the towel—actually moving my sights onto others who spent just as much time or more with Gustave, like Renoir or even Edmond, when my idea involving Metol came up and saved the day. After all, it would be easier than sin to paint it onto the back of their stupid stamps..." (Susanne eyed Thierry for a reaction to what she was planning to say next) "...and kill two philatelist birds with one pilfered stone."

Thierry looked at her incredulously...although her idea of knocking off Martial didn't come as a surprise to him at all, since she had off-handedly mentioned matrimonial-murder as a theoretical option just a few seconds earlier. "You heard me correctly," Susanne responded. "Both of Martial's children were born already, so I didn't have to worry about eliminating any of my Bruante relatives who still needed to conceive or birth their offspring—like Genevieve, whose progeny eventually procreated a few generations down the line to eventually end up in the glorious creation of 'me'. And who needed Martial anyway, after the deed was done? He would just be in the way, poised to cause me problems if he became at all suspicious about his brother's sudden death; so poisoning them *both* made perfect sense."

Her cool rationalization left Thierry speechless, allowing Susanne to continue without interruption. "It didn't take me long to figure out how to steal the stuff from Martial's developing lab without him knowing, and get it back to *Petit Gennevilliers*. A few days later, after we had finished up between the sheets in our usual ho-hum fashion, I yawned and said: 'We need a change of scenery, darling. Making love here in my bedroom is getting downright *boring*. It's the same thing, over and over and over again. Can't we pick someplace new and exciting; someplace *unconventional*?'

"'Like outdoors—in Gustave's rose garden, perhaps?' he suggested eagerly.

"'Where's the fun in that?' I scoffed. 'Yes, it's out in the open; but if Edmond, Gustave or Isabel 'catch' us, they'll just look the other way. I was thinking of something more…dangerous; someplace where our discovery would really have *consequences*. It's the risk that gets my adrenaline, *and* the juices between my legs, flowing.'

"'I can't think of anyplace.'

"'Well *I* can. How about in your house, right under Marie's nose?'

"'But she's always home with the kids!' Jean by then was just six, and Genevieve—my very own great-grandmother—approaching five.

"'All the better,' I replied. 'Like I said, we need to inject some excitement into this sexual relationship; and I can't think of a better way to liven things up than by rubbing 'us' in your wife's unknowing face…while I rub something quite a bit *sexier* in yours.' I could actually see his libido overtake his uncertainty, so I rushed ahead with the crucial part of my suggestion. 'Sneak me into your darkroom, Martial. It would be so exciting to make love to you downstairs, while she's sleeping right above us—upstairs. I'm getting *so hot* just thinking about it!' I lifted up my dress to emphasize my excitement, tracing two fingers slowly and seductively up my naked inner thigh to illustrate— just like this."

Susanne reproduced the sexually-suggestive gesture but without lifting her skirt, eliciting an impossible-to-repress gulp from Thierry. Satisfied that she seemed to be getting under Thierry's sensual-skin, she smiled mischievously and moved on. "'I suppose it could be arranged,' Martial uttered distractedly, as he watched my hand reach its intended destination, smack-dab in the middle—between my legs. 'The back entrance gives the closest access to my darkroom,' he offered. 'I could let you in one night, when everyone's asleep.'

"'Perfect. How about tomorrow?' Of course he agreed; and so our 'date' was made.

"It was two o'clock in the morning about twenty-four hours later when (after gaining access to Martial's chemical-shop by way of the back entrance on tip-toes and with my patsy as a guide) he lifted me onto one of the developer-room counters—normally used, it seemed, for a sequence of four or five trays that he had stacked neatly to the side in preparation for our little adventure. He kissed me urgently, dressed only in a nightshirt while I murmured that for the sake of maximizing the experience, I needed to be completely nude. In response, he helped me peel my clothes off to totally-bare sexuality: my specialty. 'You too,' I instructed, pulling the shirt over his head and throwing it, inside out, in the corner with my own discarded garments.

"He started with his face at counter-top level, working towards something involving my mid-pelvis that already felt incredible. His lips and tongue drove me into a gradual frenzy, until I pushed him away and climbed expediently off the counter, straddling him on the floor. I guided him in for the big finale; and while I was expertly taking care of both our needs, I looked inconspicuously around the darkroom (being the expert multi-tasker that I am) and immediately spotted a line of chemicals nearly glowing in the eerie illumination

166

of the safelight. This would be easier than stealing candy from a baby.

"When we had finished, he lay exhausted on the floor in his usual post-coital state of deep-drowsiness. I patted him endearingly on the head and nearly had to pull him physically by an arm up onto his feet, sending him on his stumbling way back to bed with his nightshirt in hand while I assured him I was perfectly capable of letting myself out discreetly, after getting dressed. I would wager that at the very same moment Martial crawled back in-between the covers beside the unsuspecting Marie *upstairs*, I had finished putting my clothes back on *downstairs*—but only after pilfering a generous sampling of Metol. I carefully sifted the deadly powder out of the main bottle and into an empty one I had brought with me, smugly stashing it in my handbag—gone without a trace. It was that simple.

"Now we arrive, finally, to the twenty-first of February, 1894—which represents the convergence of Martial's long and drawn out role in this story with Gustave's shortened one. I knew, of course, that in all of the other *Time-Shells*, ahead and behind Nicole's native one where I had landed, Gustave had died on this day, while working in his garden. What I didn't know for sure, you see, was the *mechanism* of this untimely death."

"I don't understand what you mean."

"Let me explain, then. Was Gustave's *true* demise, in every other *Time-Shell*, a *natural* event: i.e. coronary 'apoplexy' or an arrhythmia, as history details? Or, had 'Charlotte Berthier' (Elle's alias

167

rather than mine in all of those other *Time-Shells*) 'executed' a pre-destined sinister hand in his death? Perhaps my plan to poison Gustave with developing-powder was actually *hers*, as well. If so, I had an obligation to follow destiny's plan."

Thierry nodded with satisfaction to himself. If Susanne wasn't describing a scenario dictated by Elle's ancestral memories, then he was a monkey's uncle.

CHAPTER SEVENTEEN

Susanne continued waxing poetic to her 'primate' audience of 'one'. "Having taken Charlotte Berthier's position in the 'here and now' of Nicole's native *Time-Shell*, I felt compelled to select the same day that history had designated for the termination of the famous painter's life in every other *Time-Shell*. This simply felt 'right'. If Gustave was destined to die anyway, of natural causes, then the additional assurance of poison was just icing on the cake; but if murder was meant to be, then who was I to interfere with his predetermined fate? It was logical, don't you see?"

Thierry nodded numbly, so she continued on. "I wasn't one to stay entirely on another *Time-Shell's* script, though. Martial had played his part in *this* one, and it was high time for him to exit—stage left. He would only be a fly in my ointment if he stuck around—nosing about, and potentially interfering with everything 'post-mortem' that meant something to me, such as lifestyle, wealth, and acclaim. He was Gustave's sole remaining relative who, if pushed, might even try and contest my hard-earned inheritance. It would only complicate matters if he lived, so I made my plans for him to die, as well.

"I invited Martial to come visit on February twenty-first, stating that if he didn't come then, I wouldn't be available to see him until the end of March at the earliest. He and his libido agreed, planning his arrival shortly before noon for a few hours of stamp-licking followed by a leisurely dinner and then, I promised, a much more exciting session of 'licking'—of the erotic sort, make no mistake. I made sure Edmond would be out, asking him in advance if he would take some baked goods to his grandmother and visit with her until dinner. He was only too happy to comply since he and his *grand-mere* were close and he didn't get to see her much these days. It just wouldn't do to have him there as a witness to things.

"What would I do with the bodies, you ask? Absolutely nothing. Forensics hadn't even been invented, and I would claim surprise—shocked and weeping, explaining that maybe the factory glue was contaminated…tainted, somehow; a manufacturing mishap, or some sort of quality control bungle. An industrial-formulation mistake had tragically killed my two closest 'relations', and I would sue for sure, making even *more* money from my undiscovered crime to fund not only my *own* old age but the golden years of all of my lucky, unborn relatives yet to come.

"So, late at night on the twentieth, while the household slept, I dissolved the Metol powder that I had stolen from Martial's darkroom in water; grabbed a small-tipped paint-brush from Gustave's art-studio; and made my way to the permanent disarray of stamps and collector's notebooks scattered on a large table set up in the first-floor game-room.

"All I had to do was paint it onto the back of some of Gustave's newly-minted stamps, thickly stacked neatly on the top of scattered postal

170

disorder, with the tiny brush; and *voila*—the trap was set, for two. I only poisoned the top three stamp-pages, which should be plenty—enough to kill an entire *family* of Caillebottes if necessary, judging from Martial's description of the chemical's blood-cell binding potency. So imagine my surprise when the next day, waking up at my usual late-hour of eleven-thirty or so, I came downstairs rubbing the sleep from my eyes only to find Gustave busy at the stamp table already.

"'What are you doing here, alone?' I stammered. My plan to taint two brother's oral efforts rather than just one had just gone down the drain. 'Martial isn't here yet!'

"He shrugged. 'With so many new mints to organize, I just thought to get a head start,' he explained, licking the second to last un-postmarked stamp from a now-empty sheet that he had in his hand and adhering it to the open page in a collector's book whose spine was labeled with the designation: *England, new mints, 1892-1894*. 'There's more than enough work waiting for him when he comes soon. I've just depleted the third sheet; there are at least two-dozen left to go.' As if speaking of Martial's impending arrival served to remind him of the time, he pulled a pocket-watch dangling on a gold chain out of the inside vest of his waistcoat, and looked at it. 'In fact, he should be here any minute now.' Placing the watch back in his pocket, I noticed a few small beads of sweat forming on his forehead already. This was *not* a good sign.

"'How long have you been busy at this?' I asked nervously.

"'About a half-hour,' he replied, his words slightly slurred. I had no idea how long it would take for the Metol to kick in, but I was willing to wager it already had given the ominous lingual clue. And, corresponding to this thought, chaos promptly struck.

"'I feel li...light-headed, all of ...of...of a sudden,' Gustave stuttered, tongue-tied in more than one sense—the stamp stuck to his tongue and the Metol stuck to his hemoglobin...just as Martial opened the front door and let himself in.

"Martial's leisurely footsteps in the hallway became more rapid when he heard Gustave complain more loudly: 'My tongue is burning; and my chest—I can't breathe.' Martial rushed past me into the game room, while Gustave half stood, a new mint still sticking to his tongue and a sheaf of them dangling from two fingers.

"'Gustave!' Martial cried. 'What's wrong?' He looked wildly at his brother and the stamp-table, taking it all in. 'Have you been licking the new mints, without me?'

"'Yes—head start,' he gasped. 'Oh God, help me—the pain, the pain!' Gustave literally spit out the stamp that was in his mouth and grabbed his throat, terror in his bulging eyes. 'I...started without you. Can't...breath. I need air.' He dropped the sheet of new mints and overturned the table in his panic, clutching at his shirt collar and ripping it open—the buttons flying everywhere. He stumbled past us and out the front door that Martial had left

172

wide open, and we followed—Martial way ahead of me, of course. By the time we ran through the door threshold he was already in the front-lawn garden, on his knees.

"The predictable sequence of symptoms resembling coronary apoplexy took place right there, in front of our very eyes, in the midst of some still-dormant rose bushes and a planting of winter crocuses just starting to bloom on that unseasonably warm day in February. Gustave was on the ground, gagging and coughing next to a nearby bush, emptying the entire contents of his stomach onto the soggy ground. He was writhing and moaning, doubled up with agony on the brown and brittle remnants of last year's ground-cover, the strangle hold of death starting its ominous count down. Martial stood frozen in his tracks for the split second that it took for the seizures to begin; and by the time he ran down the steps and into the garden: five seconds at the most, his brother was dead.

"So it was that Gustave Caillebotte died on 21 February 1894, in his garden at *Petit Genevilliers*— in Nicole's native *Time-Shell* that I had hijacked...*and* in all the others: every single one. Who's to say that it was even the Metol at all? It was simple fate that took him, I'm telling you—in the here and now, behind and in front; in any and every *Time-Shell* you choose to examine. So it wasn't murder, really—just the hand of God."

"Whatever you say," Thierry muttered, disturbed by Susanne's deranged justification of down-right parricide.

"Martial didn't see it like that, though." Her eyes were bright—almost laughing with devilish delight. "He looked at me with hate in his eyes, rushing back up to the porch while screaming: 'What have you done?'

"'I have no idea what in the world you're inferring,' I answered indignantly.

"'You poisoned him—with Metol! I know you did; and that's why you were asking what would happen if someone ingested it. He was licking stamps when this happened! You must have stolen some from my darkroom the other night. What did you do? Paint it onto the back of the new mints after dissolving the powder in water? Or did you just sprinkle it on?'

"'You are completely nuts,' I said. 'Crazy as they come.'

"Then the horrible realization must have hit him. 'You intended to kill me, too!'

"'Don't be ridiculous,' I countered, turning my back on him and walking back into the house. He followed, close on my heel.

"'I was supposed to be sitting right next to him, licking the very same stack of new mints. If he hadn't started early, we would have *both* been pushing up daisies now.'

"'Listen to you, Martial. Why in the world would I do such a thing?'

"'To gain control of Edmond's inheritance early. I've seen you fretting over the household ledger and Gustave's bank statements. His hobbies are expensive.'

"I decided to take a different tact. 'Prove it!' I suggested. I walked over and gathered up the sheets of new mints that had been scattered willy-nilly on the floor when Gustave had overturned the table. I knew they were 'clean'. 'Have these tested; or better yet, lick some yourself,' I challenged. 'Nothing will happen, because your theory is nonsense.'

"He snatched them out of my hand. 'I'll have them analyzed all right, and I'll see you hanged.'

"His efforts to prove a poisoning ended nowhere, of course—even after months-and-months dragging into years-and-years of legal nonsense; and Gustave's death certificate, in the end, maintained that he died of 'natural causes' due to coronary apoplexy. So history, Charlotte Berthier, and Susanne Bruante were *all* triumphant." She beamed in recalling her slam-dunk success. "You can well imagine," she bubbled, "that I thoroughly enjoyed stacks and stacks of money, and a most luxurious lifestyle for just short of two years…until Elle intervened."

CHAPTER EIGHTEEN

"It was easy for me to imagine Elle and Martial's interaction that day when he came to call on her at her house in the city to offer up my ID badge: the one he had pocketed without me realizing, that regrettable night at *Petit Gennevilliers*. In fact, I can actually *see* their interaction in my mind—an explanation, his offer, an idea planted, her acceptance—almost like a memory."

This admission was not surprising to Thierry in the least, because he was sure it *was* a memory...inherited in the replicated nucleic acids of perfectly-duplicated DNA passed down to her, generation-after-generation—originating from *both* of her blood-relatives. Susanne then proceeded to recount the interaction between two people she claimed to be her great-great-great-great grandmother and great-great grandfather on separate branches of the Bruante-Caillebotte family tree, exactly like a scene from a movie screenplay.

"There was a knock on Elle's door a tad over two years after Gustave had kicked the bucket; and when she opened it, there was Martial asking for just a few minutes of her time. She motioned him in cautiously and they sat down across from each other at her small kitchen table.

"'I might very well be able to reunite you with your missing daughter,' I can hear him say, using those exact words.

"'How dare you,' Elle replied with indignation, starting to rise from her chair to escort him out the same way he had just been let in. 'You know as well as I do that she's dead. I *told* you so, shortly after I barged in on you and your birthmark-free mistress that night at *Petit Gennevilliers*. She confessed it *all* to me, just like I said.'

"'I *know* what she told you; but it's all a lie. You see, I learned some very interesting information back then, that I prudently decided to save for a time like this...when it might be put to better use. Please sit back down, Elle; because what I'm about to tell and show you could very well lead you to Nicole—who I promise you, is *not* dead.'

"Elle sat back down, reluctantly. "Charlotte Berthier is *not* who she claims to be. She comes from the future; and essentially, your daughter traded places with her—unintentionally, but not entirely unwillingly either, as it turns out. I'd dare say that Nicole is living happily, at this very moment, in the twenty-first-century, under a different name.'

"'Whose name?'

He tossed a strange rectangular item face-up on the tabletop between them. '*This* name. The Charlotte Berthier we know is actually a woman whose *real* name is Susanne Bruante. She's related to you somehow, given the last name...but I have no clue how. She hasn't been at all forthcoming in explaining the specifics of her ancestry.'

"Elle picked up my ID badge with curiosity. 'What in the world *is* this?' she asked, bringing the piece of plastic closer so that she could examine the photo of me taken nearly ten years past, in the future, more closely. She rubbed the strange material between her fingertips, unable to recognize the alien texture. I can actually *feel* her running her fingers over the smooth, strange reflective surface covered with lettered writing organized in straight official lines; and *see*, as she saw, the miniature photograph of someone who looked just like Nicole, Charlotte, and herself: Elle…in *color*, no less.

"'It's something called an Identification Badge—abbreviated '*ID*',' Martial explained, 'made of a material called 'plastic' that hasn't been invented yet…from the future. Look closely, and you'll see that it's not just *anyone's* 'ID' badge. Examine the picture, *and* the name. Go ahead—*look*!'

"Under the photograph which she analyzed carefully, she read out loud in a semi-daze: *Susanne Bruante, Assistant Director of Acquisitions and Special Exhibits, Musée d'Orsay—the tenth of March, 2008.* 'Could it be a forgery?' Elle asked. She held the badge gingerly between two fingers; but the feel of it, smooth and hard and real, screamed out 'authentic', which her sense of touch corroborated.

"'Impossible. The technology doesn't exist in our time right now, to make something like this. Susanne Bruante comes from the future, I tell you,' Martial repeated. 'I'm sure of it…because she told me as much and provided this invaluable item as proof.'

"Elle shook her head slowly, refusing yet at the same time beginning to believe that the inconceivable must be true. It was starting to sink in. 'How did she get here?'

"'The same way Nicole got *there*. They both have a certain abnormality in their genetic make-up that reacts powerfully with time, drugs, and sex.'

"She looked thoroughly confused, prompting Martial to explain. 'Nicole drank absinthe laced with laudanum many years ago, in 1876, while she and my brother: René—her lover—were shagging. The hallucinogens interacted with her body chemistry, opening a hole in time. Nicole slipped safely through to the future; but poor René, who didn't have the same kind of constitutional alteration, was crushed to death by the force of the *Time-Tunnel*.' Tears welled in his eyes. 'My dear, innocent brother.'

"Elle stretched out her hand across the table and lightly touched his, in a gesture of empathy for their shared losses. 'I'm sorry, Martial.'

"'Thank you, Elle…truly. Susanne was the one who came back later, instead of Nicole…because you see, Susanne *wanted* to be here; and Nicole, I guess, was much more suited to a life *there*.'

"I can see Elle, in my mind's eye, trying her best to keep her outward demeanor calm and collected, in the face of something so utterly unbelievable. 'So, if I understand you correctly, my daughter is alive and well, somewhere in the future?'

"Martial nodded. 'In Paris, to be exact. She arrived there in the year 2011.'

"'And you learned all this from Susanne? She just offered up that information?' Elle shook her

179

head, unable to suppress her skepticism. 'You understand, Monsieur, that all of this seems most…' (she struggled for a diplomatic word) '…unlikely.'

'"Look, we were drinking absinthe together, and it *affected* her—kind of like a 'truth-serum'; and after the initial conversation, when the cat was out of the bag and prowling around in full view, she eventually filled in all of the details and showed me the ID badge. She was so far gone by then that she forgot all about it, and I stole it. I'd be willing to bet she blacked out the experience, and may not even remember she showed it to me; and if she *did* recall her 'big reveal', she probably thinks she put it back in her jewelry box.'

He paused and studied her face. 'Look, I know exactly how you feel,' he said, 'because a few years ago I was 'you', baffled and skeptical when confronted with the same evidence. Susanne said it's a 'digital image', made by a machine called a 'computer'. They have all kinds of technology in the future, it seems. Life there is easier.' He gazed at her with a strangely playful smile. 'You should consider going.'

'"Going?' He was crazy, Elle concluded. 'What in heaven's name do you *mean*?'

'"I think there's a reasonable chance you could actually go to the future and find Nicole, is what I mean. Are you interested?'

'Of *course* I'm interested…theoretically; but what you're proposing isn't possible.'

'"It's not necessarily impossible, Madame. You see, Nicole had to inherit her sensitivity to absinthe and the 'time travel' consequences of ingesting it from someone—why not you?'

"'We *do* look similar.' Despite herself, she had started to nibble on the bait.

"'Yes, you do—*identical* in fact; although appearance isn't necessarily the determinant. Look at Susanne compared to her great-great-great grandmother: Nicole. The two of them are reproducible in appearance—virtual copies of 'you'; yet, Susanne didn't inherit Nicole's ability to open up a hole in time. The inherited talent is apparently located 'inside' somewhere, rather than 'outside' on the surface.'

"'But that doesn't add up, Martial. How in the world did Susanne get here, if she isn't capable of opening up a 'hole in time'…as you put it?'

"'She used *Nicole's* hole. You see, your daughter has two altered 'genes' (this is the term Susanne uses); and Susanne only has one. You need *two* to open up a *Time-Tunnel*. When your daughter is exposed to potent hallucinogens, her 'aura' interacts with a so-called *Common-Object* to make the connection.'

"'What's a *Common-Object*?'

"'Something that's present in both our time and in the future—or in the past, depending on your reference point. Susanne pushed Nicole out of the way during the 'time-transfer', and jumped into the 'tunnel' Nicole created before it closed. Susanne apparently acquired the ability to travel safely through the passageway without being crushed; but someone like me, for instance, wouldn't survive the journey—or so she says.'

181

"'So who's to say *I* wouldn't be crushed, if I went through a time-tunnel?'

"'You won't have the opportunity to go through one to begin with, if you don't have the necessary genetic alteration to open one up to begin with. You see, the painting won't respond to you and become a time portal after you drink absinthe, if you don't have the same double-'gene' alteration Nicole has. If the door opens as a reaction to 'you', then rest assured you'll be able to enter and pass through unscathed.'

"'And this *Common-Object*?'

"'Is a painting that Susanne still has, stored in a secret closet under the stairs. It's called *The Origin of the World*.'

"'I know that painting; it's obscene!'

"'Which is exactly why it will serve our purpose, perfectly.'

"'*Our* purpose? I don't understand.'

"'Listen closely, and you will. It's *that* particular painting, and that one *only*, that will theoretically give you access to the correct *Time-Shell* where Nicole is currently residing—affiliated through a process that Susanne calls *Recollection*. You see, *that* painting, since it was used twice before to open a tunnel between our time and the other, should 'recall' the exact same connection again. At least this is what she told me.'

"'Go on.' Now Elle was truly intrigued.

"'I'll give you the ID badge, which Susanne doesn't know I have, to make the exchange. Once she knows it's gone and you're in possession of it, she'll definitely want it back because it has the potential to make her life extremely difficult. Use it to lure her here, and make the agreed-upon exchange.'

"'So your plan is for me to request that *The Origin of the World* be returned to me, for 'safekeeping' of some kind?'

"'Sure. You want it back, let's say, to protect Nicole's reputation, in exchange for the ID badge. Go ahead and tell her you got the badge from me, and that we're prepared to partner in her financial destruction. She'll have all kinds of wild thoughts, imagining how you and I might use the badge to contest her identity and her precious 'Charlotte Berthier' inheritance. As for the painting, she keeps it hidden away with a multitude of other erotic pieces in a secret closet, under the stairs.'

"'I know precisely where it is. Remember, I lived at *Petit Gennevilliers* for a while before Charlotte...I mean Susanne...came on the scene.' She paused to think his proposal through. 'So let me get this straight. If I have the same susceptibility to hallucinogens as my daughter; *and* if I use the same painting that she used to travel to the future—the same one that Susanne used as well, to get 'here'—I might very well be able to find Nicole. Is that what you're saying?'

"He smiled pleasantly. 'Exactly. It couldn't be easier! Here; take *this*, too.' He pulled out a small flask from his waistcoat pocket. 'If you have the correct double-mutation, this should get you 'inside' the canvas and out to the other side, where your daughter, I trust, will be waiting somewhere in that correct and precise twenty-first century *Time-Shell* to greet you.'

He leaned across the table and pressed the small bottle and the piece of plastic into her palm. 'What's in the flask?' she asked.

'"Absinthe: the purest, most potent wormwood extract on the market, with a touch of laudanum added, for extra measure. I picked this up in Switzerland, adding a dram of opium distillate that I brought back with me from the Far East. You should drink the entire contents, standing in front of *The Origin of the World* with a certain *additional* passenger present as well...' (he winked) '...and with any luck, you'll *both* be greeting Nicole on the other side before you know it.'

'"*Both* of us?' Then realization dawned on her. 'Susanne, you mean.' She smiled broadly. '*Now* this makes perfect sense. It's revenge you want...same as me; but why?' Her eyes narrowed to slits. 'What happened between you two, anyway?'

'"Plenty. Murder, for one.' Elle's eyes widened. 'You heard me. She killed my brother, using *me* as an unknowing accomplice, in a way. She pilfered something poisonous called Metol from my film developing lab, and painted it on to the back of some postage stamps for Gustave to lick. I was an intended victim too, and would have ended up in a matching gravesite next to my brother, if the timing of the crime hadn't been sabotaged by Gustave's impatience to get the job done, just about a half hour before my scheduled arrival.'

184

"'That's insane!'" Thierry couldn't help but think that the sentiment was correctly stated.

"'Evil is more like it,' Martial said…about *me*, can you imagine? I *really* don't agree. Like I said before, Gustave probably would've died anyway. I just made sure it happened as history intended…in my adopted *Time-Shell,* just as in all the others."

"Of course," Thierry responded, careful not to contradict her rationalization.

"So, Martial went on to say that he'd been dismally unsuccessful in his legal efforts against me—just as I had predicted. 'I couldn't prove she poisoned the stamps,' he explained to Elle; 'so I need another way to get back at her. This solution would be perfect, if it works. I'd get rid of Susanne for good, get my brother's estate back from the conniving bitch that stole it, and give it back to Edmond—as Gustave really intended. I need to make my amends for the unintentionally role I played in my brother's death.'"

Susanne looked pensive. "In the end, Martial made it *all* up to Edmond, and *more*, by marrying off his daughter: Genevieve, to Edmond's son-by-Isabel: Marcel. In this way he consolidated the Caillebotte fortune under one marital-roof. It was very smart, really."

"Brilliant," Thierry confirmed, dryly. The entire clan, it seemed, were conniving in various, differing ways.

"So, Martial went on to tell Elle: 'It's a win-win, for both of *us*; so, what do you say?' He held out his hand, as if they were shaking on a contract.

"Elle shrugged, and took his hand. 'Why not…it's a deal.'

"So that's what happened, behind the scenes—a blow-by-blow accounting," Susanne said, concluding that chapter; "and a few days later, I received Elle's note."

CHAPTER NINETEEN

"It was March first in 1896. The letter had arrived by post a few days earlier, revealing that Elle had my *Musée d'Orsay* ID badge—given to her by Martial Caillebotte, of all people. Talk about a shock. I'd forgotten all about the damn thing, printed in 2008 on day one of my employment, and inadvertently transported with me through the time-tunnel almost ten years ago. Before receiving the note, I hadn't even realized that it was missing. If Martial had it, there was only one way he could have gotten it. I rushed straight up to my bedroom to double-check my jewelry-box and confirmed what I had so abruptly come to suspect. Sure enough, it was gone.

"I could have *kicked* myself. Yes, I had told Martial much too much, that night when the laudanum-instilled absinthe had loosened my tongue; but showing him actual proof that I came from the future, to prove my real identity as 'not' Nicole, just to pre-empt my soon-to-be nemesis: Elle, in the race towards first-disclosure? What a big mistake. Sharing that small rectangular piece of twenty-first-century nostalgia was a stupid drug-induced slip-up that I sorely wished that I could undo. Impossible, right? Wrong, I remember thinking...because gripped in my hot little hand, materialized in the note penned by Elle requesting an exchange, it appeared that I was being offered that very thing: namely, the equivalent of a 'do-over'.

"Elle had asked to meet in her apartment on the first day of March, to exchange the ID badge for a certain painting. The 'give and take' hinged on the obscene rendering of her daughter's crotch depicted in *The Origin of the World*: Courbet's erotic masterpiece—the very same one that was safely stashed in the secret closet under the stairs, where I had arrived nearly a decade before.

"'I want it back,' Elle had written. Why? Because Nicole's mother, who was apparently as narrow minded and short-sighted as the judges of the Grand Salon, didn't want the infamous painting to ever be seen in public. With age often comes paranoia, they say. *No skin off my teeth*, I quickly decided. I really didn't need the painting anymore, since there was no chance in hell, at this late date, that I would ever try to use it to 'get back' to my original place in time, in the twenty-first-century. I didn't have the correct double gene mutation anyway. If the price of retrieving my precious ID badge and keeping my true identity secret was that damned painting, then I would gladly pay.

"There was, of course, one downside to giving up the *Common-Object* that I had used to travel across the void of time. With the painting in my possession, I could at least police the entry door, and act accordingly if a certain unwelcome relative ever happened to arrive.

"But now, I realized that I really didn't need to keep the painting 'under surveillance' anymore. Nine-and-three-quarter years had come and gone, with no sign whatsoever of Nicole. She had probably settled happily into her new life in the future with her precious John. I had to admit, though, that the whole 'lovey-dovey' thing between the two of them, as nauseating as it was, had probably kept Nicole firmly planted in the future, preventing her from looking back to her past and trying to return here from the twenty-first century.

"So it was an easy conclusion that I could safely make the trade: a by-now useless painting in exchange for a very useful badge that could do plenty of damage in the wrong hands; and although you could call it blackmail, I was willing to submit and comply to the not-so-subtle twist of the arm. Why? Because having that little piece of plastic back in my possession, to destroy, would preserve my inheritance. The last thing I needed was someone raising suspicions about who I really was; because Charlotte Berthier was named in Gustave's Will, *not* Susanne Bruante. Elle stated that she would turn the little piece of plastic over to the authorities if I didn't want it, suggesting that 'other interested parties' might enjoy the novelty of the trinket, if the original owner didn't agree to make the trade. So what choice did I have, really?

"So it was that I finished my breakfast on that inauspicious morning, dabbed my lips with a napkin, and reached down to pick up the package: a carefully wrapped-in-brown-paper portrait of someone's below-the-belt anatomy that I had retrieved from the back of the closet under the stairs just before breakfast. I called for my carriage, got in, settled down in the leather seat, and dozed during the nine-mile ride. About an hour later, I stepped out accepting the driver's hand for assistance and told him to wait. 'This won't take long,' I told him over my shoulder as I walked up the short path to Elle's front door.

"One knock, two then three. Where the hell was she? I peeked through one side of double-paneled glass and seeing nothing but shadows I knocked again; and after a long delay, I finally saw some movement inside. A full minute later, Elle came and opened the door—slightly glassy-eyed, I remembered noticing, but obtusely thinking nothing of it at the time. She motioned me into a small foyer leading directly into a hallway to the right, and to stairs on the left leading to the upper-floor. She closed the door behind me a little clumsily, turning around in a semi-stagger to lean, grinning almost maniacally, with her back on the wooden part of the paned entryway.

"I looked her up and down, facing her while shifting the weight of my paper-wrapped bargaining-chip held tightly against my body under one arm. When she asked: 'Is that my painting?' and actually slurred the words to the absurdly obvious question, it occurred to me that she must be drunk. It really didn't surprise me in the least that in her isolation she may have become a lush; but if I had only realized early on that it wasn't alcohol that had altered her senses but absinthe and laudanum instead, I would still be back *there* dealing with a certain legally-troubling name discrepancy instead of *here*, literally locked behind bars arguing with doctors about identity issues of a very different medical-sort."

"I feel for you." Which Thierry did—from a treating medical-professional's standpoint, that is.

"So, I responded by lifting the package vaguely in her direction, while at the same time asking: 'Where's my ID badge?' She patted the breast-pocket of her blouse, missing the mark—blatantly uncoordinated in her altered-state. 'Let's make this quick,' I demanded brusquely.

"Elle's color was pale and her cheeks were drawn. Honestly, the woman didn't look well; so maybe she was ill, I thought, rather than inebriated. Drunk or sober, sick or healthy—her mental and physical status was really of no concern to me because I had come for one purpose, which didn't remotely involve superficial inquiries into the well-being of one of my distant, and aging, ancestors. Better to just get in and out as quickly as possible, I thought, especially if the woman had something contagious. 'Hand it over,' I ordered, simply.

"'Not so fast,' Elle responded, her expression resolute despite her visible malady and the continued garbling of her words. She pointed with a wavering arm to the package I still held under my arm. 'Unwrap it first; then we'll talk.'

"So I unwrapped the ultimate in erotic: a painting of Elle's own daughter's unspeakable and secret spot, through which I would soon learn Elle hoped to be transported, with any luck, back to the owner of the real thing—and take me with her. I let the paper float to the hallway-floor, holding up *The Origin of the World* for Elle to examine. 'Satisfied?'

"Elle nodded her approval, then pushed herself away from the door, with considerable effort it seemed; walking unsteadily and without a word down the hallway, bumping a shoulder obliviously into me while passing without even a single *pardon* or *excusé moi*. She was two (if not three) sheets to the wind, it seemed.

"*Oh well*, I thought; if the old gal wanted to throw a few down every now and then, the more power to her. She lived in a house that was barely large enough for a mouse, alone and with only rare visitors it seemed; so a glass or two or three of wine, or even something stronger, probably helped considerably to kill the time. Good for her—*now let's get on with it*, I thought.

"'Am I supposed to follow you?' I asked her, unable to disguise my annoyance. When I got nothing in response except for Elle disappearing ahead of me to the left, into another room which I would soon recognize as the kitchen, I rolled my eyes and followed, with the painting held tightly in the crook of one arm. No ID badge, no painting—it was as simple as that; so I would keep my bargaining chip close in one hand until I held the item I wanted in my other.

"I made a ninety-degree turn into the kitchen and found Elle standing next to an empty space on the counter, supporting herself with both arms and with her back turned towards me. She had cleared a large open-area there for the painting, so that it could be propped up facing the room—the floor-space empty, since she had clearly planned for the portrait's arrival by pushing her small eating-table out of the way, against the wall and into the corner.

"'Put it there,' Elle demanded in a guttural tone, her gaze unfocused and distracted it seemed, perhaps with her own internal demons. She pointed indistinctly to the vacant spot to her right, on the countertop.

"Sick or drunk or whatever, I didn't like Elle's tone. 'I don't take orders from anyone,' I responded with disdain.

"Elle shrugged and turned around gingerly, holding on to the counter the entire time as if the room was in motion and might throw her off balance at any moment. 'Have it your way,' she replied. 'After all, I don't need the painting half as much as you need what I have stashed right here in my shirt-pocket.'

"She patted her breast in an inept gesture that said 'safe and sound and still mine, drunk or sober.' Not that it would be that difficult to wrestle it away from a sloshed, by-now well into her early sixties family-matriarch who could barely stand, at the moment; but having it on her person was psychologically savvy. A physical struggle would be distasteful, to say the least. 'In fact, I don't really 'need' the painting at all,' Elle went on to tell me, her pupils strangely dilated. 'It would be nice to keep it out of the public eye; but it won't be the end of the world if that doesn't happen.'

"She had a point. I 'needed' what Elle had, whereas Elle merely 'wanted' what I had. My motivation to retrieve and destroy the ID badge was much greater than Elle's inclination to re-acquire and sequester the erotic depiction of her daughter. There was a lot at stake here, potentially—for me at least; so I decided to swallow my pride and play nicey-nice.

"'Alright. I could care less where you want me to put it.' I walked over and propped the painting up on the counter, fitting it perfectly into the spot Elle had cleared away for it. God knows why she wanted it there, of all places: out in the open where everyone could see it. It just goes to show, I thought at the moment, that Elle didn't have many guests these days. 'Satisfied?' I didn't wait for a response. 'You *should* be! Now, give me the badge, if you please.'

"Elle nodded 'sure thing', weaving her way across the small distance between us with a deliberate cautiousness that almost seemed too exaggerated, her hand groping her breast like a protective lover until she finally found the pocket, sinking her thumb and two fingers in. Was she faking the whole 'under the influence' thing? Nonsense! Drunk was drunk; and this woman was wasted—for sure...I *thought*. There was no reason in the world for paranoia.

"Now Elle was standing in front of me, uncomfortably close, exhibiting the classic disregard for boundaries that inebriation can often cause. As she pulled my badge halfway out of her pocket, I could smell it now...distinctly—the heady stench of ethanol, with just a hint of licorice.

"Wait—*licorice*? It wasn't wine or gin or brandy; the smell was absinthe—it *had* to be. My initial reaction was 'that's no surprise' since

194

absinthe was the semi-illicit beverage of choice in Paris circa the 1800's; but my next thought, galloping rapidly on the heels of composure, was pure panic—because given our family history, ingesting too much absinthe could be...well, *dangerous*.

"It was with that split-second, telling pondering when I recognized what was happening in a sudden instant of clear-sighted recognition. Elle had played the game perfectly up to this point, giving the impression of simple drunkenness while in reality the combination of absinthe and laudanum had taken her on a much more troubling 'trip'. I could see from Elle's mind's-eye perspective now, as clear as if I was in her head. Even as she found herself besieged by hallucinations and bizarre distortions of the physical world around her, she had managed to keep a firm, albeit wavering, grip on reality; and now Elle found herself, by way of focused determination executed through the haze of unreality, standing nose-to-nose with the woman she intended to take *with* her forward in time: *me*.

"In a flash, I saw and heard Elle and Martial conspiring against me, and knew that with myself and the ID badge added to the painting, my conniving relatives had engineered a triple-play of *Common-Objects*, virtually insuring that if Elle harbored the correct double-mutation, she and I would *both* be rocketed back to the correct place and time, where Elle hoped to be reunited with Nicole; and Martial, in turn, would finally get rid of me, once and for all. Revenge was sweet, for *both* of them, I thought—as at the same time, the whirlwind of vengeance began to open up in the painting.

"I saw Elle turn slightly, still right up in my face—just enough to confirm the wavering shimmer on the painting's surface, which was rapidly enlarging, millisecond by millisecond; while at the same time, I tensed my muscles and drew in my breath—the perspiration glistened on my brow. Our gazes locked in an instant of unspoken confrontation: the prelude to a simultaneous 'quick draw', rapidly executed but in seeming slow motion. I wouldn't go back, I *couldn't* go back; so I turned intending to run back towards the door, but Elle stopped me with lightning speed—both hands gripping me tightly by the shoulders.

"She pulled me forward, falling backward with a seemingly choreographed smoothness—me-with-her and her-with-me; but we didn't hit the floor. Instead, I found myself hovering in the air in front of the painting: Elle on the bottom and me on the top of a pressing face-to-face embrace.

"I had observed it all before, ten years ago in the art museum: the rippling surface, a hazy harbinger of nothingness leading to elsewhere; a quickly expanding maelstrom, white and powerful, that would draw us in, momentarily, through a vacuumed tunnel of blackness to the other side; a yawning abyss, created by chemical meets physical—a living thing, almost, focused and intent; a virtual mouth, ruthless and unsmiling, that would suck us in with a single breath then swallow us whole, deaf and blind to pleas or bargains or complaints or screams.

196

"As I watched the painting in helpless horror, the void between Courbet's rendering of Nicole's legs grew larger and larger in the sudden span of a moment, like some terrifying dilating pupil matching Elle's—intent on propelling us both like dust in an electromagnetic windstorm into the future, reuniting Elle with her missing daughter, and myself with a life I had purposely left behind a full decade ago.

"The painting, beckoning us in with a sudden sucking force, literally swept us through the open hole, headfirst into the windstorm, conjoined like a single entity, deeper and deeper into the void, leaving Elle's Paris...*my* Paris, far behind in a fraction of a millisecond.

"The wind roared in our ears as the swirling and tumbling force of time uncoupled us. Down and down, farther and farther in, closer and closer to the other side we sped surrounded by the whiteness of a burning inferno—hot on my skin, close to scorching but not quite, pressing in on me from all sides with scalding urgency. 'I'm coming, Nicole,' I heard Elle yell triumphantly. 'I'm finally coming...'

"And then it all went black."

During those last few lines, Susanne had leaned back in her chair, visibly exhausted from reliving the experience; because delusion or not, the events that she described were nonetheless incredibly traumatic in their remembering. It was as though her seemingly-endless supply of mental energy had been thoroughly drained after the plug had been pulled with her heady narrative.

197

Thierry, mindful of Susanne's sudden burnout *and* the time: six o'clock, quietly turned off the recorder, thinking that it would take weeks to thoroughly analyze what she had just provided in the eight-hour audio file. He was by no means complaining, because the data she had furnished was nothing less than amazing. It was finished...*she* was finished. Susanne's unbelievable, incredible story was finished.

PART THREE

*The poetic **PERSONA** is not Shakespeare himself
(and as such) the Sonnets themselves
resist straightforward narrative.*

Hannah Crawforth
An Introduction to Shakespeare's Sonnets
In:
<u>British Library</u>
Discovering Literature: Shakespeare and
Renaissance
13 July 2017

CHAPTER TWENTY

She wasn't crazy—far from it; but let them think she was. If any conclusions could be drawn from today's little exercise, it was the confirmation that she could gain the right sort of productive attention as an interesting psychiatric case, simply by telling the truth and being her usual deliciously irresistible self.

This 'Thierry Duvalier' had certainly been the right man for the job. Kudos to the brilliant Dr. Lefebvre, who had engaged a green-eyed, dark-haired specialist in dissociative identity disorder, of all things, to help facilitate her grand exit from this place. There was no way in the world that she had the 'multiple personality' variety of wacko: an illogical diagnosis of exclusion since all of their other treatments had ended in therapeutic dead ends. Never mind that she did, periodically, have fluctuations in mood, or attitude, or perspective...call it what you will; this was normal, after all, for someone in her situation. Being subjected, as she had been, to extreme isolation and endless scrutiny for four months now in this prison of a looney bin would have wreaked the same or even more havoc on *anyone's* psyche. In fact, it was actually a testimonial to her mental health that she had been able to remain sane for all this time when everyone around her was either nuts (her fellow detainees), or hyper-focused on nuts (the moronic hospital staff).

Her performance earlier today was a sort of 'dress rehearsal' for opening night on the psychoanalysis couch in Brussels. Susanne's exhaustive recounting of the 'facts' had been conveniently peppered with the 'fiction' of a true-to-life individual 'living' inside her. Who was this kind, vulnerable, and unassuming character? Nicole Bruante of course—the actual family member who had been Susanne's counterpart in what was for all intents and purposes someone else's past in 2011, rather than her own. Her time-traveling great-great-great grandmother was no threat to her now though, resting peacefully in a Chicago cemetery with a gravestone that erroneously identified her as Susanne Bruante.

The 'real' Susanne (*yours truly*) was so talented that she could call up Nicole at will; so convincingly that even *she* believed at times that a true personality swap had actually occurred. This ability, which she had perfected in the empty hours of boredom that consumed her in confinement, was no different than an actress thoroughly immersing herself in a theatrical role to the point that the character she was playing took on a life of her own. Dr. 'Personality Disorder' had been her private audience of one today, witnessing her seamless back-and-forth play-acting charade—taking the bait and swallowing it hook, line and sinker; and now *this* fish named Susanne Bruante was going to be freed from the goldfish bowl called *Pitié-Salpêtrière*, all because of her delicate handling of the interview that had ended just a few hours ago.

She rolled over in bed, her mind racing even though her body felt sapped and tired—the result of reliving ten years of experiences compacted into an eight-hour, comprehensive mostly one-sided discourse. She couldn't prevent herself from obsessing compulsively, thinking and rethinking the events that had already happened, and those that might happen yet.

The neuropsychologist from Belgium was definitely attracted to her, as most men with very few exceptions were, although today's well-planned escapade suggested that he would be a tougher nut to crack than some of her past conquests: the most notable being her great-great grandfather Martial Caillebotte, whose middle name had been 'malleable'. Now *he* had been the ultimate patsy, allowing himself to be led by the nose by his blind lust for her—ultimately providing the means to his own brother's end, without even realizing it until it was too late.

Thierry Duvalier was a different breed altogether, hiding behind his professional ethics like a shield and using them to quietly fend off her advances. Although his doctorly morals could represent a potential roadblock, Susanne had faith in her persuasive abilities and felt certain that she was fully capable of barreling through the obstruction by playing the mentally-ill victim whose psychiatric disorder pleaded for the healing hand of her caring physician. There was no question that today's first experience with the difficult-to-entice Thierry escalated her game-plan into challenge mode, whereby she was determined to win over his mind

202

as well as his body to gain the treasured prize: an eventual return to her true home in nineteenth century Paris; and God help any competitor who stood in her way, she might add.

Could the pretty young psychiatrist who had summoned the famous bachelor-researcher emerge as a romantic challenger? This notion, which had occurred to Susanne suddenly as a semi-obsessive afterthought on the heels of her first encounter with Thierry Duvalier, had jockeyed its way from the back of her subconscious to the front, and now represented a nagging worry that she was in the process of rationally extinguishing. There was something sexually engaging about Dr. Genevieve Lefebvre that Susanne couldn't quite put her finger on, except as a distinctly familiar aura that she recognized as disturbingly similar to her own.

Sometimes you needed to 'be one to see one', and Susanne's internal night-goggles had spotted that shadowy simpatico in her attending psychiatrist long before the compelling Thierry Duvalier had entered the scene. Perhaps it was this sixth sense-recognition of the woman's insidious sensuality that had paired the two of them (man-meets-woman) together in the paranoid recesses of Susanne's mind, with some additional vexing contributors such as the fact that they were both single, happened to be about the same age, were each unusually attractive, and shared in the same profession as doctors with an in-common mental-health subspecialty.

Yes, there was no question that they would make a disconcertingly handsome couple out on the town, in the workplace and in the privacy of the boudoir, with the images of the latter playing havoc in her brain like a scene from an X-rated movie that—try as she might to avert her eyes—she just *had* to keep watching. She could easily imagine the blond and blue-eyed beauty stripped to erotic perfection, laid bare on his bed somewhere—her compelling milk-white skin and the naked swell of her breasts touching softly against the hardness of Thierry's olive-toned chest, which pressed down on her exigently from above. She could actually feel the rhythmic dichotomy of male moving with female; hear the uttered symmetry of man blending with woman; smell the heady fragrance of X impassioned by Y; and taste the delicious climax of their secret 'boy-meets-girl' rendezvous—taking place, perhaps even now, in his hotel room after the dinner and drinks (proposed on the pretext of professional necessity, of course) had long since concluded. This nightmare scenario could be happening at this very moment, while Susanne tossed and turned in her sterile, asexual hospital bed.

She hoped that this was just her paranoia speaking, especially since her intuition assured her that neither Thierry nor Genevieve were bold enough to wriggle out of their professional straight-jackets on the first date (should this even occur)—unless of course they knew each other from some sort of common past...medical school, perhaps; or, the rigorous hospital training that followed? Regardless, they would be separated by distance come tomorrow, when Thierry returned to Brussels and Genevieve stayed behind to tend to her zoo of crazies in Paris. This was Susanne's cue, a kind of 'enter-stage-left' directive whereby *she* would very soon have the advantage of geographic proximity to her co-star, in effect stacking the odds in her favor when she was transferred to Thierry's research hospital in Belgium. Yes, indeed, the potentially back-stabbing Dr. 'Understudy' would be physically eliminated when the show went on the road and settled in for its next step: a Tony Award-deserving performance in Brussels.

Her strategy actually *did* read very much like a playbill. In the *Prologue* (already 'curtain-called'), Susanne had expertly hoodwinked the well-meaning neuropsychologist, resulting in her impending transfer from the ultra-high security psyche ward at *Pitié-Salpêtrière* to what she felt confident would be the minimal security neurologic research facility at Brugman University Hospital in Brussels. Once there, she envisioned the set opening on *Act One*, which would tell the tale of Susanne Bruante cooperating with Thierry Duvalier's evaluation process, convincing him with her best scripted lines and actions that she was truly inflicted with DID. She planned to expertly finesse the gradual 'replacement' of Susanne with Nicole—the highly sympathetic alter-ego that Susanne would lead her new team of idiotic specialists to believe had become the dominant personality, as a direct result of their highly-effective treatments.

The Nicole 'character', once established, would headline *Act Two*, posing as the helpless victim of a devastating psychiatric syndrome and in so doing, truly earn her new attending physician's empathy.

In the meantime, Susanne's knock-out body would subliminally undermine Thierry's professionally-protected masculine libido while at the same time, wide-eyed Nicole would manipulate his emotional side, working both angles in synergistic partnership *so* much more effectively than Genevieve ever could. She could even imagine a pretend theatrical reviewer's accolades: *Ms. Bruante has outdone herself in this ingeniously conceived psychological romance that twists and turns through the corridors of reality and illusion.*

Of course Susanne was intelligent enough to realize that to a mind-reading peeping Tom it might seem like she was creating a complex rationalization for explaining away the fact that she actually *was* inflicted with DID. <u>Telepathic Interviewer</u>: *Ms. Bruante, isn't this personality 'shell game' just a cover for the real disorder?* <u>Susanne Bruante</u>: *Of course not. Just think of me as producer, director and award-winning character-actress all rolled into one.*

She had to admit that she was particularly looking forward to the sex scenes in her theatrical production—because yes, her 'play' would break all the rules with an explicit depiction of this forbidden theme. After all, her favorite type of recreational pastime had been glaringly absent from her agenda these past six months in this horridly boring deprivation tank that called itself a hospital, where going it alone under the covers had long since become a lackluster substitute for the real-deal. But she would just have to be patient and play it by ear,

206

gauging Thierry's susceptibility to her irresistible X-rated femininity as *Act Two* concluded.

Act Three: the beginning of the rest of her life, required either her release or an escape from Brugman University Hospital, the details of which she reviewed over-and-over again, in her insomniac's sleepless mind.

CHAPTER TWENTY-ONE

Of course a 'cure' and a discharge from the hospital with Dr. Duvalier on her arm as an escort would be the preferred opening to *Act Three*; but one way or the other, with or without her physician-pushover, she would make her way back to Paris and to her great-uncle Henri.

The dialogue and action had yet to be written for this concluding act of her storyline, due to her inability to gather more than tidbits of information about her living family: an unfortunate consequence of her confinement to a locked and freedom-restricted psychiatric ward. She knew from speaking with Dr. Lefebvre that Henri Bruante was demented but still living in his own home in central Paris thanks to the assistance of a private duty nurse, but the questions that remained to be answered were numerous and intertwined.

For instance, how severe was his dementia? (Her plans favored at least moderate without the agitation that often came with the diagnosis, because too mild might equate with less pliable whereas too severe would limit his ability to physically cooperate).

Did he still have the asset in question: a particular family painting called *Waking Nude Preparing to Rise* created by Gustave Courbet himself, that Henri had been refurbishing in 2011—actually finding a letter hidden in the canvas-backing, penned by Nicole in 1876 'confessing' her identity as the nude model for all of Courbet's erotic paintings? (Her best guess was 'yes' since the piece was an heirloom and had special meaning for a family archivist like Henri).

Was it still 'on-site' in the house that had doubled as his art restoration workshop, in the Saint Germaine des Pres district on the left bank of Paris? (She couldn't imagine that it would be anywhere else, given the fondness he had for both the painting and its model).

And last but not least, why was finding the painting so important? (Because it provided an essential link to her family's past *and* the *Time-Shell* 'era' where she truly belonged...and intended to return).

She understood that there was no way she could gain access to *The Origin of the World*, which was still sequestered away undergoing intensive damage-repair—but no matter, because she felt certain that *Waking Nude Preparing to Rise* could easily serve as an acceptable alternative leading her back, more-or-less, to 'home'. Of course there were other paintings that would do just as well, but none in as convenient a location, presumably, as the family antique. Needless to say that she would rather not have to make an outing to *Musée d'Orsay* or *Musée de l'Orangerie*, the doting niece pushing the doddering uncle dutifully in a wheelchair; squaring him *en-face* with an alternative time-sensitive masterpiece featuring their very own Nicole as the 'bare-it-all' model—the entire eye-popping magic-trick transpiring in an undesirable, all-too public place.

Which led to the ultimate Henri-centric unknown: his chronotonin gene 'status'…and how, if a mutation happened to be present in this particular male relative at all, it would interact with her own. In her mind, she reviewed the simplistic genetics lesson that Dr. John Noland had given the small group of time-travel conspirators: herself, Uncle Henri, and Nicole, ten years ago. The gene encoding chronotonin was 'sex-linked', meaning that it's carried on the X (female) chromosome. A man inherits one of his mother's two X chromosomes and their father's single Y, giving him an 'XY' genotype for 'maleness'; whereas a woman has two X chromosomes (XX) passed on, one from each parent, making for full-fledged 'female'.

Two chronotonin mutations are needed to open a *Time-Tunnel* (case-in-point: Nicole, known as a double-mutation 'homozygote'); while harboring only *one* (for instance, Susanne herself) could not provide enough 'juice' to create a *Virtual-Hole*, but would in fact allow the 'heterozygote' single-mutation carrier to pass through the here-to-there connection unscathed. All of this had been tested not once or even twice, but *three* times beginning with Nicole's initial fledgling journey, leading her from 1876 to 2011, followed by Susanne's round-trip experience.

Susanne knew that Henri, being an 'XY' male, either harbored the sex-linked chronotonin mutation on his lonely X chromosome, or he didn't; but even if he *had* it, her now-demented great-uncle Henri would be just as incapable of opening a *Virtual-*

Hole as she was. So, why did his chronotonin gene-status even matter? Because maybe…just *maybe*, the two mutations required to open the door in a *Common-Object* leading her back to the past didn't *need* to exist simultaneously in one person.

What if her mutation *added* to someone else's, activated by hallucinogens while in close proximity to the family painting, could function in the exact same time-traveling fashion as the twin mutations residing in a single person, like Nicole? John had never mentioned if he had ever investigated this separate-but-additive gene-duality idea in lab rats; but as Susanne continued to ponder her hypothesis, she couldn't help but wonder if her journey back to the future with Elle had actually represented the ultimate 'human' experiment providing proof-positive evidence to back up her theory.

There was no way to know for sure since Elle's genes had never been tested; but perhaps her great-great-great-great grandmother had harbored only *one* mutation rather than two, lending credence to Susanne's 'additive rule'…*and* also explaining why Elle hadn't returned to 2021 after ricocheting back to 1896. If Susanne's conjecture was correct, getting high all alone with only *The Origin of the World* to keep her company would be a solitary and uneventful experience for a certain theoretical *single* mutation-carrier relative named Elle residing now in nineteenth century Paris after returning there like a boomerang, for sure.

All she would have to do is acquire a healthy cache of hallucinogens from one street dealer or another and feed them to Henri and herself while

211

her single-mutation stood by right next to his, ready for action—while making sure that *Waking Nude Preparing to Rise* was in the general vicinity. She and her alleged DNA alteration would hang lovingly on his shoulder and *voila*—both she and her fellow hoped-for heterozygote: Uncle Henri, would be transported back in time to the late nineteenth century, where she could resume her life more-or-less where she had left off.

And Henri, of course, could get to know Elle: his great-great grandmother. Was she worried that poor, demented Henri would find himself stranded in the nineteenth century without his private duty nurse to give him daily sponge baths? Not at all; because in such a close-knit family, there were always 'community' solutions. Susanne was thinking that Elle might be willing to take on that role, either 'there' in the past after Henri's arrival; or (better yet) 'here' in the present—their single mutations adding up to double: the exact amount required to buy a two-for-one ticket punched 'double-time' by nature's art-loving biochemical conductor, back to the future where Henri had started out to begin with.

But Henri might *not* have inherited the sex-linked translocation variant from one of his maternal time-travel 'capable' ancestors. If that was the case, Susanne's situation became much less hopeful for sure—but not *hopeless*, by any means. She might be forced to seek out *another* relative: for instance, a cousin named Claudine conveniently living in Paris, or Nicole's daughter residing in not-so-convenient Chicago; but before going to all that

212

trouble, she might just try getting completely wasted all by her lonesome in front of an Impressionist *Common-Object*.

You see, she had *another* theory: one that contended that John was dead wrong about a single-mutation carrier's limitations. If her belief held true, she might very well be able to 'go it' alone by ingesting an inordinate amount of the illicit fuel that she hoped would jump-start her genetic alteration and propel her like a rocket through *Waking Nude Preparing to Rise*. Never mind that John had told her all those years ago that because she harbored only one mutation rather than two, that she would *never* in a million years be able to open a *Virtual-Hole* in a *Common-Object*, regardless of how many magic-mushroom 'buttons' she popped into her mouth.

What did *he* know, anyway—a ridiculed and now dead outcast-scientist who used outdated genetic testing technology performed in the dark-ages of science more than a decade ago, in the era where medical false negatives were not that uncommon? Susanne could *easily* be that kind of case-in-point. But accurate or not, even the great John Noland would be the first to admit that even the soundest of theories are often disproven when they are thoroughly and objectively tested.

Had anyone done the necessary experiments in humans? Of course not! So maybe *she* would volunteer herself as that first pioneer, and give it a go with an especially heavy dosing of angel dust mixed with a double-fistful of LSD tablets, which she hoped would be enough to overcome those presumed 'limitations' of her single rather than double DNA mutation. One thing for sure is that it couldn't hurt to try before she hassled with the greater uncertainties and logistics of slumming it with the likes of her prostitute-cousin Claudine, or seeking out little-miss Noëlle Bruante-Noland in the heartland of another continent.

And then there was another fly in the ointment that couldn't be ignored. What if Dr. 'Tall-Dark-and-Handsome' didn't bid on her sexy auctioning merchandise, choosing another 'item' instead? Granted, blonde-over-brunette would contradict his stated preference, but who's to say the cute and single Dr. Lefebvre didn't visit the salon routinely to create a very convincing misimpression of flaxen that could be reversed to her natural-auburn on-demand? Yes, she had to admit that sweet Genevieve, regardless of her *true* hair color, was a potential problem that was already causing some serious playwright's block. No matter. She would just have to put her imaginary manuscript on the shelf for a while until the creative obstruction passed.

There was no question that the stars would need to align just so; but if they did, she could already envision herself hitchhiking back to Bohemian Paris of the late 1800's using Henri or herself as the vehicle—but *only* if she could arrange for *Waking Nude Preparing to Rise*, the incomparable Susanne Bruante, *and* her demented potentially chronotonin-producing great uncle, to be in the same room together after she fed the unknowing Henri a portion of illicit hallucinogens equivalent to a shot or two of absinthe.

All things considered, her expertly conceived script was more or less ready for opening night, having just been picked up today by a major production company called 'Thierry Duvalier, Incorporated'. The plot would soon be set in motion...so let the show begin.

CHAPTER TWENTY-TWO

Their date—couched only in part as a business dinner—occurred, as previously scheduled, shortly after the conclusion of Thierry's day-long interview-style examination of their mutual patient: an enigma that they were both convinced was afflicted with an unusual variant of DID that the brilliant neuropsychologist had named Confabulatory Identity Confusion, or CIC. Gennie fully expected that they would dine until well after midnight, with professional collaboration serving as the excuse for diving into the non-professional waters that they were both equally anxious to re-test, after a fifteen-year hiatus. She owed him an explanation along with an apology too, which she hoped to deliver in the most intimate way imaginable…if he would allow her.

She arrived a little bit earlier than their 8:00 reservation at the Michelin-rated restaurant at Thierry's hotel, sitting at the bar while waiting for him dressed in a sexy yet tasteful black dress that she had intentionally chosen for its comfortably form-fitting cut, conceived by a designer who had probably had Gennie's exact body-type in mind. The shoulder straps which hung on her fragrantly-lotioned bare shoulders traversed her perfumed open-neck in a V-shaped descent to finally meet at the mid-point of her delightfully eyebrow-raising, bra-less cleavage.

The silky material hugged the figure-eight outline of what many men would consider the ideal

216

feminine physique, curving downward—in and out and slightly in again—to trace the sensuous lines of her waist and hips, unmarred by panty lines given the absence of interfering undergarments. Clothing ended and skin began at mid-thigh, where the eye-catching trajectory continued down the straightaway of her bare, long legs: arguably her most appealing asset. In that dress: the only barrier between completely nude and the admiring world; and with her manicured nails detailed in soft lavender on enticing display in open-toed four-inch heels, there was no way in the world that Thierry would be able to concentrate on 'business' with no pleasure interjected.

"You look stunning," he commented, taking her hand lightly with two fingers in true gentlemanly fashion to help her down from the barstool, and guiding her with his palm briefly on her lower back to the *maître-d's* podium, where he confirmed their reservation. A moment later, they were sitting at a corner table, the wine-list in hand.

After agreeing on a bottle of Bordeaux, Gennie embarked on her well-practiced 'speech'; and this time he didn't interrupt but waited patiently while she had her say. "John was my very first, you see. We started dating in high school, when we were both sixteen; and until you, I had never considered being with anyone else. When I started to fall for you, I got really scared. That night in the call-room, you were a beautiful temptation; but by the time we had reached the moment of truth, when going all the way would seal my infidelity as 'official', I just couldn't do it. Guilt intervened, you see."

John quietly nodded his understanding as Gennie continued. "I was horrified that I had let it go as far as it did. My ten-year obligation to John drove me out of that call room and away from the potential for something beautiful and meaningful between us, I'm afraid. I'm really sorry." She took a deep breath…of sincere regret. "I felt, at the time, that John deserved the chance at 'forever' that he claimed he wanted. As it turns out, he had stepped out on me *way* before then, and so many other times after. I learned the truth about his repetitive unfaithfulness with a slap in the face: a pregnancy—and *not* mine."

She saw Thierry's eyes widen in disbelief. "That's right," she confirmed in an indignant tone. "Can you believe it? He had actually 'knocked up' one of his many girlfriends behind my back. Thank God I hadn't married him; and *double*-thank God we didn't have any children together, is all I can say."

Thierry took her hand kindly from across the table. "This is a terrible story. You must have felt totally betrayed." She nodded silently, and squeezed his hand. "What happened between us all those years ago is water under the bridge; and now we're standing together at the very same overpass. Will you jump into the water with me this time, Gennie? We could start right where we left off."

She laughed lightly. "I'm game if you are; but just a warning—I'm a terrible swimmer."

"Well I'm approaching Olympic caliber, so I should be able to help you along."

Their dinner began, then, in earnest, with a leisurely candle-lit perusal of the Classically-French menu followed by some surprisingly comfortable chit-chat over escargot and foie gras. The business portion of their dinner date was executed exclusively during the main course: seared grouper for her and a nicely-prepared chicken cordon bleu for him.

"I'm convinced there are other personalities clamoring for a voice inside her, with at least one of them attempting to emerge during my evaluation. I think it might be nineteenth century Nicole, materialized from Susanne's ancestral memories of her."

"So CIC remains your working diagnosis, after your marathon session today?"

"Definitely. The first step upon transfer will be to intensively study her subconscious with hypnotherapy using a past life regression technique. If my suspicions are confirmed, I'll be able to lead her through many of the experiences she only eluded to in today's interview, plus many more I hope. This way, we can sort through and organize her inherited recollections to corroborate the existence of the characters and events that she describes."

"How about your clinical trial using the mnemosyne receptor blocker that we discussed earlier?"

"That should wait until we've completed a thorough data-mining of her ancestral memories. If we block her receptors beforehand, even reversibly, then those recollections could be lost forever. We just don't have enough experience with *AXP34125* in human subjects to know if this agent will permanently affect memory and if so, to what extent."

"That makes sense."

"Would you agree that the timing of her transfer will depend primarily on the flexibility of the French authorities?" he asked her with a worried furrowing of his brow.

She waved away his concern with her fork. "They could care less at this point. You see, the team of art restorers have had great success in repairing the damage she caused to the Courbet painting and Degas sculptures, so the legal implications of her museum hysterics have essentially been eliminated. They are no longer threatening criminal charges at this point."

"That's a relief. I wonder then—does this change your viewpoint at all on supervision?"

"Meaning?"

"Well, she's confined in a high-security psychiatric facility here, which is providing an intense level of supervision that I won't be able to match at *Brugman*—especially if she's admitted, as I'm planning, to the neuropsychological clinical research unit. Yes, we'll have nurses and orderlies overseeing her day-to-day care there; but subtract from the security picture all of the video monitors, key-card access panels and restricted entry and exit doors that you have here. There could be ample opportunity for her to wander off if the staff becomes distracted by their various other patient-care duties."

"But where would she go, with no ID card, driver's license, passport, or most importantly money?"

"True." He paused to take a sip from his wine glass. "Then why, may I ask, have you maintained such a high level of security surrounding her stay here at *Pitié-Salpêtrière?*"

"Mainly because our facility doesn't *have* a low-security option, the reason being that the majority of our patients are severely disturbed. In actuality, the restrictions on her liberties are designed to protect *her* as much or more than her fellow detainees, which circles back to the reciprocal policy: namely, that we are obligated to insure that she doesn't pose a risk to herself or others. Hence, the careful monitoring."

"The question then becomes...*does* she?"

"Pose a risk to herself or others?"

"Yes."

She shook her head. "No, I don't think so. We've ruled out depression and anxiety, which are the usual diagnostic triggers for suicide; and I think you'll agree that she isn't exactly lacking in the self-esteem department either. In my experience, a narcissist like Susanne thinks *much* too highly of herself to inflict self-harm."

"That covers 'herself'...but how about 'others'?"

"We've established that she isn't psychotic in the classic schizophrenic or bipolar definition of the term, and she hasn't displayed any of the classic hallmarks of a psychopath—and believe me, we have *plenty* of them here! Additionally, she hasn't exhibited any violent tendencies at all since the first few days of her admission. My professional opinion is that I think you're safe on both counts."

"That's reassuring." She noticed that his brow was now smooth and relaxed rather than wrinkled with concern. "Would you care for another?" he asked her, pointing a finger at the empty *Canon La Gaffeliere* bottle that the waiter had just drained in the refilling of both of their glasses.

"No thank you, I'd rather save my alcoholic-reserve for a digestif or two with desert."

He nodded agreement and re-focused his attention on his nearly-consumed chicken cordon bleu, but only momentarily. Immediately after the waiter had politely retreated, Thierry put his utensils aside and looked her straight in the eyes with the most compelling and intense hazel-green that she had ever seen. "So I was thinking that you deserve some professional recognition in all this, if only for coming to the not-so-obvious conclusion that Susanne may have a variant type of DID." It seemed that he was now getting straight to an additional, unexpected item on the 'business' agenda. "Even if your contribution stops there, I intend on acknowledging your insight; but what if you became an *official* collaborating physician?"

"In what sense?"

"Well to begin with, I could make you a contributing author on any publications that result from our work together on this case; but that would require…your 'contribution'—physically, perhaps?"

His eyes literally twinkled. This was an offer that she'd be an idiot to refuse, but she needed him to spell it out. "Go on," she replied as coolly as her rapidly over-heating emotions would allow.

"Well, we could certainly involve you remotely by way of video-conferencing, but psychotherapy doesn't lend itself well to this method. I was thinking that if we could find a way for you to be present in Brussels at least part-time, then you could become an integral member of Susanne's treatment team. You could lend an important psychiatric viewpoint to my neuropsychological one."

Her heart started to beat frantically, but she feigned an outward calm. "This would have to involve an academic appointment at *Brugman* though. Wouldn't that be a challenge to negotiate?"

"You seem to forget that I have some 'pull' in administrative arrangements such as this." That was an understatement, coming from the internationally-recognized Neuropsychology division-chief at *Brugman* and someone who would probably be awarded the Nobel prize in medicine shortly. In fact, Thierry Duvalier would easily be able to 'pull' a freighter with his pinky-finger using the kind of heavy-duty influence he had at his disposal. "This wouldn't be the first time that I've sponsored faculty from another institution for temporary privileges at ours, you know. If you're agreeable, I can start the process when I return to Belgium tomorrow."

That he would go to such lengths to collaborate with her was extraordinarily generous, and represented a once in a lifetime opportunity. The underlying romantic repercussions couldn't be ignored, either. "I don't know what to say…" she began, intending to complete her sentence with a gracious *except thank you and yes,* if he had only given her the chance.

"Well you don't have to decide at this very moment," he interrupted kindly, the statement obviously meant to clarify that what he was offering her was a 'no pressure whatsoever' proposal. "I realize it's a very big decision that would require the approval of your administration here at *Pitié-Salpêtrière*, and would involve relocation to my adopted city at least for a few days each week. I could find you a university-sponsored apartment that wouldn't cost you much, very close to the research facility…*and* to my own place of residence."

This is the exact point where the business discussion ended and the deliciously personal part of their evening began.

CHAPTER TWENTY-THREE

"So I imagine we would see quite a bit of each other, if this all worked out?" It seemed difficult for her to fully catch her breath.

"If I answer 'this is exactly what I had in mind and I truly hope so' would that work *for* me, or *against* me?"

She reached across the table and placed her hand gently on top of his. Her skin touching his sent shivers up and down her spine and accelerated her heart-rate to a double-pounding. The intimate setting made the skin-on-skin contact feel much different than the simple hand-holding they had enjoyed early this morning. "It would definitely work *for* you," she responded quietly.

He turned his hand over so that he could entwine his fingers in hers, a maneuver that made her breath catch. "Is that a yes, then?"

"Yes," she whispered, realizing as she said it that this one word of affirmation held in its simple three letters a virtual world of meaning: both literal and implied. Yes, she would accept his proposition that they collaborate on the Susanne Doe case; yes, she would agree to work temporarily in Brussels; yes, she would take an apartment close to his so they could see each other as often as possible; and yes, she would fall madly in love with him—now, finally, picking up where they had left off fifteen years ago. So they ordered a flourless *torte chocolat* and shared it with one fork rather than two, as a meaningful symbol of their now obviously burgeoning revisited romance.

They retired to the lounge, equipped with a small bar and more comfortable seating, where he enjoyed some cognac and she a port (not just one) over God knows how many hours of conversation. She listened semi-enthralled while he described a series of relationships that had all apparently ended because of his 'career-takes-precedence-over-everything-else' mentality...and, as it turns out, because he had never quite gotten over her. "I had no idea," she said, with guilt-tinged sadness. "Why didn't you ever try to contact me?"

"Maybe I *should* have; but I thought you'd made your choice...and that was that. You can't force someone to love you, Gennie. That has to come naturally, springing from mutual feelings— and I suppose I was convinced that the emotions associated with our brief interaction were strictly one-sided."

"Well, they weren't...*far* from it."

"I had no idea," he said using her exact words from seconds ago, with a perfectly matching mixture of self-reproach and melancholy. To Gennie, the phonetic duplication seemed especially apropos given their lost-but-now-found simpatico. "So, as an escape from the heartbreak..." (she cringed to hear him use the word...because the last thing she ever wanted to do was hurt him) "...I totally devoted myself to my career. But now, I've decided that it's high time to adopt a drastically different attitude."

"How so?"

His normally quick and pressured speech slowed down to almost leisurely due to the amount of alcohol that he had consumed so far. "Well, I'm in my early forties and I've already created my professional legacy." She could see and hear him focusing on his articulation, which confirmed her impression that he was tipsy, despite his admirable handling of an impressive amount of VSOP. "I'm long overdue for a meaningful re-focus on my personal life."

"Perhaps you need a career-minded woman who fully understands your professional commitment, which I'd wager to guess started a full decade-and-a-half ago; someone who can help you ease into a more balanced lifestyle," she suggested. In fact, she had just such a person in mind.

He was quick to agree. "Yes, but someone like that is hard to find," he teased.

"Sometimes when you least expect it, you discover what you've been searching for in the most unlikely of places."

"Like in a lounge at a Ritz Carlton hotel well after midnight, in the heart of Paris?"

Her second port had convinced her that continuing this playful banter ran counter to their re-discovered affinity and the honesty of their conversation so far; and so she decided that now was the perfect time for a more candid, forward approach. His gaze seemed to agree—telling it straight, plainly beckoning her with a certain shade of enchanting bedroom-green that enveloped her like the embrace of the passionate lover that she knew he was…if their aborted call room experience

227

from years before held any measure for her to judge. He had taken her to the brink back then, in a way that few men had been able to do since—but she had resisted the full-fledged 'fall from grace'. That look promised to lead her to the brink again; but this time, she felt certain that there would be no retreating…and no going back.

He placed his hand on her bare leg, tentatively at first, just a few inches above her exposed knee on her outer thigh; and when this salvo was not rejected, he leaned over for a re-testing of their mutual desire—a second kiss, so much different than this morning's. With eyes closed she felt his lips moving tenderly on hers, literally crashing into her like a high pressure zone intermingling with her low, creating a virtual maelstrom in the climate of her already sweltering libido. The resulting physical effect had by now reached the critical point, where she must now stop or else succumb—giving in to the deliciously inevitable. *Give in!* her entire being screamed. And why not? Her heart and mind told her in unison that there was no reason in the world that she shouldn't.

"You two need to get a room," the waiter interrupted. Looking up, she noticed that the place had cleared. They were the only customers left. "Seriously," he said, with a wink. "We're closing."

"We've *got* a room," Thierry laughed, pulling her up with one hand and leading her playfully across the lobby, up the elevators, and down the hall to room 1293. He swiped his card, swung the door open…and then, with no warning, swept her off her feet and into his arms.

Before she knew it he was actually carrying her across the threshold, as if they were newlyweds. He laid her gingerly on the bed, while kicking the door closed with one heel with a theatrical flair. "Too melodramatic?" he asked.

"No; more like perfectly romantic," she countered in a low voice—husky with desire and vaguely trembling with anticipation. He lay beside her and kissed her neck, lips, and ears so tenderly that she actually started to weep.

"What's wrong?" he asked, brushing some strands of hair away from her face with his fingertips and the wetness from her cheek with the back of his hand.

"Oh Thierry," she whispered. "Nothing...nothing at all. Make love to me, please—right now."

So he did. He stripped first and then peeled off her dress as she lay on the bed: a model of pure erotic perfection. He unstrapped her heels and lay his naked body directly on top of her yearning vulnerability—the firm, milk-white swell of her breasts: below, touching softly against the hardness of his olive-toned chest: above. Then they were moving together, the rhythmic dichotomy of male-in-female a softly blended symmetry occurring *now* as it should have *then*, with all the pent up intensity of so many waiting-years. The heady fragrance of X impassioned by Y filled the room, until they were both drunk with the intoxicating aroma of each other until, with deliberate and delicious slowness, they reached the pinnacle of masculine-meets-feminine together—his wetness surpassed only slightly by hers, commingling in the warm interior of her deepest sexuality. This was the compelling sex-scene that had been playing in her head for fifteen years now—every move choreographed and practiced in her fantasy, now becoming reality. 'Take one', in the call room years ago, had been canned for incompleteness; but 'take two' was a keeper—and he was too.

By now it was a quarter past two, and he was dozing beside her, his hand folded in hers, while she lay wide awake—her thoughts racing. She had a powerful premonition that this man from her past was now her destiny. At dinner and after, she had found herself almost alarmingly comfortable sharing with him her most private likes and dislikes in the realm of the intimately personal. But after some internal back-and-forth earlier, she had decided not to reveal her closet pleasure…just yet.

Was she worried that he might judge her? Yes, of course she was—it would be a lie to deny it. Many men, especially those with a self-centered mindset, had the tendency to lash out with misdirected accusations and jealousy as a reaction to their own insecurities. She had a sense already that he wasn't cut from this type of narrow-minded mold, yet it would be much safer to withhold this small piece of sensitive information for a while until she knew him, in the present, a tad bit better.

Was she ashamed? God no! Her body was a beautiful work of art that she thoroughly enjoyed sharing, portrayed on canvas by one painter this way and another painter that way—the focus shifting from one prohibited body part to another, from piece to piece. There was nothing on earth that compared to being stripped magnificently naked for a late evening sitting, with creative eyes focused on what was considered taboo by the outdated norms of general society. The exercise always sent the thrill of forbidden exposure trembling through her perfect *au naturel* frame.

She did *so* enjoy her clandestine pastime. Along with the physical pleasure, she savored the psychological dichotomy of the entire concept: namely, that a serious and respected physician with a sharp and intelligent mind could at the same time be defined in private as a totally physical being, transformed in that exquisite moment of primitive nudity into the definition of female sexuality and the ideal object of universal artistic desire. And the beauty of it all is that no one in the world except those she posed for (and of course her 'inner circle' of carefully chosen confidants) would ever suspect that she was in some ways living two separate and radically oppositional lives.

It was actually this yin and yang that sustained her in life's darker moments, when a patient's ailments seemed entirely unsolvable and particularly resistant to her best efforts. In these moments she would retreat into the reassurance of another world altogether, where those professional problems did not exist and her intellect was unlikely to dwell on anything but the simple joy of the artistically erotic.

Oh yes, she fully recognized that it was truly ironic that the case they were about to share together featured a mentally-ill woman who, in her fantasy-world, believed that *she* was a nude artist's model. Well Gennie really *was*, with her naked form (identity undisclosed) on display in more than just a handful of Parisian galleries, which in a way gave her a certain personal insight into Susanne's psyche. If shared experience—true or fabricated—counted, it could theoretically be beneficial to the eventual therapeutic outcome to have a psychiatrist/nude model continue her involvement in this case as a contributing psychotherapist.

He stirred, opening his eyes and smiling at her with them. "Let's get under the covers and sleep," he suggested.

"It's late," she murmured between kisses, "and I have to attend on rounds at eight. I should go."

"Stay. Don't leave me, like before."

"Oh, my poor darling," she said, taking him in her arms again. "I'm here for good." She pulled the sheet and blanket out from underneath, and covered them both with the reassurance of shared silk and cotton. "I'll stay..." (*forever*).

232

CHAPTER TWENTY-FOUR

Thierry Duvalier had never been happier. His entire life had changed shortly after returning from his trip to Paris, which had culminated with something more than just a date with a woman from his past: the stunningly beautiful, intellectually engaging, and rediscovered love of his life, Dr. Gennie Lefebvre.

He had quietly pulled some strings the moment he returned to Belgium and soon after, Gennie had been generously granted an eighteen-month sabbatical from *Pitié-Salpêtrière*—astonishingly allowing her to reside in Brussels full-time rather than just a few days a week: their original hoped-for plan. True to his word, he found her a one-bedroom apartment in a complex owned by the University located a mere five-minute walk from his own townhome. The convenience of proximity would make it easy for them to work together and more, if the stars aligned as he hoped they would.

Six weeks later, in mid-August, he found himself excitedly helping her settle into her new flat, offering a hand with the unpacking—an activity that resulted in the not-so-accidental 'exposure' of Gennie's interesting sideline. After the fact, she sheepishly admitted that her request that he empty *that* particular box had been intentional, as a way for him to conveniently discover her hobby.

She had slipped the ten-by-twenty-inch oil-on-canvas into a long pillowcase for protection, carefully placing it between the cushion of blankets and sheets in one of her moving crates to prevent damage during the relocation. When he had innocently uncovered the rectangular item that she had fully intended for him to 'light upon', the simple fact that it depicted a nude woman lying prone with her full-frontage facing the viewer was enough to give *anyone* an embarrassed mixed-company sort of pause; but a split-second later when he did a double-take and instantly recognized the model, he could feel the blood rush into his cheeks with double or triple the initial intensity.

She was standing at his side, looking over his left shoulder in what, for him, felt like an awkward shared inspection of the tastefully erotic painting. Her reaction to viewing the 'nude' with a newfound critic seemed quite the opposite, if her nonchalant and perfectly relaxed demeanor was any indication. "It was quite difficult maintaining that pose during the sitting. I specifically recall that my arm kept falling asleep."

She made these comments in a surprisingly matter-of-fact tone, indicating that in contrast to his situational discomfort, *she* considered their concurrent viewing of an artistic representation of her perfect naked body as the most natural thing in the world, and not awkward in the least. Indeed, as he studied the positioning of her extremity he could well imagine the uncomfortable pins-and-needles sensation that must have accompanied the sustained supporting of her head on that delicate limb, one palm on a rosy cheek cradling that exquisite face leveraged on a bent elbow. In the scene her eyes were slightly averted and her long hair streamed downward in a golden waterfall which did little to distract him from those astonishing stripped-to-explicit details that would normally be enjoyed in one's imagination only.

He was holding the naked bodyscape in both hands at arm's-length literally enthralled by the view until she walked from behind him to in front, breaking the spell by gently taking the painting from him and placing it carefully on the floor propped against the wall, being careful to face it outward rather than in—the choice made deliberately it seemed, allowing for continued visibility in an implied statement of principle. 'I'm proud of this and I don't care what people think' was the message he heard, underscored by the boldness he read in her eyes—which were now staring him down in a playfully defiant request for his feedback, whether it be good or bad.

She exuded a self-confidence reflected not only in her comportment but also in the way she bravely put herself out there by sharing a potentially shocking aspect of her personal life with someone she really barely knew (although they were getting familiar with each other very rapidly, he had to admit). Not only was she taking a risk by revealing this type of sensitive information to a person whose moral disposition and openness to the world of unapologetic self-exposure had yet to be explored or determined, but it was a seriously dangerous gamble for her to disclose her lack of inhibitions in the no-clothing arena to a collaborator with whom she would be working shoulder-to-shoulder in an intimately professional environment for a full year-and-a-half. It was chancy, to say the least—and he truly admired the chutzpah.

They were facing each other now and she took both of his hands in hers, almost as if they were preparing to dance. Well in a way they were, and now it was high-time for him to take the lead. "I love it," he said; and it was true—he really did. "It's a powerful statement of freedom and beauty, and I'm so happy you decided to share it with me."

He drew her towards him, placing both arms around her waist while she busied herself with buckles and zippers in the narrowed space between them. With her hurried assistance he stepped into a quick and total nakedness; while with his, she shimmied out of jeans and panties and stripped off her t-shirt and sports-bra in what appeared to be a single, easy movement. He eased her, breathtakingly nude, onto the carpeted floor right in front of the instigating portrait, feeling her beckoning skin conjoining with his in a kind of unrelated yet consanguine unity that spoke to destiny's desire. His lips caressed the line of her neck, the swell of her chest and the slope of her navel—ever so gentle, yet the effect was anything but calming. She rolled him almost frantically onto his back while maintaining their face-to-face contact, joining their bodies with primal purpose at the center-point—her face pointed upward with eyes closed in a private yet shared ecstasy that, due to her wildly tenacious efforts, would very shortly bind them together in fluid-unity.

Her body and his were one, and there was no going back. "I'm in love with you, Gennie," he blurted out before he could stop himself, the words spilling out from above as involuntarily as his passion did from below. "I loved you back then, and I love you now...more than anything else in this world."

He knew full well that it was inadvisable to make such a premature declaration at this early stage; yet, was this so different than her trusting him with her own sensually-sensitive secret just a few minutes earlier? She had had an intuition that he was of the same mindset, and in a similar fashion he had just applied the reciprocal hunch.

She collapsed on top of him and placed her head on his pounding chest, unresponsive to his commentary at first while she caught her breath and allowed her own trembling body to recover from their shared nirvana. He thought that perhaps in her silence she was contemplating some sort of deflecting rejoinder, but when she looked up at him with eyes that said 'me too' rather than 'so sorry' he knew that he had done little damage to their evolving rekindled relationship with his impulsive outburst.

"I feel the same way," she whispered, putting an exclamation point on her statement by taking his face in both her hands and preventing further discussion by engaging her lips and tongue with his own until finally she rolled off, lying next to him and assuming the identical pose as in the painting— her face propped on one arm with the entire length of her body facing-front in tantalizing contact with

237

his left side. He rolled over towards her and reflected her positioning so that their post-coital moments could take place in a cozy rapport of up-close and face-to-face.

They enjoyed a non-conversational moment breathing in unison until finally he broke the silence after lowering his shoulder onto the floor and shaking out his supporting arm, since it had fallen asleep. "I see what you mean about holding that particular pose."

"It doesn't take long for full-blown pins and needles, that's for sure." She too had given her supporting arm reprieve, stretching it out above her head which she was now resting on a makeshift pillow created by the juncture of her shoulder and slender biceps. Her back faced the painting but from his opposing perspective he enjoyed a perfect view, which she acknowledged by looking over her shoulder to follow the line of his gaze such that hers now rested on the same focus. "Do you really like it?"

"It's truly amazing." He examined the beautiful lines of her painted body—his gaze moving from top to bottom and back again; and then repeated the visual exercise but this time admiring the real thing. "The artist reproduced every inch of you with incredible precision. What did he call you?" The confused look on her face demanded clarification. "I mean the name of the painting."

She laughed lightly. "Well *she* referred to it simply as *Nude Reclining*."

"She?

"Yes, 'she'—at least for *this* one; although you *are* correct that most of the artists that choose to paint me are men."

He had incorrectly assumed that he was looking at the only artistic representation of Gennie's nude body; but now it seemed with her use of the plural that modeling disrobed was an activity that she enjoyed repeatedly, making it something more than just a one-time whim. She must have seen the realization dawn on his face. "Enjoying the concept of 'nude' is an inherited proclivity, you know," she said, feeling in a way that an explanation was in order. "I already mentioned that my great-great-great grandfather was the famous nineteenth-century painter Jules Joseph Lefebvre. He was noted for his countless renderings of beautiful nudes, reflecting his love for the genre—expressed artistically from the opposite side of the canvas though, of course."

"You don't need to make excuses for something as awe-inspiring as 'you'," he said, waving a hand in the general direction of the flesh-and-blood model and the adjacent visually-striking rendering of herself. "Honestly," he added, his eyes and words ever so sincere. "But on a separate note—don't you agree that the emerging similarities between yourself and our unique patient are adding up to 'truly bizarre'?" He didn't pause for a response before elucidating. "Not only does Susanne share the same predilection, imagined or real, for the nude artistic posing; but she's also convinced she's a blood relative of not one, but two, famous French artists and their families: namely, Courbet and Caillebotte."

She nodded agreement. "No one would argue that this *entire* situation is curiously ironic. I'm sure that for you, discovering that your former love-interest and intern—someone who rather abruptly became not only your significant 'other' but also a professional colleague—is in many ways a partial reflection of your latest research subject...must be particularly disconcerting, to say the least. I hope the nude modeling 'angle' doesn't color your work-related feelings towards me; *or* present an insurmountable relationship-hurdle." She looked him squarely in the eyes, looking deeply for his reaction. "Does my hobby bother you?"

"Oh my," he laughed; "not at all. I'm just letting it all sink in—coincidences and all."

She sat up, relieved; so he did too, sitting cross-legged and thoughtful with his hands in hers and their fingers symbolically entwined.

"You're not like other men," she commented softly.

"Meaning?"

"For one thing you're open minded." She rolled her eyes. "You'd be surprised how uptight most of them are when it comes to *this* sort of thing." Gennie waved her hand in the general direction of *Nude Reclining* as the conceptual source of her frustration with certain members of the opposite sex.

"Is there anything else that sets me apart, aside from my liberal mindset?"

"Fishing for compliments, are we?"

240

"I'm afraid you caught me practicing one of my favorite pastimes."

"Okay, I'll bite. In addition to being amazing in bed—*and* on the floor, I should say; you don't seem threatened by my little guilty pleasure."

"I see no reason why guilt should factor into this discussion at all, or why you posing nude would be intimidating to someone who isn't directly involved in the undertaking."

"You see, *that's* where you and 'most men' disagree. For them, the concept of erotic exposure in the name of art, with *my* naked body's 'signature' sprawled licentiously on the canvas, triggers a kind of 'man-becomes-werewolf' transformation."

He raised his eyebrows in a request for elaboration. "It usually starts out with a mildly-injured yet perfectly tame: 'how could you?'; and then ends up later with the all-claws-out, accusatory line: 'how dare you!' scripted, it seems, for Lon Chaney himself. They make it all about them when it's not about 'them' at all! It's about *me*, and I refuse to let them impose their brand of high-horsed morality on my free-spirited one."

"That type of finger-pointing is just a defense mechanism driven by their own insecurities."

"You'd make a good psychologist."

"Very funny."

"The point is; those jealous types outnumber their non-jealous counterparts ten-to-one."

"It sounds like you've enjoyed a particularly unhealthy sampling of the nine-out-of-ten 'distasteful' majority."

241

"You might say that. But *you*, I'm happy to say, taste delicious."

He laughing quietly at her bedroom-humor. "I'm not the jealous type." And he really wasn't. He was secure enough in himself to recognize that his 'value' in matters of the mind, soul or heart existed separately from the actions of a significant-other. Just as she had said, it involved *her* not *him*; and the nude modeling was obviously a source of immense satisfaction...so why should it bother him?

Well it *didn't*; just the opposite, in fact. Although he was just getting to *really* know her, he felt that soon if not already her happiness was linked to his own, which meant that if baring it all and allowing an artist's-only viewing of her alluring naked body made her heart soar, then by all means she should continue to revel in this occasional *non-*guilty pleasure—and with no excuses required.

"I had an inkling you were one of the good ones, which is why I picked you," she proclaimed with a grin.

"I thought it was the other way around."

"The one doesn't exclude the other. Haven't you ever heard of 'love at first sight'?"

"Who hasn't! I fell in love with you at first glance, fifteen years ago—case-in-point. And you?"

"The same...although it took a second glance to seal the deal!" She leaned over slightly to kiss the tip of his nose in a syrupy show of affection. "Love at first sight, I believe, is really just another way to describe instantaneous mutual selection. I picked you, and you picked me—then and now; and here we are."

And 'here' was exactly where he wanted to stay…forever.

CHAPTER TWENTY-FIVE

Things had been going swimmingly—that is, until *she* showed up.

Susanne had been transferred by long-distance ambulance just a few days after Thierry's initial visit, quickly settling into her new hospital environment where locked doors and security systems were as foreign as she was. Her private room was basic hospital issue, offering a television and a picture window for entertainment which meant that she looked forward to the twice-daily neuropsychiatric 'sessions' with her quietly-sexy new doctor, if only to break the cycle of boredom.

Of course there were occasional nurses and orderlies wandering in and out to lighten her isolation, but she hadn't paid much attention to them until now, about six weeks after her arrival, when it seemed apparent that identifying and enlisting an unknowing co-conspirator in her escape would be a necessity. Her plans to seduce and manipulate the hard-to-read Dr. Duvalier just got blown to pieces by the materialization of her paranoia; because yes, that *tête-à-tête* taking place in the privacy of Thierry's hotel room after a 'strictly business' dinner-date probably *did* transpire in just the way she had presciently envisioned—or something close to it...if not in Thierry's five-star flophouse in Paris, then in some other apartment or rented condo that the now-visiting Mademoiselle Professor would come to call home, right here in Brussels. It was a shame, for sure; but already

Susanne had started to formulate a back-up plan because if she was anything, she was adaptable.

Thierry had explained during the initial examination on arrival that her treatment would proceed in two phases: the first delving extensively into her psyche using psychoanalysis and deep-dive hypnotherapy, and the second involving some new drug that he seemed particularly excited to experiment on her. He was convinced that this investigational agent would effectively treat a bogus disorder that he called Confabulatory Identity Confusion, or CIC, that he believed had led to a delusional and complex fantasy rather than a real time-traveling adventure. She had no problem playing along with phase one, which was well on its way by now to an aborted conclusion since she would have to institute a change in plans and 'get the hell out of Dodge' as soon as possible—but phase two? Forget it! There was no way in hell that she would agree to be his guinea pig, even if she *was* 'the perfect research subject'.

Yes, she had overheard him use those very words, standing outside her doorway speaking with nerdy excitement to that harlot posing as a professional collaborator, who had signed up for a full year-and-a-half of sex-on-the-side using 'research' as the excuse for what was sure to be a particularly raunchy affair, occurring entirely at Susanne's expense. Some crazy blood test had apparently revealed that 'the perfect research subject' had record-setting levels of a memory peptide coursing through her veins (*go figure*), but this make-believe substance was truly irrelevant to reality. Scientists like Thierry lived and breathed for their fanciful theories and presumptions that were really just (to borrow the enemy's favorite term) 'confabulations'. Wasn't it truly ironic that Thierry viewed *her* as delusional, even labeling her with some made-up disorder when it was really *him* and the entire community of medical scientists who should be studied on the Freudian psychoanalysis couch.

Hypnosis was actually nothing like she had anticipated. She understood after experiencing her first induced trance that the classic scene featuring a gold watch swinging like a miniature pendulum just inches from some amenable subject's glazed-over eyes was just a Hollywood cliché, bearing no similarity to the actual process which she had to admit he executed quite expertly. At the time he put her 'under' she was fully engaged in their little game, making her abundantly more susceptible to his past life regression procedure than she would be now when little-miss 'spread your legs' had crashed their private party.

"'Ancestral memory mining' is really a more accurate description than 'past-life regression therapy'," Thierry had explained as she had willingly taken her place on his leather office recliner for the first time, sinking into its soft embracing comfort with eyes closed while he led her with quiet voice and calming words, down-and-down-and-down a spiral staircase into the depths of her mind. Finally, after infinity circled with dizzying purpose into yesterday she reached the bottom, where the air hung moist and humid with

246

centuries curling like smoke around the steamy millennia of the distant past. She was fully 'under'.

"Tell me what you see."

"A hallway of doors," she heard herself murmur—unexpectedly trance-like, to her surprise. There were dozens and dozens of them—some with antique latch-handles and others with ornamental knobs; some made of exquisitely carved wood and others fashioned from gold and displaying extraordinarily-intricate inlays. Entry to the rooms behind could be gained, she realized, by individual keys hanging on hooks attached to each door-frame.

"Pick one," he suggested, his voice far away and disembodied like her own subconscious.

She felt distinctly detached from herself: completely devoid of identity in a bleary-eyed world where she wasn't Susanne at all, or anyone else—for the moment. The essence that wasn't her knew immediately, however, which door to select, and who she would become as soon as she stepped over the threshold. "That one," she mumbled.

It was barely more than a weathered plank with an iron keyhole, conveniently located first in line to her right. She picked the key off its hook, inserting it smoothly into the lock and turning it one 'click' clockwise, which immediately gained her entry via creaking and rusty hinges into a meagerly furnished room equipped with an easel, adjacent painting supplies arranged haphazardly on a small table, a wooden high-backed chair intended for use by the artist, and a platform raised to more-or-less eye level on an entanglement of boxes and wooden blocks just a few feet opposite the painting-station.

"Where are you?" the subliminal voice inquired.

"In Jean's studio." She always called him by his first name whereas everyone else referred to the famous painter by his third: 'Gustave'.

"Courbet?" her unconscious guide asked.

"Yes," she confirmed lazily, the word echoing in her head and bouncing off the walls of her mind. "I remember every second of this beautiful day—when we conceived our son: Edmond." She paused for a moment, walking perfectly naked over to the open window to look out on the familiar courtyard of trees, their leaves dripping teardrops from a muggy August rain while in the distance she heard the far-off approaching rumble of yet another sultry thunderstorm.

"Who are you?"

"Nicole Thérèse Bruante." And she truly was. Every molecule, atom and particle of her being sang this long-lost identity, exhumed in a strange other-world of melodies taking place somewhere beyond the grave in her until-now forgotten ancestral memory-bank.

"Describe what you see, hear and feel." The suggestion to narrate settled deep inside her like a fertile impregnation, taking on a life of its own. From here on out she would require no further subliminal prompting.

"It's August tenth in 1866, when Jean finished that amazing painting of me that he called *The Origin of the World:* the name reflecting the tool of womankind's fertility—so blatant in depiction yet subtle in meaning. My womb would actually be

248

filled with life on that day, bearing out the symbolic title."

The sights and sounds of that re-lived moment washed over her as she turned, recalling that he was standing right there with his back to her adjusting the canvas on its easel. She took a few steps forward, wrapping her arms around his neck from behind to peek over his shoulder on tip-toes, her nudity pressed against him in a distinct recollection of desire that she knew would be fulfilled shortly—right there on the posing platform, as soon as her lover brushed the final strokes of paint onto his shockingly-explicit *en-face* rendering of her breasts and genitalia. "It's extraordinary," she commented, her words echoing off the walls of the past *and* the present—the strange duality memorialized by the scratching sounds of pen-on-paper scribbled far, far away in that other world where medical research ruled.

"Of course it is—because it's *you*, my love."

She felt honored to have been chosen as the model for such a groundbreaking erotic masterpiece. Nothing quite like it had ever been attempted, mainly because it required a boldness of spirit on the part of both the painter *and* the subject that most individuals lacked; but also because her Jean was on a mission to normalize something that in private everyone viewed as glorious and natural, while in public they denounced as perverse and abhorrent.

"It's so hypocritical," he used to comment in idle studio-conversation while he painted and she posed. "Mankind's source of life, where *all* of us originated, should be honored and celebrated, not shunned and demonized—*wherever* it happens to be encountered. Your carnal anatomy and everything it stands for is gorgeous, awe inspiring, and thoroughly deserving of open praise, whether it's on display under the bedsheets, out there in the bustling streets, or right *here...*" (he waved a paintbrush first at the 'real thing' and then at his work-in-progress: a one-of-a-kind philosophical statement that his short-sighted critics would later label as pornographic) "...where your exquisite femininity will be captured in time for all the world to enjoy."

She was saddened by the in-hindsight knowledge that *The Origin of the World* would be banned from exhibition, sitting unseen in her attic room along with all of Courbet's other explicit nudes, relegated to her safekeeping after her lover was exiled for the remainder of his life to far-off Switzerland, as punishment for his leadership role in the Paris Commune.

Still looking over his shoulder, she took a moment to admire the nearly-finished sexually-provocative portrait of her private (correction: intended to soon be *public*) parts. Her ample breasts dominated the upper dextral quadrant, seen at a tilted angle and with the right one forming a rounded prominence directly under the canopy of a sheet that was placed just-so, failing miserably in its intended job of concealment. Her left one, equally enticing, stood with aroused vigilance in the shadows created by the same inadequate camouflage, beckoning the viewer to imagine what might happen next in the scene immediately

250

following this frozen moment in time, when a determined but trembling hand dares to remove that bed-clothed source of darkness.

Next her gaze journeyed down the sloping lines of her torso to rest for a moment on the flat valley of her stomach, marred only by the gentle inward kiss of her navel. This was one of her favorite erogenous zones that Jean often explored with the light touch of his fingertips, lingering only briefly before traveling south into prohibited territory. Her pubic underbrush functioned below much as the bedsheet did above: as a particularly ineffectual veil that did very little to shield this enticing but forbidden zone from being examined by her traveling eye. Her right leg was positioned in a straight line extending into the lower sinistral corner of the painting, while her left leg rested flat and at a ninety-degree angle to exit from the opposite right-lower side, opening her pelvis to reveal the secret details of her gender in a front-and-center exposé that Jean executed in classic realist style—since after all, he *was* the father of this artistic movement. He had even speckled subtle drops of moisture onto the portrait's cynosure so that to those viewers who were particularly attentive, her excitement in the pose would be clearly evident.

"He asked me at that moment to position myself on the pallet for one last session, since the piece was nearly finished," she heard herself describe, knowing somewhere in the back of her mind that in another time and place entirely, her words were being fastidiously transcribed into a notebook for someone's future reference. All that mattered was that 'portrait in time', where her newfound identity was crystal-clear and everyone else (including a stranger called Susanne and her doctor, whose name she could not remember) existed as mere shadows lurking in the far corners of her subconscious.

She kissed the back of Jean's neck in acknowledgement that it was time for work, navigating around the painter's island to settle onto the platform. Despite the summer atmosphere that hung warm inside the small room, the first contact of her clammy skin on the bare wood felt cold on the flat of her back, if only for an instant. She let her legs fall open using identical posturing to match the painting, which came quite naturally now since their 'sittings' for this piece had begun when spring had barely started to age into summer. She loved the indelible contribution to erotic posterity that this project represented, and would truly miss the daily opportunity to make her mark on the underground world of the sensually artistic.

"Posing like this always makes me want you," she whispered, knowing in the back of her mind that her uttered words would be heard not only *inside* the memory she was in the process of reliving, but *outside* as well—in a sterile office located in the bowels of a hospital where someone vulnerable and vaguely unstable was being analyzed like a bug in a bottle.

"You'll have me soon enough."

That promise was soon fulfilled. The cloudy daylight was starting to darken into night when he smiled, dropped his paintbrush into a jar of acetone, took off his painter's smock and declared *finis*.

He lit some candles and an oil lantern while she watched him strip to naked in the days when he was still slim rather than overweight—her own body primed and ready lying explicitly on the platform, intensely unwilling to break the pose until she felt the relief she needed in that hungry focal-point of model's body and artist's picture. He descended upon her, strong and hard and with an exigency that matched her own until she felt the wave of creation—yes, the planted seed of her only child, Edmond Bruante—crashing inside her onto the sands of an alternate reality that she recognized as her own and *not* her own…and that's when he woke her.

"Open your eyes, Susanne," Thierry Duvalier commanded. When she did, her identity came rushing back, and with it a cocky skepticism that she painstakingly concealed—because after all, she had a plan that required her to play the part of a 'woe is me' victim who desperately needed her doctor to save her from the confusing and terrifying world of a patient who suffered from multiple personality disorder.

This had been the first of many hypnosis sessions over the span of about four weeks, and also the most powerful. Subsequent trips for the most part focused on her nineteenth century memories, although a few took her back further in time when she opened doors leading to millennia gone-by rather than centuries. She couldn't argue that these potent recollections could very well represent

253

inherited DNA-encoded flashbacks stolen by way of meiosis from her various ancestors, just as Thierry claimed; but there was no way in the world that she had jumbled all of those recollections together in some type of confabulated story-line that Thierry excitedly referred to as CIC, almost like he was drooling over a playboy centerfold. His masturbatory theorizing would soon ejaculate prematurely to no fruitful conclusion however, because she was actively plotting her escape—and the exit-door now seemed to be partially propped open.

CHAPTER TWENTY-SIX

Her name was Margot: an attractive nurse with walnut-colored hair, brown eyes and a facial structure that more-or-less matched Susanne's. From a distance, in poor lighting, or even theoretically on an ID card, Margot and Susanne could pass on quick glance as interchangeable—an observation that Susanne noticed on their first meeting, keeping that wild card in her back pocket for later use as the poker game progressed. Better yet, Margot it seemed had a distinct preference for women, making this inclination known to Susanne in a conversation one night when she was working as the nurse in-charge that was so blatantly flirtatious that it was laughable. Susanne at first passed over this fertile field of potential manipulation, but now it seemed that planting a seed would be a necessity.

"This is getting old," Susanne commented to Margot one morning during nursing rounds, about eight weeks after her arrival during the first week of September.

"How do you mean?"

"Imagine if you were in my position, all alone in one hospital or another these past six months with no options for physical relief...except for what I'm able to provide on my own."

"That must be terrible." Margot sat sympathetically on the edge of Susanne's bed, taking her hand in a gesture that had palpable double-meaning. Yes, it was professionally considerate, but the gentleness of her touch and the suggestive way she pressed her palm against Susanne's could also be interpreted as a direct personal proposition.

This was Susanne's opening. "You can't imagine. What I wouldn't give for just one night with someone *else* touching the right spot." She ran her index finger slowly and evocatively up and down Margot's adjacent digit as a not-so-subtle way to imply the self-evident solution.

That was the seed, and it took surprisingly little time to grow. A few days later, when the census on the research wing had conveniently dwindled down to a single, lonely and conveniently needy patient named Susanne, Margot switched her daytime assignment for the nighttime—beginning her 12 hour shift with a coy 'it's just me and you tonight; *please* ring the call bell if there's anything at *all* I can do for you,' and ending it with a post-coital giggle, hug and kiss at end-of-duty morning's bed-side.

It actually *had* been tremendously satisfying to be pleasured by someone else; and since Susanne could easily swing both ways, hosting the admittedly talented Margot under the sheets had provided hours of past-due enjoyment that she found herself looking forward to repeating a few times at least before she kicked her new plaything to the curb. It was during one of these night-time rendezvous (number three, to be exact) that Susanne nonchalantly suggested the outing meant to facilitate her escape. They had been 'seeing' each other for about a month now, so the time was ripe.

256

"Take me on a date."

"Like to the cafeteria?" Margot suggested, lying naked by Susanne's side under the hospital-sheet. "I think that could be arranged."

"Don't be ridiculous. I mean a *real* date, somewhere out *there*." She pointed towards the window, to the city beyond. "Maybe a club? Preferably women only, if you please."

"How would *that* work, with you not exactly being free to come and go at the moment?" Margot sat partly upright on the small hospital bed causing the covers to slide off her upper body, revealing her voluptuous naked breasts topped with an inviting pink hardness.

"It seems to me that you could easily sneak me out in the middle of the night down the back stairway," Susanne said, while provocatively circling her finger around the circumference of the nearest tense nipple. "You know as well as I do that they never check in on me after eight o'clock, and you'll have me back *long* before morning rounds. They'll never miss me."

So a week later, when a particularly unconscientious nurse named Belle had the night duty, Margot did exactly as Susanne had suggested. Fortunately, the clinical research unit was accommodatingly set apart from the main hospital, lending itself flawlessly to Susanne's escape plan.

It was midnight when Margot brought a modest sampling of party attire from her wardrobe, helping Susanne select a short black skirt speckled with sequins, a tight-fitting maroon-colored blouse cut low in the front to showcase her cleavage, and sexy stiletto heels with open toes. The clothes fit her perfectly (this was no surprise, since they shared nearly identical builds), which meant that the other unchosen items relegated to the transporting backpack would too. Unknowingly, Margot had in reality packed Susanne's luggage, which would sit ready and waiting in the getaway car.

"Put the heels on when we get outside," Margot whispered over her shoulder, holding her own pair dangling from two fingers as they stepped into semi-darkness, five rooms down from the brightly-lit nursing station located at the opposite end of the hallway from the back-stair exit. Belle was absent from her post most likely reading a magazine in the back room, making it easy for them to find their silent way to freedom—careful to inch the heavy steel door open just enough for them to creep through on bare feet, easing it closed without a sound, and then making their way down to the bottom of the stairwell. Here, they repeated the process with the even-sturdier door to the outside, but only after Margot deactivated the electronic lock with a simple swipe of her ID card. The early October, 'Indian-summer' night was a warm and vast world of endless, unrestrained latitude—such a contrast to the confinement of the sterile, climatized hospital rooms that she had grown accustomed to, both here and in Paris.

"My car is parked right over there," she said, still in muted tones even though there wasn't a soul in sight. They ran through dew-topped grass still holding their shoes until reaching Margot's Fiat spider convertible: the ideal selection of 'wheels', as if Margot had picked the vehicle model specifically with Susanne's mode of liberation in mind. "How do you like it?" Margot asked, throwing the backpack containing Susanne's future change of clothes, if all went according to plan, into the storage bin behind the two bucket seats and plucking the key from her clutch.

"It's perfect." And she meant it. She could already see herself alone behind the wheel of the sporty roadster, betting that Margot wouldn't call the police as her first reaction to the theft since it would immediately implicate her in the escape of a high-profile mental patient. She could well imagine the sheepish lesbian sitting with her lovely legs crossed, giving her statement to the officer in charge who might in turn pass her robbery case judgmentally over to another detective as an entirely different matter altogether.

She would certainly lose her job if not her nursing license as well, if her role in aiding and abetting Susanne's hospital extrication and disappearance became known. Even if Margot's hesitation to report only gave Susanne a three or four-day head start, that would be more than enough time to locate Uncle Henri and to manipulate his good-nature *and* his dementia to her advantage. She only needed to 'be' Margot for a short period of time, until her family resource in Paris could assist with a more full-blown version of her hoped-for incognito a century and a quarter or so in the past.

Susanne lowered herself into the passenger seat, putting on the eye-catching borrowed heels while Margot started the ignition, driving them down the back alley and turning the corner into the midnight streets of Brussels. "I'm taking you to my favorite place." *That's good*, Susanne thought, *"because at least you'll feel at home when I ditch you there*. "I should warn you that we'll get plenty of offers to hook-up." She took Susanne's hand over the center console and gave it a quick squeeze between gear shifts. "No matter what ends up happening though, I promise that we're in it together. Are you okay with that?"

She was *more* than okay with that! In fact, it would be so much easier for Susanne to slip out unnoticed if Margot was preoccupied with the promise of two or three for the price of one. Instantly, this brilliant idea became an integral part of her escape plan. "Oh, definitely. This is so exciting!"

They reached the club in a matter of minutes, since the streets were all but deserted. Brussels was nothing like Paris, giving a sleepy and laid-back impression as opposed to the all-night manic-vibe of the city of lights. She pulled up to the valet, powered off the engine and handed her key to the attendant.

"Welcome to *Seulement Femmes*." It was somewhat ironic that a club named *Only Ladies* would staff their parking service with a young and obviously heterosexual man. He hungrily eyed them both as they climbed out of the low-rising convertible showing off ample leg and thigh. Margot handed him a €20 bill (one of many it seemed to Susanne's eavesdropping glance, nestled in her clutch along with a few credit cards—*more* than enough to finance an escaped patient's upcoming trip) which he accepted with a broad smile.

"My name is Jean Paul," he beamed, ripping the stub off the valet ticket with a dramatic flair and handing it decisively to the Fiat's owner. "I will be waiting for you at the retrieval podium right over there next to the entrance until four AM." He winked, as if he was in the 'know' about their *true* romantic preference: for *him* in their bed, rather than for each-other. It was ludicrous. Never mind that they were just about to enter a ladies-only club arm-in-arm as a couple, which was as clear an advertisement of their presumed sexual orientation as if they were wearing a sign hanging from their necks. "Have a great time."

"Oh, we will," Susanne replied, winking back—because after all, *she* wasn't as gender discriminating as Mademoiselle 'Hardcore *femme-sur-femme*', who at the moment was gently tugging on Susanne's interlocked arm in the general direction of the entry door. One thing for certain was that playing *this* game was way more fun, *and* productive, than pretending to be the victim of some made up psychiatric disorder, trying unsuccessfully to chisel away at the granite ethics of a certain single-minded neuropsychologist. In the end, Dr. Genevieve Lefebvre actually did Susanne a big favor by showing up to the festivities unannounced and uninvited.

"Come on Susanne—you're going to love it."

Inside, the Euro dance music pounded rhythmically to a packed house. Their first stop was the bar, where a thin blonde with her hair shaved close but only on one side served them drinks. They danced, drank quite a bit more, and made out in the corner next to (and before much longer *with*) another steamy couple, creating a perfect storm of inebriation and the promise of something considerably more promiscuous than expected, that ripened to absolute perfection after about two hours of partying. Margot was far down the road of wasted and absorbed in something more than drunken conversation with her two new friends, so the time was definitely now.

"I need to freshen up." She nonchalantly put her hand on Margot's clutch, which was sitting on the table in front of her, just waiting to be 'borrowed'. "I'll be right back."

Margot nodded absently without a word of objection, her hand on candidate number one's bare leg under the table while candidate number two had taken up a strategic position next to Margot on her other side. "Don't be long, my love," she mumbled distractedly.

It was incredibly easy to blend into the crowd and walk out the door rather than into the bathroom, while oblivious Margot (who was now engaged in a passionate kiss with candidate number two) remained clueless to the double-cross. Well, at least she would have a couple of shoulders to cry on when she realized what had happened. She opened the zipper, taking stock of the contents which included phone, money, credit cards, a driver's ID and cosmetics while fishing out the valet slip and handing it to Jean Paul.

"Where's your sexy friend?" he asked.

"Otherwise engaged. I'm afraid she's going home with someone else."

"Ah, too bad." He quickly jotted some numbers down on a piece of paper and handed it to her. "Call me if you're lonely later." He didn't wait for a response, but disappeared around the corner to fetch her sporty little Fiat. If she wasn't in such a rush to flee the scene of her evolving missing-person's drama, she might have actually taken him up on his offer.

A moment later he was back, standing next to the Fiat with his hand on the opened driver's side door, waiting politely for her to climb in. Since he had received his monetary tip on arrival, she decided to give him something a little bit different now. Instead of brushing past him she stopped, put both arms around his neck and kissed him—long, wet, and deep. "I'll call you soon," she lied as she climbed into the convertible, started the ignition and sped away.

CHAPTER TWENTY-SEVEN

It had been an easy trip, all things considered. She made it out of the city and into the outskirts of Brussels using google maps—provided courtesy of Margot's cell phone, which had been so simple to unlock using the passcode that Susanne had memorized while watching its owner enter it late one night during the world's most boring photo-album slide-show of nieces, nephews, and pet cats: galore. By that time, it was well after sunrise, and with it came a brief stop for fuel and a bite of fast-food at the petrol station.

She didn't linger for very long, taking advantage of the semi-deserted roadway for a good hour until the volume moving steadily towards Paris got heavier. The drive to the Parisian outskirts, which would normally take three-and-a-half hours, took closer to six because of traffic combined with four more stops: the *first* to purchase some necessary items (including a piece of luggage, a mini-wardrobe of everyday clothes to supplement the clubbing-bag that Margot had kindly prepared for her, and a full supply of toiletry items and make-up); and the second, third and fourth to visit ATMs with the end-result of three maximum withdrawals putting €1500 of cash conveniently into the back pocket of her newly-purchased blue jeans—to use for some pricey street-purchases necessary to her travel-plans. Having Margot's credit and debit cards (the latter ridiculously easy to 'activate' for electronic access using Margot's birthday as the

PIN...can you imagine the stupidity?) made her initial re-entry into society a cake-walk; but she didn't plan on staying in this century for long. Her sights were set on the past, where she intended to relocate at her earliest convenience.

Getting from the edge of the city into the heart was a nightmare, with a bumper-to-bumper traffic jam extending her time behind the wheel by yet another two hours. This delay meant that her door-to-door travel time from *Seulement Femmes* to the *Île de la Cité* parking garage (where she had decided to 'store' Margot's vehicle either for future use or to be eventually retrieved by the police) had taken an unbelievably-grueling eight hours—successfully accomplished but with some alarming, split-second nod-offs due to operating on no sleep for close to a day-and-a-half. She left the suitcase in the trunk, retrieving the backpack from the storage compartment and transferring two days' worth of clothes and the toiletries into it; and just like a vacationing twenty-something with her bag slung over one shoulder, she exited the shadowed garage into the bright afternoon sunlight of her native city.

It was maybe three-o'clock when she sat at an outdoor café in the fourth *arrondissement* overlooking the Seine, enjoying a double espresso, a *croque-monsieur* and a delicious serving of *crêpes Suzette* for dessert while she reoriented herself to the layout of modern Paris, using the mobile google maps 'app' as her guide. She located Henri's residence in *Saint Germain des Prés* in the sixth *arrondissement* on the famous left-bank, double-checking the street directions to *10 Rue de Bac* (although she remembered quite well how to get there) before she tossed the phone into the river. Although she felt certain that Margot wouldn't go to the police on her own accord to report the theft of her vehicle and her identity anytime soon for fear that it would expose her vital role in facilitating Susanne's disappearance, it would be much safer to eliminate the risk of GPS tracking *now* before the authorities eventually linked Margot to her escape.

Because she predicted that very soon they would. She could well imagine that someone like that cocky valet Jean Paul, who had obviously been hoping for a threesome with two sexy semi-lookalikes only a short twelve-plus hours ago, might be the identifying 'witness' responding to internet photos of a missing psychiatric patient, making an animated phone call to the Brussels police precinct with his description of the runaway and her accomplice. This way, with the phone gurgling its signal to 'silent' at the muddy bottom of Paris' watery landmark, the trail would stop here rather than at Henri's house, where she would camp out just long enough with her demented great uncle to locate *Waking Nude Preparing to Rise*.

Once there and with the painting in her 'sights', she would initiate 'plan A'—slipping Henri some pricey 'medicine' that she would gladly take too, and wait for the effects to declare itself. If he was a cooperative 'patient' then they would *both* be on their way to the nineteenth century; and if he wasn't, she would promptly retire to the stripped-to-naked privacy of the guest room with the painting as her voyeuristic-bedfellow. She found herself almost hoping for 'plan B' as a sexy-preference instead, since it involved the self-administration of a few more servings of the entertaining antidote to her own hoped-for time-sensitive genetic disorder, ingested while she self-administrated a very *different* sort of concurrent-remedy between her legs.

At least in 2011, the area surrounding the Montmartre district was the place to go if you had an addiction to feed—or so she had heard, since she had never been a frequent visitor to the land of the high-flyers; yet, something unreachable in realm of remembered-then-forgotten whispered a familiarity with the concept that she tried unsuccessfully to brush off like a nagging, biting fly. Not being one to linger on memory-lapse lane, she made that little detour on the way to the Latin district to find what she needed, boarding the metro train and getting off at *Place Pigalle* where she wandered down a side-street until she located a grouping of junkies huddled around a dealer. She elbowed her way to the center unconcerned about 'cutting the queue' if there even was one, nearly accosting the pusher who had just pocketed some cash in exchange for the sale of a bag of pills. "I need some heavy-duty dope," she demanded.

He gazed back at her with the same lustful look that every man that she could ever recall had always given her. "It'll cost you, baby." His black eyes within sunken user's sockets looked her up and down, resting for a moment on the *Esprit* logo scrawled suggestively in cursive across the double-bulge of her T-shirt before they moved upward to an

267

almost-thoughtful study of her facial features. "Haven't I seen you somewhere before?"

She sniggered at the clichéd pick-up line. "Forget it, pal. I'm way out of your league."

He ignored her brush-off. "Have you ever posed or performed—uh, you know…nude?"

She laughed. This guy was really pushing it, so she would just have to push back. "Plenty of times," she teased, stringing him along during a suggestive pause before delivering the all-too-true punch-line. "For the reasonable price of an entry ticket to *Musée d'Orsay*, you can enjoy me from every conceivable angle modeling in the buff. I'm plastered all over the walls of that museum."

He seemed genuinely confused by her response; but honestly, she didn't have time to explore the cognitive limitations of a moron, even if he might be a closet art-aficionado. "Look, enough small talk, Picasso. Can you or can't you get me the stuff I need? I've got plenty of money, so why don't we get down to business?"

He shrugged off her impatience and put on his nicest 'I'm a full-service retail operation' sales-smile, showing her a mouthful of decaying teeth. "Okay darling—what did you have in mind?"

"I need something with a major psychedelic punch…and something a little bit milder, too. You see, my friend can't handle as much as I can."

"How about a harmless little baggie of acid pills and a big-girl's helping of angel dust?"

"That sounds about right." She reached into her back pocket and pulled out about a third of her hefty stack of euros. "How much?"

"For the 'premium' package—five hundred?"

That sounded a little steep but she had no reason to quibble—because it wasn't her money anyway, and where she'd soon be going she wouldn't need the balance. "Sold," she declared, counting out the price of her freedom and slapping the bills on his dirty, open palm. In exchange, she didn't have to wait long to be handed a brown paper bag that it took him no time at all to prepare from a squatting position near the storm drain—the contents selected from an impressive cache of merchandise guarded carefully by a burly business associate whose bulge of a handgun hidden under his belt was as visible and potentially as dangerous as the one she couldn't help but notice sheltered behind his zipper. And just like that, she sauntered off to her next destination, her backpack (with the 'goods' tucked away inside) slung over one shoulder, and with a dozen addict-eyes fixated on the irresistible sway of her perfect *derriere*.

She traveled back to central Paris by retracing the same outbound Metro route but in reverse, except that she got off at the University of Paris station instead of *Île de la Cité*. She walked down the same streets that she remembered from who knows how long ago, passing the *Saint Germaine* cathedral that was actually used as an abbey in Susanne's other lifetime, and finally arriving in front of the house on *Rue de Bac* that she knew all too well. The art restoration sign had been taken down and the front display window was now curtained, so she figured she'd use the ground-floor entrance in front to announce her arrival, rather than climbing up the side stairs to the upper level. In the old days her great uncle had lived above his art restoration studio, but now that he required a permanent house-guest to change and feed him, she assumed the old business space had been converted back to residential.

She rang the doorbell and a girl in her mid-twenties (most likely the live-in medical aide that Susanne had heard about) answered. She was dressed in street clothes, but this didn't mean she wasn't on duty. "Can I help you?"

"Does Henri Bruante still live here?"

"Yes."

Her soft and pliable brown eyes engaged with Susanne's in a way that only a sympathetic and trusting healthcare worker's would. This would be easy. "I've traveled a very long way to see him. He's my uncle."

As the nurse's eyes opened wider, so did the door. "By all means, come in!"

Susanne stepped over the threshold and into what used to look like a warehouse in her memory, but had now been re-converted into a conventional partitioned living space—just as she had anticipated. They were standing in a foyer leading into a spacious sitting room, where the girl's easy demeanor reflected a no-questions-asked attitude. "He's napping now. Would you like to wait in here for a while until he wakes?" She motioned into the living room, where a moment later they were sitting almost knee-to-knee.

"I'm Georgette," she offered, "his 'private duty'. It's really an easy assignment since he's so sweet and really doesn't need very much care, but it gets tedious sometimes staying here all alone. I do get one day off a week though, which helps." She smiled brightly. "He doesn't have many visitors, so I'm actually happy for this rare distraction."

"It's a pleasure meeting you, Georgette. You can call me..." (she thought for a moment, realizing that an escaped health-system convict would be wise to keep her true identity hidden) "...Eve—Eve Montagne." She had no idea where that name had come from, popping into her head in a flash of dissembling certainty—but no matter. It seemed to come to mind naturally, so she would just run with it.

Her nod acknowledged the lie without even a minor hint of suspicion. "You said you're Henri's niece?"

"Well, a great-great niece, of sorts..." (she added two generations to account for her unusually-youthful appearance induced by reverse-aging for nearly ten years while living in the distant-past) "...from his sister's side." Using a non-Bruante surname meant that her pretend heritage should be derived from a female relative, so linking herself vaguely to some unauthentic family member seemed as good a pick as any. The girl, in any case, had no knowledge of their family tree, so in reality it didn't much matter. "I'm not sure if that would technically make me more of a cousin?" She shrugged. "Regardless of what you label our relationship, he's always been like an uncle to me."

Georgette, as expected, didn't seem to be a stickler for relationship-details. Her eyes wandered to 'Eve's' backpack. "Do you have someplace to stay?"

She decided to twist the inquiry into an invitation. "*Here* would be wonderful! You are so very kind to ask."

There was a moment of awkward silence while Georgette seemed to be processing Susanne's 'quick-draw' acceptance of her unintentional offer. "There's an unused guest room upstairs," she thought out loud in what quickly turned into a confirmation. "I'm sure Henri would love to host you for a day or two," she added uncertainly.

Susanne in fact remembered that bedroom well. "That will do just fine, Georgette." She decided to take the opportunity now to 'schedule' some privacy. "When is your day off?"

"Not until Sunday."

"That's five days away. I'll tell you what—how about I stay with Henri tomorrow while you take some time to yourself? He and I can catch up, and the agency doesn't even need to know."

"That's so kind of you." She jumped on the unexpected opportunity like a cat attacking a ball of yarn. "I think I'll take you up on that."

And that's when a voice: *his* voice, called out from the adjoining room.

CHAPTER TWENTY-EIGHT

"Who are you talking to?" Henri yelled mildly—his voice raspy with age.

Georgette glanced over at Susanne and whispered: "Don't be upset if he doesn't recognize you. His monthly injection helps quite a bit, but it doesn't usually last the full four weeks."

He must be taking Thierry's wonder drug, Susanne thought. She knew that mnemositide (which had been hailed as the drug of the century, helping millions of patients with Alzheimer's to live more normal lives) was an intramuscular 'depot' injection that slowly leeched into the bloodstream from its fleshy reservoir in a timed-release fashion. Judging from Georgette's comment, she gathered that sometimes the dose would be depleted early depending on physiologic factors that she didn't need to understand. Leave the hocus-pocus to the doctors, and the real-life business of taking advantage of Henri's affliction to the ever-resourceful Susanne. "Are you saying he's due for a treatment?"

"Tomorrow night. That means that he's pretty much at his worst right now; but if you stay until after his next injection, he'll be at his best!"

Susanne had no intention of staying past tomorrow, unless *Waking Nude Preparing to Rise* was not easily accessible and/or her experiments with Henri, herself and an excess dosage of psychedelics didn't give her the life-altering results that she desired. In that case having Henri more

273

lucid on freshly-administered medication might be better anyway, so he could help her figure out what to do next. If anything, Henri had always been blindly loyal to family and with a special soft-spot for his favorite great-niece.

"Joelle?" Henri called again from the other room.

Susanne met Georgette's gaze and furrowed her brow quizzically, deciding to play dumb when she knew full well that Henri was confusing Georgette with his long-dead older sister, and her *own* grandmother. "Who's Joelle?"

"His sister. It's one of several names that he seems to recycle when it's almost time for another injection. Nicole and Susanne are two others: deceased relatives from the past, I think."

Now things were starting to get more interesting. Susanne stood up. "We're coming!" she yelled, while at the same time winking at Georgette. "I'll pretend to be one of those other two," she suggested to the nurse under her breath. "That way I won't upset him."

"I do that all the time. At this point in his medication cycle, it's really not worth arguing identity because it'll get you nowhere anyway."

Susanne tried not to look overly elated at the opportunity to impersonate herself. "Let's say *bonjour*, then." She smiled conspiratorially. "'Susanne' can't wait to see her uncle!"

On entering the room, the first thing Susanne noticed, with excitement and satisfaction, was the painting she had come all this way to hopefully find, hanging right there on the wall directly facing the bed just a few paces from the footboard. It couldn't have been placed more perfectly if she had planned the interior design herself. She sighed internally, relieved that 'condition one' in the countdown to her successful journey had been so easily fulfilled.

The room was small, with its original use a study judging from the desk pushed tightly into one corner and the set of bookcases sitting side-by-side taking up too much space in the make-shift bedroom. "The stairs are difficult for him now," Georgette commented by way of explanation for the clutter of furniture.

Susanne nodded her understanding as she walked over to Henri, taking his hand in the best show of insincere kindness that she could muster. "Hello Uncle Henri." She paused and looked over at Georgette for a moment just to create the desired dramatic effect. This false-yet-true identity game would be amusing to play. "It's Susanne." She felt like a double-agent in a spy novel.

He squinted, as though this method of correcting blurred vision would somehow help him to identify her. "Susanne? Is that really you?" She had the distinct feeling that he really *did* recognize her, despite the profoundly confused state of his seriously demented mind.

"Yes it is. I'm here to visit with you, just for a day or two."

"It's been so long." He studied her face with a vague flicker of perception. "I thought you had died."

She was impressed with this surprisingly lucid comment. Whether he thought that she was Nicole posing as Susanne, now dead and buried in Chicago after her life ended with John's in what was described as a terrible car accident, versus the real Susanne (aka herself) absent these past ten years after disappearing through a *Virtual Hole* in *The Origin of the World*, his comment could be considered appropriate. "I survived," she explained—a response that would be applicable to *either* the real Susanne, or the imposter. It was definitely best to keep things ambiguous, for now.

"What a nice surprise," he said in a flat tone of voice strikingly devoid of emotion. She imagined that it was not at all unusual for an Alzheimer's patient to exhibit inappropriate affect as a defense mechanism to deal with just this type of identity confusion. This calm denial that his mind was gone was so much better though than the alternative: namely, the typical aggressive agitation demonstrated by many patients afflicted with this form of dementia. It was fortunate however that Henri appeared to have the perfect behavioral variant of the disease that would be amenable to manipulation. She could easily imagine him allowing her to administer the psychotropics tomorrow without muss or fuss, much like feeding candy to a helpless and cooperative baby and waiting for the sugar-fix that would propel them back in time to kick in.

"Are you hungry, Henri?" Georgette asked, having hung back in the door threshold.

Henri looked past Susanne at Georgette and nearly beamed with nostalgia. "My dear sweet sister, how I have missed you. Do you remember how to make the camembert and spinach quiche that I loved so much when I was nine or ten?"

"Of course, Henri." Georgette met Susanne's gaze and shook her head sadly as if to say 'what did I tell you?' "There's still some left over from yesterday's dinner that I'll go heat up for you now."

"You're my angel, Joelle."

"Let me help you," Susanne offered, following closely at the nurse's heels, wanting to minimize unnecessary exposure to her great uncle just in case his ramblings hit upon some telling truth that would make his live-in caretaker suspicious that 'Eve' was someone else entirely.

"Have you eaten?" Georgette asked politely, turning to face Susanne when they had crossed the threshold and were standing once again in the living room. "There's enough for three."

"I'm still full from lunch. What I could really use instead is sleep." She counted out thirty-six hours, more or less, since she had awoken yesterday morning at five AM. She was literally exhausted, and needed some shut-eye more than quiche at the moment.

"Oh, of course—I'm sure you're exhausted from your trip. Where did you say you've traveled from?"

"I hadn't said." She used the time it took for her to retrieve her backpack to decide on a location much farther away than Brussels—not only to explain the premature fatigue and early bedtime, but

277

also to cover her tracks in case Georgette happened to have access to missing-persons bulletins over the next few days. Oddly, a city that to her knowledge she had never visited popped into her head, almost as seamlessly as the name 'Eve Montagne' had; but it would certainly fit the bill, being about three times further from Paris than Brussels in distance. "Hamburg," she declared decisively.

"I've always wanted to visit Hamburg."

Me too. "You should—it has the largest red light district in the world." God knows why that little piece of trivia had worked its way into the disingenuous conversation. "I'll host you sometime if you come to visit," she added with a lascivious smile. "You'd be surprised how one 'skin show' in public can lead to the equivalent in private."

Georgette's reaction was deadpan. "Let me show you how to get upstairs now so you can rest." It seemed that Georgette was no Margot, judging from her nonexistent reaction to the blatant sexual invitation. It was just as well though, since Susanne truly *was* exhausted.

Georgette led the way through the kitchen located adjacent to the living room and through a small bedroom that was obviously hers, and into a small back foyer to the same stairway that Susanne remembered when the ground floor had been tantamount to a small warehouse. At that time, the entire space had been devoted to Henri's art repair and renovation business as a workroom, while he lived upstairs in three small first-floor rooms.

"Thank you. I can find my way around up there, if it's anything like it used to be years ago."

She climbed the stairs after exchanging 'good nights' with Georgette, crossing the upper-level living-room tidied up to sterile since it was no longer lived in; passing Henri's old master-bedroom heading for the second one, where she used to stay on occasion in the old days—when she was the Director of Acquisitions and Special Exhibits at *Musée d'Orsay*, and he had been a well-respected and talented art restorer, not that long ago. Then, throwing her backpack on the second pillow and stripping off her clothes to her preferred state of completely nude, she climbed between the musty-smelling sheets to fall immediately into a sound and purposeful sleep...resting, quite literally, like the dead.

CHAPTER TWENTY-NINE

The past day and night seemed to last forever as the authorities searched for their missing patient. All leads at first came up cold, but now—only about twenty-four hours since Susanne had gone missing—the police had finally uncovered a clue that could help locate her.

At eight AM yesterday on the morning of Susanne's disappearance, Thierry had almost caused Gennie to spill coffee on her laptop when he burst abruptly into her office. "She's gone," he declared, dropping with desperate dejection into the chair next to her desk.

She thought she already knew 'who' because otherwise he wouldn't have been in such a panic, but decided to ask the question regardless. "*Who's* gone?"

"Susanne." He hadn't even paused to take a breath. "Missing, without a trace. And we were making such great progress, too. In today's past life regression, I was going to explore the last cache of her 'Courbet' memories in a final hypnotherapy session, prior to starting her on *AXP34125*."

By now, Gennie was as aware as Thierry that Susanne had inherited just as much in the way of DNA recollections from the father of realism as she had from Nicole Bruante, since they were *both* her distant relatives—even though the exact familial relationship still remained elusive, given the enduring mystery of Susanne's true identity. "You're over-reacting—we'll find her."

280

"I hope you're right." He shook his head regretfully. "We definitely underestimated her resourcefulness."

"That's true; but at least we know she won't get far with no ID, money, credit cards, phone or mode of transportation."

His countenance brightened slightly in reaction to this comment. "I hadn't thought about that."

"That's why you have me." She got up and sat on his lap, kissing him tenderly for a moment as a gesture of support, and more. 'We're in this together,' the caress of her lips had said, 'no matter what happens.'

"She'll require much closer monitoring when we readmit her." He seemed calmer and less panicked now, thanks to the attention she had given him.

"For sure; and when we do, we'll have to seriously refocus our efforts to actually *treating* her psychiatric disorder on your clinical trial."

Thierry and Genevieve had made a mutual decision to delay the initiation of pharmaceutical therapy for Susanne's CIC syndrome while they gathered the fascinating data from Susanne's past life regression sessions. Once her mnemosyne receptors were blocked by *AXP34125* (an oral agent given daily in tablet form), they would be unable to mine the depths of her psyche for the ancestral memories that formed the basis for her complex confabulations. Although withholding treatment had seemed like the right decision at the time, Gennie wasn't so sure now. Yes, there *was* the benefit to humanity to consider, since their research on

Susanne had without question furthered the scientific understanding of multiple personality disorder; but at what price? Now a mentally unstable 'psychopath' of sorts was on the loose, and they'd have to retrieve her promptly in order to avoid a repeat of the incident at *Musée d'Orsay*, or worse.

"I agree. Our psychiatric research will be furthered just as much by analyzing her response to mnemosyne blockade anyway. We might even discover who she really is—if not immediately, then eventually after her blood levels of *AXP34125* reach therapeutic."

A worried look had passed briefly over his face again, which wasn't at all difficult for her to interpret. "She'll turn up somewhere, Thierry— probably right down the street at some café, trying to seduce someone or other into helping her."

Well, that's close to what actually happened. Fast-forward to today, when Thierry once again barged into her office but with a very different 'take two' version of excited. "The police had an on-line response to the missing persons alert last night."

Photographs of Susanne had been posted all over the internet. "And...?"

"A valet at a lesbian club saw her there with another woman: a regular named Margot Charbot. It turns out Margot is a nurse—right *here*, in the very same inpatient research unit where Susanne was admitted!"

"You have *got* to be kidding!"

"She apparently convinced Margot to take her out on a 'date'."

282

Knowing Susanne quite well by now after being her treating psychiatrist for more than half a year, Gennie could well imagine how Susanne had managed to shrewdly feign romantic feelings for a nurse who had probably made her sexual orientation and personal vulnerability clearly known to Susanne from the very start. Who knows, but she may have even had *sex* with her, right there in the research ward under everyone's noses—in a supply closet or perhaps in her own hospital bed in the middle of the night. To actually sneak Susanne out and trust that she wouldn't take off meant that Margot had fallen like a brick for the insincere commitment that Susanne had probably promised.

Which led to the following question: what kind of psychologically-unstable and manipulative mind would come up with such an outrageous yet deviously-imaginative plan to break herself out of a mental institution? The answer that immediately came to mind was: a bloodline descendant of the ethically-barren Charlotte Berthier: aka Noëlle 'Elle' Bruante. If Susanne's 'memories' of 'Charlotte' killing her own grandson's lover: Gustave Caillebotte (who had trusted her to function as a 'beard' to his true hidden sexual orientation— the deed accomplished by the criminally-inspired method of instilling poison in the form of photographic developer onto the back of postage stamps for him to lick) was true, then the familial sociopathic 'gene' had certainly been passed down as well, through six or more generations to rest side-by-side next to those murderously-cunning recollections. "Do you think Margot is harboring her?"

"No. The valet parked the car that they had arrived in together; but guess who came out alone to retrieve it?"

"So Susanne stole Margot's *vehicle*?"

"So it seems…along with her credit cards, ID, and phone." So much for Gennie's theory that Susanne was out there wandering the streets of Brussels, geographically crippled by the lack of financial, motorized or technological support. "Margot just gave her statement to the police. It seems that she refrained from reporting the identity and property theft when it happened since she was worried it would be traced to her affiliation with Susanne. She was afraid of losing her job and her nursing license."

And rightly so. Poor Margot could now be counted as yet another victim of the centuries-old Bruante-Berthier genetic legacy where nothing is sacred, morals are negotiable, and the boundary-line between decent and indecent is hazy and blurred. "Can we speak with Margot? She might have some ideas about where Susanne may have gone since it appears they were romantically close."

"That was my thought exactly—and also why I came to get you. The police are holding her at the precinct for us."

They took the car that had been sent for them, arriving at the station to find Margot waiting for them in an interrogation room. "She's free to go when you're finished," the officer in charge told them after introducing himself by his last name:

Desgraviers—because of course Margot had not been charged with any criminal wrongdoing, but would most certainly be faced with heavily punitive disciplinary action shortly, not only from the hospital administration but also from the Belgium board of nursing.

Detective Desgraviers was a muscular man in his thirties whose three-day-beard gave the distinct impression of stylishly-intentional rather than lazily-unshaven. "We have our fraud team checking for credit card purchases and ATM withdrawals using Mademoiselle Charbot's banking cards, which should give us an idea of where your patient is heading. We'll also 'ping' her phone...although my guess is that your patient probably tossed it by now, after making good use of GPS navigation over the past twenty-four-plus hours. I'll share whatever location information we find with you before you go."

Entering the room, they took seats on either side of the emotionally frazzled nurse rather than across from her to give the impression of empathy as opposed to confrontation, in an effort to create an atmosphere conducive to cooperation. Looking Susanne's 'collaborator' up and down as casually as possible, Gennie understood immediately why Susanne would choose Margot as her dupe.

The woman was certainly attractive, with dark hair, brown eyes, and a body-type that roughly matched Susanne's, explaining why Margot had been Susanne's selection as the most likely candidate to provide a no-questions-asked 'ticket to ride'. Susanne could easily pass as Margot in any quick-glance ID-inspection situation, and could be anywhere in the European Union by now posing as a vacationing twenty-something, given the open border policy of Schengen. Margot's face was still red and blotchy from crying, but it appeared that the worst emotional outburst was probably over as the young nurse sat up in her chair with a determined look on her face, seemingly ready to make her amends by helping in the search-and-retrieve endeavor.

"Hi," Thierry began. "I'm Thierry Duvalier."

"I know who you are." Of course she did, since on more than one occasion she had been on duty in the research unit when Thierry had made his rounds. "Please accept my apologies, Dr. Duvalier. Even though this sounds unbelievable, I fell head-over-heels in love with her and my emotions clouded my common sense."

"We understand," Gennie said, even though she really didn't. Margot had grossly overstepped professional boundaries by getting involved with a patient and facilitating her escape from the hospital and out into the community. Although Gennie was fairly certain that Susanne wasn't a risk to herself or others, the type of extreme manipulation that she had just exhibited could very well be a red flag indicating that more guileful and potentially violent behavior simmered insidiously below the surface. "I'm sure we'll find her…with your assistance."

The nurse looked from Gennie to Thierry, and then down at a spot on the floor, visibly embarrassed by her crucial role in Susanne's disappearance. "Of course. Just tell me what I can do to help—anything at all."

"To start with, do you have any idea where she may have gone?"

"Usually, I was the one sharing personal information rather than vice versa." Margot bit her lower lip. "We even looked at photos together on my phone, and like an idiot I made no effort at all to hide my passcode from her." Knowing her phone PIN had given Susanne immediate access, once she had fled, to every resource imaginable ranging from navigation apps to internet location services, making her trip to wherever it was that she was heading as easy as typing in the destination and applying a heavy foot to the gas pedal.

"Think carefully. Did she mention anywhere or anyone with even a slight hint of nostalgia?"

"Paris, of course." She paused for a split second to think. "And an uncle. I don't recall his name…it could have been Enrique, or maybe André?"

Gennie and Thierry looked briefly at each other. "Henri?" they both suggested at once, saying the name together as if rehearsed.

Margot's face brightened. "Maybe—or rather, yes. I'm quite sure now after hearing you say his name that it was Henri."

It *had* to be. Henri was one of the handful of living Bruante relatives that had come up in their identity search a few months ago; plus, he lived in Paris which was close enough to reach quickly and easily by car. It made sense that she would choose him as her first contact after gaining her freedom. Chances were good that she was still there; but even if she wasn't, Henri was as good a place as any to start in tracking her trail.

"Thank you Margot; you have been incredibly helpful."

Before leaving the station, Thierry confirmed with Detective Desgraviers that Margot's credit cards had been used to purchase fuel, food and clothing along the highway leading from Brussels to Paris, and that her debit card had been used repeatedly to essentially drain Margot's modest checking account.

"How in the world did Susanne access Margot's account to withdraw cash?" Gennie asked, doubting that the debit card's owner would have knowingly shared the access number with her bed-partner, even in the throes of passion.

Desgraviers shook his head. "She told me that she set the PIN with the six digits of her birthday. It's an all too common practice, and one that in this case cost Mademoiselle Charbot about €1500."

That was a load of cash that could buy Susanne's anonymous freedom for at least a few weeks after she jettisoned Margot's credit cards. What a shame. By sharing something as basic and seemingly harmless as a birthday, Margot had unknowingly turned over complete access to her finances including bank funds to a near-complete stranger with major psychological and mental health issues.

"Where does the 'money trail' lead?" Gennie inquired, knowing the answer in advance.

"Paris."

"And phone location services?" Thierry added.

"The device is no longer signaling; but the last entry is logged in *Île de la Cité* right in the heart of the fourth Arrondissement.

"At the bottom of the Seine, I'd be willing to bet!" Gennie interjected.

Desgraviers smiled. "Our thoughts exactly. We've notified Parisian authorities, who will take up the search from there."

"Thank you detective." Thierry shook his hand. "We appreciate everything you've done to locate our patient."

They quickly left the station and hailed a taxi. "You didn't tell him about Henri Bruante."

"That's right. I'm sure you'd agree that it would be far better for *us* to find her before the police do." It was true that their chances of taking her back to *Brugman* rather than being forced to readmit her to *Pitié-Salpêtrière* on French soil was far greater if they located her first and escorted her personally back to Brussels. He turned towards her as the cab pulled up to the curb. "Will you come with me to Paris?" he asked.

"You know I will." Her reputation was as much on the line as his, since Susanne was still under Gennie's care indirectly as Thierry's collaborating specialist. "In fact I'll book our train tickets right now.

CHAPTER THIRTY

Susanne had been wakened a little while ago by Georgette shaking her bare shoulder, while bright sunlight streamed in through the partly-cracked blinds. "Eve—it's time to get up."

She had opened her eyes and saw that Georgette was dressed for an outing, equipped with a light jacket appropriate for early October draped over the crook of one arm, and a purse hanging from the opposite shoulder. She propped herself partly up, disoriented, and rubbed her eyes. "Is it late?"

"No, early—eight o'clock, to be exact." She had slept about fourteen hours, straight through.

She stifled a yawn. "I promised you a full day off, so away you go."

"Thanks. Henri has eaten and he's watching television. There's soup in the refrigerator you can feed him for lunch, if you don't mind. I'll be back by three o'clock at the latest—see you then!"

Hopefully not. By mid-morning or even earlier, Susanne hoped to be lunching with an Impressionist artist or two up on nineteenth-century Montmartre hill.

She had decided to put some clothes on— because even though it would be great fun seeing an old man's reaction to her naked body; and even *greater* fun emerging nude somewhere in the painting's past with a clothed forgetful companion in tow, she thought better of it mainly because Henri, in his current state of confusion, might be less likely to cooperate with her if she offered him his 'medications' in the buff. For a patient like Henri (or for anyone who subscribed to the irony of a societal norm that considered the perfectly natural state of undress to be shockingly unnatural), any deviation from the usual routine could lead to a behavioral crisis that wouldn't lend itself well to easy manipulation. She'd save the naked time-traveling concept for later, should she be faced with going it alone in the privacy of this very bedroom, in the event that Henri failed to react to the handful of 'Lucy's' that she would give him shortly.

Now that Georgette was out the door and out of the picture for the foreseeable future (*and* the quickly-approaching past), Susanne opened her backpack and pulled out the brown paper bag, dumping its contents carefully onto the bedsheet to select what she needed for 'take-one' of her medical-thriller's climax. Her 'pusher' had provided a large zip-lock baggie containing about ten LSD pills, and three smaller ones filled about a quarter of the way each with colored powder ranging from dirty white, to brown sugar, to dark chocolate in tone, which he had explained away as varying grades of purity.

'Variety is the spice of illicit life' he had said, pointing out the lighter color as more-or-less purified and the darker as mostly un-cut angel dust. 'The darker should give you a more primal trip— reaching far down into the reaches of your brain; while the lighter usually provides a safer, crisper journey.' She had purchased all three since she couldn't predict how much potency she would need, and she had plenty of cash on hand to buy what she hoped would be a multitude of effective options to eventually (by trial and error if necessary) guarantee a successful voyage.

She opened the large bag and plucked out four of the acid tablets. *This should be enough to activate Henri's mutation...if he has one*, she thought to herself, figuring that one or two might be enough to get him high as a kite but would probably be inadequate as a stimulus for his hopefully-present Bruante time-traveling mutation. She would need double the dosing, she calculated, to make his 'trip' a productive one. She took the remaining LSD tablets with her—stuffing the bag in her back pocket for easy access, since she planned on getting high herself, immediately after Henri's dose kicked in so as to activate *both* of their mutations concurrently. She left all three baggies of PCP on her bed as potential last-resort propagators of her second go-to stratagem: 'plan B', if 'plan A' did not transpire as planned.

She went downstairs to find Henri staring blankly at the TV which sat on a small dresser immediately underneath *Waking Nude Preparing to Rise*. She walked over and turned it off, which effectively turned him 'on' by removing the mindless and monotonous distraction of the digital screen. His face suddenly became animated as he focused on hers approaching him from across the room—eventually ending up well within his recognition range when she sat next to him on the edge of the bed. He took her hand and squeezed it with concern. "Where have you been, Eve?"

She couldn't help but startle slightly when he used her randomly-selected alias, given to Georgette as a way to cover up her real identity. She relaxed though when she realized that he must have overheard her introduction to the private duty nurse yesterday from the other room; or else and more likely, he had had a de-briefing of sorts from Georgette this morning as she left on her shopping spree, telling him that 'Eve' would be in charge until her return in the mid-afternoon. Regardless, the lucid expression on his face was a little bit more than disconcerting since he actually seemed to recognize her as the person belonging to that name, despite the fact that he had conversed with her only yesterday 'posing' as her actual self: Susanne Bruante.

"I've been upstairs, asleep," she answered in the most matter-of-fact tone of voice imaginable.

"That's not what I meant. You disappeared ten years ago, at least!"

That would certainly go along with 'Susanne's' period of absence from the twenty-first century, which immediately put her mind at ease as it related to Henri's muddled name-confusion. "You're right, Uncle. I've been away for a long, long time; but I came back yesterday because I've missed you. I'm your great-niece: Susanne."

The lucid calm, disconcertedly sane, left his face like the passing eye of a hurricane. "You aren't Susanne—she's dead!" he claimed aggressively—his raging dementia rushing back, full force, into his expression. "You look just like Eve: Nicole Montagne's daughter. Your mother was Susanne's

293

half-sister: the illegitimate, disinherited one." Susanne frowned—totally confused by Henri's rantings. "I *know* it's you!" he added assuredly. "There's a family tree, in my closet—get it out and I can show you."

For a moment a shiver of fear passed through her, as though perhaps the ravings of a confused Alzheimer's patient might actually be true. She quickly recovered though, deciding that she would need to go along with his delusions in order to prevent him from becoming more disquieted. She would retrieve the Bruante lineage, though—just as he suggested, mostly to appease him.

"It's *true* Uncle…I'm Eve," she said, while walking to the closet and opening the door. "You see, I was just testing your memory with a name-game and you passed—with flying colors."

"I knew it! Those doctors got it all wrong; my memory is *fine*! It's on the top shelf," he added, as an aside.

She found a rolled up scroll of industrial-paper just where he directed, pulled it down and walked back to the bedside with it in her hand. That's when he looked her up and down curiously, like he was examining a cherished item lost but recently found to make sure the object still retained some singular, recalled characteristics. "Where have you *been* all these years?" He had already forgotten about the family tree, which she set aside on the floor next to the bed.

"I've been living in Hamburg…" (she chose the same city she had mentioned to Georgette yesterday, just in case Henri had overheard more

294

than just the name of her assumed identity), "…studying art history there, and funding my schooling by working in the entertainment business." She could almost see herself dancing around a pole, then taking a customer or two for a 'ride' in the sinfully-private back-room every so often to supplement her stripper's income. These days, a lot of students were forced to make ends meet that way…so why not 'Eve'? It appealed to Susanne to imagine herself employed in such a sexy sideline anyway, so why not match her made-up relative's inclinations to her own?"

His face assumed a more pleasant countenance in reaction to her logical explanation almost immediately. "That's lovely my dear. I'm so happy to see you."

She had had enough of the pleasantries; now it was time for some serious recreational drug use. "I have some medicine to give you, Uncle. Georgette left it for me to administer."

He shrugged in a way that said 'whatever you want.' He had always been a trusting soul, but the dementia seemed to make him twice as naïve. He closed his eyes and opened his mouth like a baby bird waiting for his feeding, so Susanne popped in the four '*mellow-yellows*' (actually orange, as acid tablets were normally colored) and handed him a glass of water that was sitting on the nightstand half full, most likely intended for just this purpose—but with administration of prescription pills rather than street-bought substitutes in mind.

She took two of the LSD pills herself, fishing them out of her back pocket baggie and swallowing

295

them dry; which meant that now it was just a matter of 'watch and wait' within the *Time Portal*-vicinity of *Waking Nude Preparing to Rise*. It was surely close enough, hanging on the wall not even twelve feet from Henri's pillowed head; so she kissed Henri on the cheek, wrapping her arms around him and settling on the bed beside him, as if she was a little girl cuddling with her favorite stuffed animal. "I'm just going to lay with you here for a minute. Do you remember how close we were when I was little?"

"I didn't know you when you were little." By now, the waxing and waning recollections of a man inflicted with a memory disorder didn't trouble her; yet, it seemed like a strange comment—since according to everything she had read about Alzheimer's, distant recollections were preserved to a much greater extent than the recent.

For a moment, though, Henri's confusion actually caused her to question her *own* childhood memories, which were glaringly devoid of a father given that she had been essentially estranged from her own long before he had died accidentally when she was sixteen—the gap filled, in part, by her lovingly-paternal great-uncle. But now was not the time nor place for that kind of painful nostalgia. The LSD should be kicking in by now, interacting with Henri's cryptic biology as well as her known body-chemistry, to potentially generate that gaping hole in the painting that she knew all too well, from her travels there and back again.

She hugged him tighter yet while watching the canvas out of the corner of her eye, feeling her

uncle's muscles relax and tighten and relax again—
an indication that he had departed this reality for
another one entirely, achieved by the magic of those
four little agents of psychedelia. His trip seemed a
pleasant one at least, with eyes darting here and
there under closed lids accompanied by mumbled
banter and silly non-sequiturs taking place in his
own private Wonderland, perhaps in conversation
with Alice herself. This went on for a good fifteen
minutes before she disengaged with the tripping
Henri, pushing him away towards the wall with
undisguised disgust; muttering "enough" under her
breath while pouring the remaining contents of the
plastic bag: another four pills, into her palm.

"I'll take the two-for-one special: one way to
the nineteenth century, please," she announced
sarcastically as if bargaining over a ticket-purchase;
then proceeding to gulp down the rest of the LSD
tablets. "*Now* we'll see what family affinity can
achieve." She swallowed them in a handful,
washing them down with the remaining water since
dry wouldn't do for so many; lying there with her
drugged-up uncle, waiting to join him in
hallucination-land where they would board the train
together heading to the past.

The painting started to throb like a heartbeat,
the side of Nicole's facing pounding large then
small then large again; her face leering and her lips
jeering, mouthing the words that she heard
insidiously whispering in her head like a hissing
serpent's tongue: '*He doesn't have it.*' Nicole was
right—Henri *wasn't* a mutant; and she was wasting
precious time lying here next to him when she could

almost certainly overcome the impotence of the LSD alone by adding some PCP potency.

So she got up and marched right over to the uncooperative painting, nearly ripping it off its wired hooks with a determination that she felt rising within her as surely as the internal certainty that with the right mixture of chemicals she could overcome her genetic limitations. She climbed to the upper-floor with *Waking Nude Preparing to Rise* under her arm, navigating the stairs that seemed to move like a drunken escalator under her feet. When she reached her bedroom she placed it propped up on the mattress of her guest-bed against the headboard after moving the pillows to the foot-end so that she would at least be comfortable when she laid herself bare. And that's what she literally did, stripping out of her clothes as provocatively as if she had an audience.

She closed her eyes as she seductively disrobed, envisioning the thrill of being the center of lustful attention with a roomful of gazes focused on her gradual transformation from clothed to nude, in what strangely seemed to be as real as true memories. After the rapid disposing of her outer garments, she unhurriedly removed the sexy bikini-stringed bra, tossing it away as a prize for some imagined adoring fan after the deliciously lingering tease had been completed. Next she shimmied out of her G-string panties with tantalizing deliberation, finally revealing the maximum amount of 'intimate': a customary but costly privilege for her assembled admirers who came back night after night to enjoy the public and sometimes private nirvana of her singular 'bare-all'.

Her flesh reflected sexually 'primal' in the heat of the sweat-producing spotlight as she danced naked with the pole as her tried-and-true lover, building up to the show's climax fueled by the cold, hard metal sliding suggestively on her warmly pliable skin. She looked down in her mind's eye at the birthmark—absent, then present, then absent again—placed yet not-placed in the most private spot imaginable, drawing attention to (Susanne's...Nicole's...Eve's?) erotic identity with the spread of two fingers that with a certain change in positioning would inevitably lead to the trembling conclusion of her uncensored performance.

She awoke from this oddly familiar daydream only to find herself in the 'real' state of her imaginings, touching her now-naked 'indiscretion' lightly in an almost sleepwalker's state of distraction. She would need to finish the job, adding sexual arousal to the gene-stimulating effects of the LSD *and* PCP, redoubling her activity so that it would end in wave after wave of the unmentionable, lapping up her groin due to the imagined-marking's proximity to a certain excitable spot that always longed for this sort of contact.

She climbed onto the bed naked, while her arousal climbed simultaneously to near-completion. She arranged the three bags of ultra-potent 'gene-enhancers' across her bared stomach with one hand since the other was otherwise occupied, so she could pick-and-choose from the contents. She had no idea what dosage she would need, so it was best to err on the side of more rather than less, just to insure success.

She had taken a total of six of the LSD pills, which had already created hallucinations. She'd just snort a generous pinch of *each* colored powder, to make the impotent mutation potent. Inhaling the dust seemed seamless and easy, to the point that you'd think she was a professional junkie the way she breathed the stuff into one nostril first, then the other, then back to the same nares where she had started. She figured the stronger the psychotropic 'hit', the more powerful its effect on her single gene mutation so she decided to take an extra two snorts of the chocolate 'flavor' since the dealer said it would burrow deep inside her psyche. She immediately felt dizzy so she pushed away her stash and lay back on the pillows to concentrate on her mounting physical needs, her feet just about touching the door-disguised-as-a-painting which she hoped would soon lead to her longed-for destination.

It didn't take long at all, before she had reached the edge of no return and plunged over to the other side. Her body relented to an ecstatic fall while at the same time, her skin burned as if she was some type of living fire, generating a cloud of heat that blew in from somewhere deep inside and emanated outward to open up a sizzling hole in the nude masterpiece. She recognized with elation the swirling vortex that led into white nothingness from her last two journeys: hot, empty, magnetic, and all-consuming. It was taking her now, pulling and tugging at the very fiber of her being and mind just as she had wished; lifting her body upward to float if only for a split-second before she was rocketed into the void in a quick and instant motion that paradoxically seemed to happen in excruciatingly slow motion.

"I'm heading home," she moaned, her voice sounding distant and disembodied, not like hers at all. She didn't resist as she tumbled into the burning hole of a scorching sun: so brilliant that it threatened to blind her, and so white that she had to close her eyes.

And when she did, that's when it all turned utterly and completely black.

She had finally arrived.

CHAPTER THIRTY-ONE

Thierry and Gennie arrived at Henri's house at about three o'clock by taxi from the train station to find a young woman in her twenties trying to fish her keys out of her purse. The task was made considerably more difficult by her refusal to put down about a half-dozen shopping bags hanging on her opposite arm.

"Is this Henri Bruante's residence?" Thierry asked.

The woman looked up from her struggles and smiled. "Why yes. I've been ringing the doorbell hoping that his niece will answer, since my keys are lost somewhere in the bottom of this clutter."

"Let us help you," he offered as they approached, taking the bags from off her arm so that she could continue the search unencumbered.

"*Voila*," she declared, putting the retrieved key in the lock and pushing the door open after hearing the decisive click of disengagement. "I'm not sure why Eve didn't answer. She offered to watch Henri for me today so I could go shopping."

"Eve?" Thierry gazed over the girl's shoulder to meet Gennie's equally quizzical gaze.

"Yes. Eve Montagne. She came yesterday, all the way from Hamburg just to visit her great uncle."

"Is she still here?" Gennie asked, stepping from behind to join Thierry in front of the door threshold.

"I certainly hope so. If she took off that means that Henri has been unsupervised for most of the day. Thankfully he's not very mobile due to the

302

arthritis, but still…" She stepped into a neatly kept living room, and signaled them to follow. She wasn't exactly the most cautious of live-in's, to invite two perfect strangers into her charge's home without asking for at least verbal identification. That probably explains why Susanne was able to get away with using some made-up name and insincere claim to have travelled seven-hundred kilometers rather than three-hundred without even being questioned by Henri's caretaker.

They stepped into the house while making the introductions that the private duty nurse had not bothered to ask for. "I'm Dr. Thierry Duvalier, and this is my associate Dr. Genevieve Lefebvre."

"Are you here to examine Henri?" she asked, obviously accustomed to occasional home-visits from healthcare professionals.

"In a way," Gennie replied. "But we're also quite interested in finding 'Eve'. You see, she may not be who she claims to be."

The girl took on a look of concern. "Really? She seemed entirely genuine."

Thierry didn't want to spook her unnecessarily, especially since Susanne had probably come and gone by now and there would be nothing gained by creating panic after the fact. "She's harmless, really. You see, she works with us." This misleading statement was not entirely untrue, and it would prevent any further emotional escalation while they continued for the moment as amateur detectives. The girl would be under enough pressure from the French police soon enough, as the unknowing first-stop facilitator of Susanne's great escape.

She nodded acceptance of the co-worker line and held out her hand. "I'm Georgette, by the way. Excuse me, but I should really check on Henri. If you'd like to examine him now, feel free to join me. Or look around for Eve instead, if you'd prefer." Georgette disappeared into the adjoining room, where they heard her speaking in a low voice to Henri.

"Why don't you search for Susanne in case she's still here while I spend a moment with Henri," Thierry suggested to Gennie, under his hand. In all likelihood their patient had already fled the scene, probably after pocketing some of Henri's cash to supplement Margot's; but then again maybe they'd get lucky and find her passed out, high or drunk in one of the extra rooms having had access to something recreational for a change. Seven months of teetotaling confinement in one mental institution or another might have been enough to drive her to a mini-binge of drink or drugs on the first leg of her escape-route.

Thierry left Gennie to her assignment while he entered the bedroom with a light tap on the doorframe meant to politely announce his entry. He found that Georgette had already pulled up a chair next to a hospital bed which had been pushed into the corner of a room that looked like it had been a study before it was converted into sleeping-quarters. Henry was a very thin man sporting a full head of unkempt white hair who looked visibly groggy and drained; yet, he still seemed able to answer Georgette's questions, albeit in a typical demented fashion.

"Where is Eve?" she asked him in a soft and soothing tone.

"Who?"

"Your niece. I left her in charge of you today."

A flash of semi-recognition lit up his face. "Oh, her. Yes—you can find her on the family tree." Thierry glanced at Georgette—puzzled; while the private duty nurse laughed mildly, bending over to pick up a rolled up scroll of stiff industrial paper which lay next to the bed. "He's obsessed with this," she explained; "studies it constantly, as if seeing the names of his relatives, living and dead, will bring back his forgotten memories." She turned back to Henri. "We know her *name's* on this tree; but where's the actual person: your niece."

"How should I know?" he replied irritably. "After she gave me those pills, all I remember is having some strange dreams. My sister was in one of them, but her face and head were stretched and distorted all out of proportion."

"Pills?"

"Yes, the ones you left for me."

"I didn't leave any pills; and I'm sure she didn't 'give' you anything, Monsieur Bruante. It's all in your mind." Georgette looked sadly over her shoulder at the 'doctor in charge' and addressed him with her take on things. "He's due right now for his monthly memory injection. He gets so confused when the medicine has worn off like this." She got up from her chair, walking out of the room presumably to fetch the syringe and needle from the bathroom or kitchen. Thierry smiled to himself, knowing that Georgette had no idea that the actual inventor of the very same miracle drug was standing right there in front of her.

"Where's my painting?" Henry was pointing to the empty space on the wall while turning his head to address Thierry as if it was the most natural thing in the world to have a total stranger standing in his bedroom to query. "It was a nude of someone in the family." He looked at a loss for words, trying to search his fading memory for a name. "Elle, perhaps? Or Susanne, or Nicole? Why can't I remember?"

Thierry couldn't comment on the presence or absence of an alleged painting, or who may have posed nude for it; but he *was* in a position to allay the confusion-related agitation typically seen in Alzheimer's patients with some comforting words of reassurance. "Don't worry, Henri—we'll figure it out together, after you've had your injection." Usually, a fresh dose of mnemositide would help almost instantaneously by restoring the blood levels of mnemosyne-analogue, bringing with it a surprising amount of clarity that would slowly taper off over the four-week release-time of the drug from the gluteal muscle reservoir.

At that opportune moment, Georgette returned with syringe in hand. "Let me help you," Thierry offered, taking Henri's hand and gently encouraging him to roll over so that his backside could be accessed for his treatment. "I'm sure you know the drill!"

Henri didn't fight it, probably because he knew the injection would help. With a slight wince, he accepted the deep sting of pain in exchange for a few good weeks of gain and then rolled himself back to supine, settling himself into the pillows with eyes closed as if anticipating some kind of magical recovery. Mnemositide wouldn't cure him, but he knew as well as Thierry did that in a matter of minutes he would suddenly remember things that were lost to him now, thanks to the wonder-drug that Thierry had been pivotal in creating.

"He said that a painting is missing," Thierry commented quietly, pointing as Henri had to the empty wall across from the foot of the bed, above the dresser and TV.

Georgette followed his finger and abruptly took in a quick breath of surprise. "Oh my—I hadn't noticed." It seemed as though this girl's special talent was in the missing of details.

Could Susanne have stolen a painting? That seemed an odd choice of theft, when ready cash would be so much easier than trying to raise funds by selling a piece of pilfered art to a dealer. "Henri, can you tell us something about the painting you had on your wall?"

"It was a painting of my great-grandmother...done by my great-grandfather."

In a flash, John recalled the scene from Susanne's past life regression where Nicole Bruante had posed nude for her lover Jean Désiré Gustave Courbet, conceiving their son Edmond right there on the wooden pallet in the artist's studio when the paint from the completing brushstroke hadn't even been dry five minutes. That painting was *The Origin of the World*. Could Henri's missing painting be *another* Courbet: an unknown, unsigned piece—the

307

very one in fact that had featured so prominently in his research subject's confabulated narrative? Recalling his interviewee's reflections, Thierry asked: "Henri, was the missing painting called *Waking Nude Preparing to Rise*?"

He hesitated, but only for a moment. "Why, yes—I believe it was."

And that's when Gennie barged into the bedroom, her face ashen and her lips trembling. "Thierry—it's not good news. You need to come upstairs, right now."

From the tone of her voice and her grave appearance, he couldn't imagine what kind of disaster Gennie had discovered on the upper floor. She was already leading the way, so he followed her through the kitchen and a cluttered bedroom that he was pretty sure belonged to Georgette, and then up the back stairs into a living area flanked by two open doors leading into twin bedrooms, it seemed. She escorted him to the left, standing aside while he brushed passed her, taking in the scene without understanding at first what he saw.

There was the painting, propped up against the headboard of a double bed situated in the far left corner of the room. The frame and mattress were pushed nearly-against the wall but not quite, leaving just enough space to accommodate one of a twin-pair of nightstands in-between hard plaster and the softness of feather-stuffing. This arrangement provided for a narrow-yet-walkable gap between the bed and the back-wall where the sheets and blankets now partly resided, having been pushed or pulled largely off and into the crevice—the bottom of which, as seen from Thierry's vantage-point standing just within the doorway, enjoyed an obstructed-view with added floor-concealment provided by the displaced linens.

The room was empty. Was it possible? It *couldn't* be, although here was the evidence staring him right in the face and screaming for validation. Had *Waking Nude Preparing to Rise* in actuality served as the *Common-Object*-substitute for *The Origin of the World*, allowing Susanne to travel back in time using some ingenious method of gene activation that overcame her alleged single-rather-than-double mutational-deficiency?

The scene that presented itself, unlikely as it seemed, appeared to corroborate Susanne's utterly crazy claim that she had lived and breathed in nineteenth century Paris for the past ten years in a swap of sorts with her distant relative Nicole, who had accidentally ended up in 2011 after ingesting too much absinthe laced with laudanum. This was impossible; yet, the declaration of truth slapped him hard on both cheeks—the one side stinging with the proposition of 'possible', and the other painfully burning with the assertion of 'probable'. Had it all been real, rather than the confabulated memories of a woman inflicted with a rare form of DID that he had dubbed CIC? He looked at Gennie desperately for clarification.

She shook her head sadly, walking over to the foot of the bed and gazing down into the gap between the bed and the back wall where the bedsheets had fallen as if it was a cleft in time that had opened and closed, pulling their patient in and swallowing her whole. "She's gone."

So it *was* true. "Back to bohemian Paris?" he asked—his whisper audibly wallowing in defeat.

She stared at him with an expression that said 'have you gone mad?' "For heaven's sake, Thierry—*no*! Look over here!"

Running over to Gennie's side, he took in the spectacle that had been hidden by distance, angle, and the confusion of twisted night-bedding. With horror, he saw a totally naked Susanne lying still and entangled in the pulled-off covers, all-but-wedged into the crevice having apparently rolled off of the bed at some point earlier in the day. Her skin was grey and pale, indicating that she had been 'gone' for hours.

Susanne had not traveled back in time at all, but to the next life instead. She was dead.

CHAPTER THIRTY-TWO

It was determined by the coroner that their patient had died from a drug overdose. Large quantities of LSD and varying danger-laden purities of PCP had been found in her blood and body tissues, indicating that she had consumed these same agents along with not-insubstantial amounts of ketamine, cocaine…and fentanyl. The three baggies of powder found on the bed at the scene were analyzed; and it seemed that all of them (but especially the dark brown formulation) contained angel dust laced with these numerous other 'illicits', designed to enhance the experience if used cautiously—in much lower doses than those ingested by the imprudent mental patient; and, of course, to encourage addiction so that the purchaser would return frequently for more.

One could only conjecture that in the afflicted woman's mentally-deranged mind, she figured that more was better; that if a pinch wouldn't do it then a hand-full would. The positioning of the painting suggested that she fully intended to travel naked through it to the past using drugs that she erroneously believed would alter her DNA and body chemistry via a fanciful gene called chronotonin. It was ironic that their patient, still very much a mystery-woman, had dreamed-up a nonexistent genetic 'hypersensitivity' to hallucinogens, while in reality she *did* harbor an inherited chemical imbalance which was probably caused by the interaction of psychedelic drugs with her body's unique mnemosyne-producing biology. This being the case, it seemed entirely plausible that the long-term psychedelic effects of past drug-use on the overdose-victim's psyche had contributed to her peptide-driven disorder as well as her far-fetched convictions—*whoever* she was.

It was a well-known fact, after all, that agents like PCP and ketamine commonly altered the user's brain chemistry and could result in permanent psychosis and mental derangement. After nearly a decade of presumed chronic exposure to these agents, enjoyed both in Paris and perhaps during a self-imposed exile in the international capital of erotic extremes: Hamburg, the subject's neurons may have been irreversibly modified, becoming especially prone to the hereditary memory-inducing effects of mnemosyne. It was a perfect storm, Thierry and Gennie theorized, that would allow for a bizarre confabulatory identity confusion that (if their data was eventually accepted for publication) would go down in medical history as the first known case of CIC—but in a patient whose true identity was still far from clear.

Who *was* she, really—the person who went by the name of the deceased wife of a once-famous astrophysicist who had dabbled in the scientific field of time-travel; a woman who claimed that the French ex-patriot Susanne Bruante, tragically killed with her husband in a recent automobile crash in the Chicago suburbs, was an imposter…and that she, herself, was the 'real-deal'? Could she have *actually* been Eve Montagne instead—a genius, no doubt, who had gotten sucked into the Parisian subculture of commercialized sexual performance and psychedelic drugs at the tender age of sixteen or seventeen perhaps, moving her studies and exploits to Hamburg—perhaps to escape a crime-scene?

Thierry and Gennie were convinced that she was, indeed, this second woman: a well-educated but erotically-corrupted individual in her late-twenties descended from Courbet, Caillebotte and Bruante bloodlines. Why else would she have given the name Eve Montagne to Henri and Georgette, if not as a subconscious 'confession' of her real identity? Naysayers argued that the name-drop was just a ploy—yet another conniving alias stemming from her somehow-intimate knowledge of that family's genealogy. Thierry and Gennie had to admit that a new 'assumed' identity of 'Eve Montagne', especially if based on a real-life individual, would do nothing less than keep the authorities and her medical team guessing.

So who was right—the two doctors who had dedicated more than six months of intensive medical efforts to understand a most fascinating case and heal a troubled psychiatric patient, or the critics who demanded proof-positive that Susanne Bruante was truly an unfortunate soul named Eve Montagne rather than some other never-to-be-identified sufferer of a peculiar medical syndrome? In the end, the uncertainty was a nagging reminder to both physicians that their ancestral memory research would by necessity remain inconclusive albeit thought-provoking, since the question of their patient's notorious family identity would forever remain wide-open.

Henri, given the advanced stage of his dementia and even with the assistance of mnemositide, couldn't recall very much of substance; so most of what they had to go by was culled in-part from the poster-sized family tree that was left at his bedside, with the rest filled-in by a hand-written family history of sorts, which he kept in his dresser drawer. The confusing details involving extra-marital affairs and illegitimate births, as they related to their patient, were indeed suggestive...but *far* from identity-clinching.

The real Eve Jean Montagne, Henri had chronicled, was the daughter of Nicole Élise Montagne, who was in turn the daughter of a thirty-something domestic servant in the Bruante household named Monique Marthe Montagne—impregnated in the nineteen-fifties by the under-age Didier Bruante: Susanne Bruante's *actual* father. Didier was merely 15 at the time, when Monique, in her gloriously seductive prime, persuaded him to engage in something devilishly forbidden. Who's to say, though, that the eyebrow-raising coercion wasn't executed instead by the young, randy teenager rather than the subserviént employee? Pressure-to-comply may have been felt by the poor woman, who felt obligated by her financial-reliance on the wealthy Bruante family to appease the sexual appetite of the youngest son.

This family scandal, whoever instigated it, was summarily swept under the rug by the matriarch-in-residence: Joelle (Henri's much older sister) by enforcing estrangement of Monique and her daughter Nicole from the family, facilitated by a legal contract accompanied by a large monetary pay-off. Didier was Henri's nephew, although they were actually quite close in age given the fact that Henri was nearly twenty years younger than his sister: Joelle—making his actual relationship with Didier's legitimate daughter, Susanne, great-uncle to great-niece. He did, in reality, become a semi-father-figure to Susanne after the now-mature Didier, a general internist who had long-since divorced Susanne's bipolar mother, was killed in a pedestrian-meets-car accident on his way to see patients when his daughter was only sixteen.

Henri had secretly kept up with the estranged illegitimate family-branch, which ran counter to his sister's insistence that the mother-and-daughter pair remain in radio-silence with their Bruante relatives forever. Monique's grand-daughter (and Nicole's daughter): Eve, was an academic child protégé who was enrolled in a five-year bachelor-and-master's program in art history at the Sorbonne, beginning her studies there at the incredibly tender age of thirteen. Her mother tragically died of breast cancer, long after Eve had somehow plunged into the world of drugs and prostitution to earn money while still in school. Her necessary extra-curriculars were most likely prompted by her mother's psychiatric disability, which rendered her unable and unwilling to provide financial support for her daughter. In all likelihood, Eve's *own* mental illness had been derived from a 'nature and nurture' predisposition inherited from her mother: Nicole Montagne, and fanned by a poisoned parental-environment to the

315

point that 'nature's' ember was eventually 'nurtured' into a blazing flame.

Although undocumented anywhere in Henri's family-history writings, the teenaged Eve, nearing womanhood at age seventeen or eighteen, could have very well been the totally-nude woman at *Musée d'Orsay*, captured on the video-feed along with two dead, naked men that made the headlines in 2011. She could have very easily been hired for a raunchy threesome orchestrated by the night security guard that went terribly wrong; but who knows for sure? Everything associated with that bizarre murder-case would be eternally left to speculation since all of the forensic evidence and investigation-documentation went missing long ago in the renovation of 'the 36' and in a bungled server migration. This meant that the genetic material of the perpetrator-versus-victim of a sordid paid-for triad could never to compared to Susanne/Eve's DNA, relegating the punctuated-identity of *both* mystery-women to a permanent question-mark.

How about the *real* Eve Montagne's DNA and fingerprints? With no criminal record in France, Germany, or elsewhere within the borders of the European Union, the use of this data was nothing less than unrevealing and unfruitful. After her alleged escape from the scene of the crime in 2011 (which truly *did* resemble a time-traveling vanishing-trick) she may have very well fled to Hamburg, the erotic capital of the world—*if* her claim to Georgette that she lived there represented the truth rather than a lie. If she was a full-fledged resident of this sensually-charged city even for a time, she must have used another alias, since no one named Eve Montagne had ever been registered in census documents or work rosters. The same absence of legal footprints, oddly enough, were applicable to Paris, beginning soon after Eve's graduation from the University of Paris in 2009, at the age of sixteen. She must have gone by another name in the *City of Lights* just as she had in *Tor Zur Welt* (aka Hamburg). Go figure.

Eve, the fugitive, may or may not have spent the next ten years nurturing a secretive assumed identity, since she didn't want Parisian police to find her. If so, she would have been tempted to dive more deeply into the seedy life of erotica in the free-spirited German city compared to her involvement in Paris, cultivating an evolving personality disorder exacerbated by an angel dust habit and a career path that led her down into the valley of the unthinkably carnal. The end-result, the dual-team of psychiatrist and neuropsychologist hypothesized, was a multi-personality identity-swapping disorder called Confabulated Identity Confusion or CIC: a unique variant of Dissociative Identity Disorder that so far affected a patient-party of one.

Even taking into account their patient's mind-boggling, destructive family history and her mentally-flawed logic, what in the world could have possessed 'Eve' to return to the scene of her escape a decade later in 2021 at the age of twenty-seven? She presumably hid out in a museum-closet after closing and then proceeded to nearly destroy the very same painting where she had witnessed or participated in a double-murder, when she was only seventeen or eighteen. It was hard to imagine why she felt compelled to revisit the place where slightly shy of ten years earlier, her panicked flight down a back-hallway and out an alarmed back door had represented a truly traumatic event in her life. Perhaps she was seeking justification and closure—hence, her inexplicable return.

And so Thierry and Gennie surmised that 'justification' took the form of a complex delusion based on ancestral memories, involving her great-great-great-great grandmother: Nicole Thérèse Bruante—a character who stood for freedom, joy and happy endings; and a more modern-day relative: an aunt (her mother's half-sister) named Susanne, a significantly more devious character, at least in Eve's mind, who just happened to work in a position of prominence at *Musée d'Orsay*. Susanne could play the villain to Nicole's hero, and provide a fantasy-framework for 'Eve's' escape from reality. The entire Nicole confabulation could have actually represented a psychological strategy for 'Eve' to remove herself from what had *really* happened in the museum…whatever that had been. If she was guilty of anything, making a distant relative the innocent bystander by time-travel was a perfect solution whereby she could entirely remove herself of any culpability…or so the dual-investigator medical-team of Duvalier and Lefebvre cogitated.

Until the very end, 'Eve' truly believed herself to be Susanne Bruante: a time-traveling distortion of the real Susanne blending memories from other

318

distant relatives including the artist-models Nicole Thérèse Bruante and Charlotte Berthier (aka Elle Bruante). These family-based characters and two nude paintings—*The Origin of the World* and *Waking Nude Preparing to Rise*—were the centerpieces of her fragmented identity for which she was even willing to risk death by overdose in a desperate imaginary gamble, attempting to return to the fantasy world where she was truly the most comfortable and at home. Sadly, what actually transpired in that upstairs bedroom at *Rue de Bac*, if not consciously but subconsciously, had tragically but clearly represented suicide.

What a waste of a brilliant mind corrupted by drugs, plagued by a rare mental illness, and inflicted with an inherited memory-accessing 'gift' that many would consider a blessing. What a waste, indeed.

EPILOGUE

Gennie had been working almost nonstop on their manuscript for three months now, providing the psychiatric and psychoanalytical backdrop to Thierry's neuropsychiatric data-analysis. The final product had just been accepted for publication in the *Journal of Neuropsychiatric and Clinical Neurosciences*; and to celebrate, they were going out to dinner. Thierry had made reservations at the Michelin rated *Restaurant Le Rabassier*: a true splurge which deviated from their usual casual fare.

It was a brisk winter night right after New Year's, the softly falling snowflakes adding little to the larger drifts pushed off to either side, resulting from the fastidious clearing of the Brussels sidewalks. The air was clear and speckled with downy white, floating on a twinkling backdrop of the same color: a brilliant punctuation of holiday lights decorating the countless vendor's booths. *Where are you?* her phone's text message-screen asked as she walked through the bustling Christmas market.

Almost there, my love, she responded.

Back table, to the right, he instructed; which is where she headed momentarily after stepping through the entry-door into the warmth of yellow candlelight and wafting heat from the noted chef's oven. She navigated in a zig-zag around a dozen or so tables until she found her seat across from him.

She sat, finding him smiling while he motioned impatiently to a small plate covered by a metal heat-

320

cover. "I ordered our appetizers." He lifted off his cover revealing a circular meat-tart covered with a 'tasteful' swirl of decorative sauce. "Open yours," he urged, nearly beaming with a little too much enthusiasm.

"You're in a good mood," she commented. "Hungry, are we?"

"Yes to both." He nearly glowed, from somewhere within his happy-place, it seemed. "I was just thinking that we make a good team, don't you think?"

"A *tremendous* team! Our journal article will turn some heads, for sure." She lifted the metal cover, and froze.

"As I said: we make a good team," he repeated, "and I'd like to make it official, from one colleague to another lover."

He got up, picked up the diamond ring from off of her plate (which quite to her surprise lacked even a crumb of an appetizer), and got on his knees right next to her.

"Now it's *really* time to turn some heads," he commented lightly, as the diners sitting at the adjacent tables all looked on approvingly while he asked the age-old question, hoping for her affirmative answer.

THE END

FOOTNOTE:
PARTIALLY FACT, LARGELY FICTION
CHARACTER GENEALOGY
(AUTHENTIC HISTORICAL NAMES ARE
HIGHLIGHTED IN BOLD)

Bruante-Berthier-Courbet 'left-half' of family tree

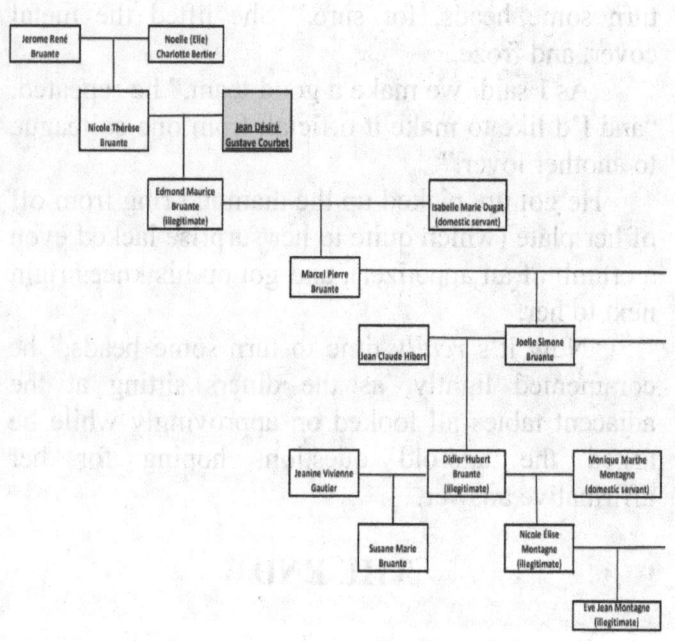

Caillebotte-Hagan/Minorette 'right-half' of family tree

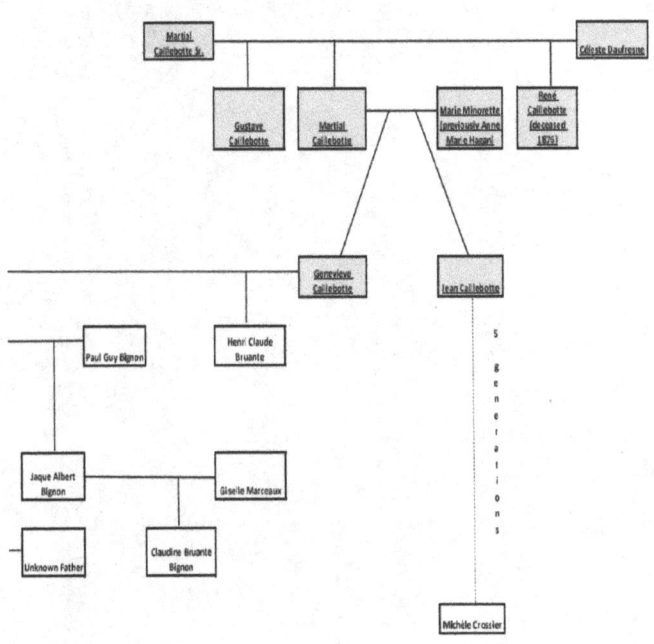